THE SOL-BECT WAR
PART 1

a Terran Shift novel

PAUL J BELANGER

To my good friend Ann Nelson, whose last name I used for a character in tribute to her and her family. I really appreciate the honest input which helped me finally complete this monster.

To my very first readers; Jamie, Marilyn, Lucille and Jean-Paul (aka Mom & Dad), and my sister Lynn.

A big thanks to my brother, Jamie, whose editing skills and input are always a tremendous asset.

A special thanks to *Vicious Crusade*, whose music, set on repeat, helped inspire and keep me going. I used the song *Final Chapter* for most of the book, and *Let it Burn* for the combat sequences. Rock on!

-- Paul J Belanger

October
2347

CHAPTER
1

G et him off me," yelled the young pilot over the command frequency. Several other pilots joined him in the yell for help, all of them knee deep in a slaughter, their own. His short-range scanner showed the area around him full of white and red dots. He had trouble picking his friends out of that mess and witnessed the blinking out of a few white dots as laser fire raked the tail of his Stiletto fighter.

He jinked left just like he was taught at the Flight Academy, but the alien ship was waiting for him and walked the laser fire along his stubby left wing. The young pilot's left engine burst into subdued plasma flame as he shoved the control stick full forward and to the right. The Stiletto responded sluggishly, full power on the right engine making the turn difficult as thrusters struggled to compensate. His caution annunciator panel lit up as the fire spread into his tail section. He screamed for help over the radio again as the fire hit his wing fuel tank and erupted in a plume of flames which flashed briefly into the void of space. He reached for the ejection handle and pulled hard as his Stiletto disintegrated violently around him. The ejection compartment's thrusters pushed it upward and clear of the wreckage as the force of the explosion caused him to lose consciousness.

The sealed ejection compartment was the entire cockpit area and contained the seat along with flight controls, instruments, and computers. Several of the alien fighters took shots at the ejection compartment as they passed by and set their sights on the United Earth fighters that remained. A few of the laser blasts connected with the armored shell of the ejection compartment, initiating a slight spin but causing minimal damage.

The alien fighters were rather bulbous in appearance and most pilots referred to them as slugs. They had relatively flat bottoms and a lip that went around the entire lower edge which housed their propulsion orifice and directional thrusters. The top portion of the ship extended upward, like an exaggerated convex lens. A metal band surrounded the upper portion of the lens-shaped top and was thought to be a window. The slugs were a greenish-black color and the only way you could determine the front of the ship was by the two extended rods that were energy weapons. They protruded halfway between the propulsion lip and the window.

"Help me," shouted another junior officer as he tried jinking left and right in rapid succession. He knew there were at least three slugs following him and the caution annunciator panel readily showed their progress in the destruction of his fighter. His right engine burst into flames and the left one soon followed as he yanked back hard on the control stick and ejected. One of the slugs pulled back to avoid the wreckage of the Stiletto and collided with the ejection compartment, destroying its craft and the compartment in the process.

"Come on," coaxed another pilot as he struggled to line up the slug he was following. "I'll get you one way or another." The slug turned to the left and the young pilot followed him. He fired a few laser blasts at the slug and was rewarded with only glancing blows. "Come on," he urged the alien, "just a little bit closer." The lasers streamed across the alien's hull and cracked the outer armor, releasing the gas from within. A few more blasts and the slug burst wide open with pieces scattered about the space in front of him. The young pilot banked hard to the left to avoid the wreckage.

"Yeah, I got one," yelled the pilot over the command frequency. An alien bomber that had been following the junior pilot quickly ended his celebration. The alien missile blew the Stiletto apart before the pilot even had a chance to realize that he had been hit.

The alien bombers, nicknamed gumdrops, were one and a half times the size of the slugs. They had one large orifice in the front of their ship that missiles were launched from. The alien missiles were accurate and left little behind to recover. The gumdrops sported a total of five energy weapon ports, two in front, one on each side, and one in the rear. The bombers were nearly the same speed as their fighters but could not turn as well, which was a good thing.

"What a mess," said Major Scott Carson over the short-range frequency. He was the leader of the sixteen fighters of Alert Squadron and directly in command of First Alert Flight. The short-range frequency had a range of roughly one-kilometer and was used to coordinate attacks at the squadron level.

"That's putting it mildly," replied Captain Julie Runzik, second-in-command for Alert Squadron. She was in charge of the Second Alert Flight of eight ships.

Each squadron was split into two flights, which were composed of four sections, each containing a wingleader and a wingman. Alert Squadron was one of four fighter squadrons assigned to one of United Earth's front-line carriers, the Ticonderoga. The UE Ticonderoga's mission was to patrol space less than twenty-five Light Years from the Sol solar system, where Earth was located, while performing escort duty for United Earth shipping.

"Is anybody left?" asked Major Carson.

"Slugs and gumdrops," replied Captain Runzik.

"That wasn't funny, Captain."

"Sorry sir, it was the first thing that came to mind. Let's see if we can clean up this section of space."

"You've got that right. Let's get busy everybody," said Major Carson as he decreased power to fifty percent and slowed for combat.

The two flights split up and targeted the gumdrops first, since they were the greatest threat. The Stiletto combat computer indicated a total of three gumdrops and fourteen slugs. It would be a very messy battle for the humans since having even odds were never really even. The odds were always in the aliens' favor.

Major Carson was the first to arrive at the group of alien ships and launched his two missiles at the nearest gumdrop. The ship's shields absorbed the impact of both explosive devices and the gumdrop changed direction away from the Stiletto it was following. The Major kept firing his lasers as his wingman followed his lead. They stayed on the alien's tail until the ship burst open in a showery mess of metal and gases. Both pilots swerved away from the wreckage and picked out the next nearest gumdrop.

"Nice shooting, boss," said Captain Runzik as she and her wingman took the next gumdrop apart. Its wreckage glanced off of her forward hull and nearly collided with her wingman. She turned to make sure he was all right and watched in stunned silence as two slugs systematically removed parts from his Stiletto with their combined laser fire. She momentarily lost her train of thought as a good friend and wingman disintegrated before her eyes.

"Julie, wake up," yelled Scott as he tried to shake the group of slugs on his tail. "We've got work to do."

Julie broke away from the grim scene and took a few shots at a passing slug before she noticed the group amassing on her tail. She could not shake them so she increased power in an attempt to gain some distance. A Stiletto shot by in front of her and came within meters of hitting her. She banked hard to the right and squeezed off a few shots on some passing slugs before turning left to return to the battle.

"Nice collection you've got going there, Julie," said First Lieutenant Carlos Mendez with a snicker. "I count four slugs on your ass."

"Four?" asked Julie in disbelief.

"Make that three, we just popped the trailing one," said Carlos as he lined up on the next one. *Pop* was fighter pilot slang for destroying a ship by cracking its hull and releasing the contents into space.

"John, get the one on the right," said Carlos over his very short-range wingman communication frequency, commonly called the wingcom. It was used for wingleader and wingman communication within twenty-five meters and was a unique frequency per team.

"Roger that," replied Second Lieutenant John Bowyer as he targeted the slug and depressed his trigger. Laser blasts smacked against the alien craft until the hull cracked open and burst apart in front of him.

"Julie, your tail is clear. The remaining slug broke off and we'll pursue," said Carlos over the short-range frequency as he lined up his next target.

"Thanks Carlos and John, I owe you one."

"Anytime, just not tonight please, I have a date," said Carlos as he turned toward the continuing battle. The enemy had lost half of its attacking force but they were still ahead of the game.

"You always have a date."

"Cut the chatter and get busy," yelled an irate Major Carson.

Neither of them responded but their conversation ceased. Carlos and his wingman, John, found four more pilots in trouble and were only able to help one of them. The others never had time to eject before their ships and their lives were removed from existence.

It took the group of Stilettos twenty minutes to finish off the enemy ships, but only after Defend Squadron arrived to assist.

*

"Status report," yelled Captain Washington angrily as he regretted letting the annoyance show through his voice. It was becoming difficult for him to maintain his composure under such hopeless circumstances.

"All alien fighters have been destroyed, sir," replied the scanner operator. "Recovery operations have begun."

Captain Jefferson Adams Washington stood on the bridge with his hands behind his back. His sharply pressed white undress uniform had four gold stripes and a star on each shoulder board. He was named for the first three presidents in the history of a country that was instrumental in the formation of what later became United Earth. His history lessons were selective so he could never recall the name of that country, except that it had contained the word *United* in it. He was a black man in his mid-forties, clean-shaven, and one hundred and ninety-three centimeters tall. He was taller than most men on the ship and had the bulk to go along with it. Some said he looked like a bear and, on days like today, he had the demeanor of one.

"Colonel, do I want to know how we fared?" asked Captain Washington as he lowered his head, expecting the worst.

"No sir, not really," replied Lieutenant Colonel Terry Nelson as he looked over the incoming reports. Terry was in his late-thirties and the Flight Group Commander for the UE Ticonderoga. He stood one hundred and eighty centimeters tall and was thin from overwork. He looked extremely tired since the last several days had been an active retreat from battle.

"The same, or worse?"

"The same," replied Lieutenant Colonel Nelson. "We lost all the replacement Stilettos and only two pilots safely ejected and have been located."

"We lost all thirty-two Stilettos?" asked a shocked Captain Washington as he stared at Lieutenant Colonel Nelson in disbelief.

"Negative sir, only one squadron was lost. The other squadron had been delayed due to several mechanical problems. They should arrive in a few days."

"Well, I guess that is the good news in this mess, if you want to push it that far, and I don't. What about our fighters?"

"Alert Squadron lost the most with nine Stilettos destroyed and seven pilots killed. Defend Squadron lost three pilots and craft."

"Shit, twenty-eight Stilettos. Why don't we just destroy them as they come out of the factory? It would save those damn aliens the trouble and at least save some lives," said Captain Washington. Lacking a target for his anger he took a deep breath and shook his head slowly.

"Keep me posted," said Captain Washington as he returned to watching the long-range scanner.

"Yes sir," replied Lieutenant Colonel Nelson as he exited the bridge. He also took a deep breath and felt like punching a wall. Maybe breaking his hand would relieve some of his anger since the enemy was not allowing them any satisfaction in that regard. Just like in any war he ever read about, the losses were always greater than the gains.

CHAPTER
2

At oh-six-oh-nine hours on the fifth day after the battle, the second squadron of replacement pilots arrived. They met no resistance en route but two of the Stilettos required maintenance after an accidental collision while attempting close-formation flying. Formation flying was one subject that had been shortened in the Flight Academy in order to get pilots through the course faster. Pilots were needed on the front lines and several areas of training were either reduced or removed to facilitate their hastened departures. The remainder of their training was to be conducted and completed in the field.

"Sir, I'm picking up a faint contact coming into range," said the Lieutenant Junior Grade working the scanning equipment on the bridge of the Ticonderoga.

Commander Frank Mito looked up from his daily paperwork. He was the UE Ticonderoga's First Officer, the second-in-command on the carrier. He stood and walked casually to the scanner.

"What do we have?" asked Commander Mito.

"Unknown object, but not geological, it appears to be man-made and has no propulsion system."

"I don't care about what it appears to be, Lieutenant, I want to know exactly what it is," replied Commander Mito. He stopped behind the young lieutenant and placed his right hand on the young man's left shoulder. He tucked his left hand into the small of his back behind his belt. The Commander could plainly see his sharp white undress uniform reflecting in the view screen and knew this would annoy the young man. But that was his job as an officer.

"Yes sir. The object is cylindrical, one meter in diameter and two point five meters long. It has markings on it that I cannot discern from this angle. There is also an active generator on board, maybe a solar power array, and very little power is being emitted. It may have a life support system and has no known exhaust signature."

"Has it changed course?"

"Negative, sir. Just floating along."

"Great. Have an Alert bird check it out. I don't want some kind of unknown explosive device damaging the Group on my watch." Commander Mito glanced at the twenty-four hour clock that was configured for Greenwich Mean Time, also called Zulu time. It displayed oh-six-thirty-six in bright red numbers. The military maintained the twenty-four hour duty day, calibrated to match Earth's cycle, even while in deep space. It simplified things for everyone.

"Alert Six, Ticonderoga," said the Lieutenant Junior Grade into his boom microphone.

"Ticonderoga, Alert Six, go ahead," replied First Lieutenant Carlos Mendez who was flying close area patrol.

"Alert Six, intercept and inspect a cylindrical object at grid forty-seven, positive inclination of twenty-two. Use caution."

*

"Roger, Ticonderoga," replied Carlos as he banked his fighter sharply. The Stiletto's twin engine exhaust ports sprayed abused plasma as it accelerated. The gap slowly decreased as the cylindrical object grew in his front window. Carlos approached the object slowly while watching his long-range scanners out of habit. The aliens they had been fighting for the past few years had learned a great deal from them, unfortunately, and it had been costing the humans dearly.

"Ticonderoga, Alert Six. The object has no exhaust port but it is generating a small amount of power. It does not, I repeat, does not appear to be a missile."

"What the hell is up with all this *appearing* crap?" shot Commander Mito over the command frequency. "Can't anyone in this Group determine anything definitively?"

"Sorry Commander. This object does not match any known self-propelled weapon. How's that?"

"Much better, Lieutenant. Now stop being a smart-ass and do your damn job."

"Yes sir," replied First Lieutenant Mendez. "Across one side of the cylinder in large white letters are *U*, *S*, and *A*. There are a couple of metal plaques with writing upon them, one is on the top front and the other is attached to the flat portion away from the carrier. From my position I can see a line which extends across the flat portions of the cylinder and down both sides, effectively splitting it in half."

"Is it emitting any radiation?"

"Negative," replied First Lieutenant Mendez. "Nothing across the spectrum nor any known destructive isotope. Indications are conducive to heavy metal shielding."

"Is it hiding something?"

"Unknown," responded First Lieutenant Mendez quickly as he checked his main display. The metal was primarily a steel alloy and thick. He detected nothing leaking from the crack around the casing. Either it was very well sealed or it was empty. The cylinder was painted dark gray and there was a small colored rectangle on the aft plaque. It had a small blue square section with white dots in the upper left corner and the rest was filled with alternating red and white stripes. He wished his imaging cameras had enough quality on high resolution to allow him to read them, but the picture was blurred. The cameras were effective for identifying ship shapes at huge distances but delicate things were beyond its capability.

"Well, if it had a proximity sensor for detonation I think it would have gone off by now," said First Lieutenant Mendez as the cylinder passed within a meter of his stubby right wing.

"Are you crazy?" asked Commander Mito, seriously wondering why this lieutenant was risking his life like this.

"Probably, but I know you're thinking about bringing this thing onto the carrier. If someone needs to risk their life it might as well be some crazy pilot instead of a ship with ten thousand people on it."

"Good point. Continue monitoring the cylinder while I contact the Captain."

"Roger that, Ticonderoga."

First Lieutenant Mendez matched the speed and course of the cylinder and pondered its contents. Most likely it was just a space trashcan that was ejected out of some space liner on a cruise to somewhere expensive. They usually shot them into a sun or black hole, where it would not bother anybody or disrupt shipping lanes. But this was war, and all the rules were broken. The entire galaxy was broken.

Carlos sat quietly in his fighter and waited. He had been flying the Alert Six position for a while now and was tasked with watching over the carrier UE Ticonderoga. He had been on the carrier only three months and his first week was spent in training until his instructor was killed during a combat mission. Then Carlos was immediately thrown into combat with a half dozen of his friends from the Flight Academy. They were all dead now, but somehow he had survived. He figured that it was due to his lack of training that he was still alive. His last instructor had died in combat so he must not have been any good. Since then Carlos did things his own way and would never follow instructions one hundred percent.

The first thing Carlos did when he arrived on the carrier was shack up with a decent-looking engine mechanic named Delilah. She sure knew how to keep his motor in overdrive. The result was less time for studying and more time for sex, and there was lots of that. Training was a futile enterprise anyway. They were all going to die soon at the rate the war was going. With or without training the new pilots were given a fighter and sent out to meet the enemy, and their maker. Most of them died quickly. A few managed to survive long enough to be seen as knowing what the hell they were doing. They were promoted to first lieutenant and given a wingman that would learn by following their example. Hopefully that kept them both alive. If not, replacements would fill the ranks.

After almost three months of combat, Carlos was halfway up the chain of experience in his squadron. He was no longer the *greenie*, he was now a battle-seasoned veteran combat fighter pilot. His superior officers did not care very much for his attitude because he enjoyed bucking the system. The thing that Carlos' higher-ups did like was that he stayed alive, and managed to keep his wingman alive in the process. The two of them had been a team for the past five weeks, which was unheard of recently. They had teamed up just after the Battle of Cori Prime, where the Group had taken the heaviest losses of the war.

Carlos never felt like he was a great pilot or anything. He just figured that he was one hell of a lucky one. Delilah was such a great pleasure to be with that that kept him very cautious most of the time. He did not want his last piece of ass to be the last piece, he always wanted more. So he was somewhat confused by his actions with the cylinder. There it sat, calmly floating through space with a purpose. Or maybe it had no purpose at all and just sat there, he was not sure. The only thing he was sure of was that he really wanted to read what those plaques had to say. The three large letters on the side were Terran but did not spell any word that he knew of. Consulting the computer's dictionary revealed nothing, but that was not telling him very much either. The Stilettos kept a very minimal database of what command personnel considered *useless crap*.

"Alert Six, Ticonderoga," said the Lieutenant Junior Grade over the command frequency.

"Alert Six, go ahead," replied Carlos.

"Shuttle coming, ETA is five minutes. Loiter."

"Roger that, Ticonderoga."

"John," said Carlos over the short-range frequency.

"Hey Carlos, what's up?" responded his wingman.

"We've gotta cover the cylinder pickup, close up and let's center our patrol here."

"Acknowledged. Coming up on your six now."

Second Lieutenant John Bowyer had been flying combat missions for only five weeks. As soon as he arrived at the carrier he was given a fighter and an assignment, and two hours later he was knee deep in an alien shit storm. Through an act of God and lots of luck, Carlos had kept him alive. The only good part about John's predicament was that he had only really flown with one pilot, Carlos. So it was easy for him to learn the man's quirks and how best to stay alive to fight another day. That was probably a bad thing. Variety gave people the knowledge to change their tactics to fit the circumstances. John never knew any different, so for him this was an easy job. He enjoyed working with Carlos and was in no rush to get a promotion and his own wingman. They made a good team.

The two fighters closed formation and began flying a slow and elongated circle ten kilometers around the cylinder while they scanned the area for enemy craft. Five minutes later a shuttle approached and began retrieving the cylinder into its cargo bay. After fifteen minutes passed the shuttle turned toward the carrier and fired its thrusters.

"Let's give them some room and roll out on the upper incline and two kilometers back," said Carlos.

"Roger," responded John as he followed Carlos' lead. Their short-range scanning equipment picked up only friendly ships and the long-range scanner, which was crap most of the time, was blank. The carrier was equipped with much more powerful long-range scanning equipment and they would have alerted the entire Group if anything were happening. It was the general consensus that they had left the enemy behind. He thanked God every day that the alien ships were a tad bit slower than they were. It had saved their lives numerous times.

*

The shuttle, built by Wong Li Corporation in a remote suburb of Beijing

China, was a cargo bay and not much more. It had no weaponry mounted anywhere and the only real windows were found in the cramped cockpit. It required only one pilot to fly it and the copilot also doubled as the loadmaster when an enlisted man could not be found. It was a rather boxy design that would win no awards. It could be configured for cargo or as a troop transport, carrying up to thirty armed soldiers. Today it had only one piece of cargo, a metal cylinder that was attached to the floor in the center of the cargo compartment.

Two individuals wearing environmental suits stood at either side of the cylinder, each watching it closely. The cylinder was strapped down at two points to keep it from floating around inside the compartment. The shuttle was not built for comfort so it contained no form of artificial gravity. Both individuals wore magnetic boots that were securely attached to the deck floor.

The flight was short and the docking to the carrier took longer than the flight had. After the loud bang and vibration of metal against metal came the hiss of pressurization, which took several minutes to complete. Pressurization contained a minor sterilization component that was designed to flush the most common forms of contaminants into space. Because of the nature of this brief mission both individuals knew they would need to spend some time in quarantine. The pilots, because they remained sealed in the cockpit and had no contact with the cylinder, might be spared that annoyance.

The shuttle's external rear door opened slowly into a small cargo hold on the Ticonderoga that was four times the size of the actual shuttle. Waiting there were four more individuals wearing dark blue environmental suits. Between them was a padded cart with six wheels used for moving projectiles or coffins, depending upon the circumstances of the day. The cart was strapped securely to the cargo hold's floor.

The two individuals in the shuttle cargo compartment unlatched the cargo straps around the cylinder. The cylinder floated easily in the zero gravity. It took less than a minute to move the cylinder to the awaiting cart. With all six individuals working together they quickly latched the cylinder to the cart. The internal door closed and several yellow lights placed around the cargo hold began flashing as the warning klaxon sounded.

"Stand by for artificial gravity," said the recorded female voice over the speakers mounted in the corners of the room. "Artificial gravity introduction will begin in twenty seconds. Secure yourself and all items to the deck at the points indicated by the metal rings located at spaced intervals."

The warning continued as the individuals waited for gravity. The process was rather bizarre at first. If you failed to attach yourself with the magnetic boots, you floated along carelessly. As the gravity was introduced you drifted to the floor and gradually felt yourself pulled as your weight slowly increased. No one had ever been injured during the process but they could be if they were trapped beneath a heavy object. They were all professionals so safety came first.

Once gravity stabilized, the yellow lights and klaxon went off. The six individuals unlatched the cart from the floor and moved it toward the awaiting door across from the shuttle. This particular cargo hold was adjacent to the quarantine section of the ship and was used exclusively for isolation purposes.

"Damn, this thing is heavy," said the man tasked with pushing it. Four of the others stood on the sides and were steering while the last one opened the doors for them. The door opener held a security ID card at the end of a plastic encased steel wire attached to his wrist. He placed the ID card in front of a magnetic strip to the right side of the door and it opened slowly with a mechanical whir.

"Quit whining and get that thing in here," said the door opener, obviously the leader of the group.

"Yes sir."

It took a couple of tries to make the corner without bumping into any walls. The room was a sterile white color and two lab technicians, wearing white biological suits, stood there waiting. Next to the technicians was a table of tools and a computer built into the wall. As soon as the cylinder and cart came to a halt the two lab technicians went to work. The others left the chamber silently and the door opener closed and sealed the door behind them. With their task completed the six men headed to the quarantine room for decontamination.

A few minutes later the monitor on the back wall shifted from the United Earth logo to a picture of Captain Washington. His eyes had the somewhat sunken look of someone that had been on duty for far too long without sufficient rest.

"Sorry to interrupt you, Major, but I need to know what we've brought onto my ship. Any idea yet?" he asked dryly, trying desperately to sound friendly despite the tiredness he felt. He took a deep breath and held it as he struggled to relax himself. Everyone had a job to do and no one could work any faster than they possibly could, especially if he started yelling for immediate response and action. This war was wearing on his nerves.

"Yes Captain," replied one of the lab technicians as he walked to the view screen with his clipboard. "It's a coffin, of a sort."

"Some dead body? But that's not the standard UE coffin."

"Well, there's a plaque on one end which looks like a manufacturer plate complete with a model number and serial number. Final Resting Space Org. of San Diego California."

"San Diego, huh? Been there ... once."

"The other plaque on top is even more interesting. It contains ..." started the lab technician before he was interrupted by a voice behind the Captain. The Captain turned his head quickly offscreen.

"Damn, sound general quarters." He turned to the view screen. "Sorry Major, I'll get back to you. They found us again."

"Good luck, sir," replied the technician as the screen went black and the UE logo returned.

"Don't those freaks ever lay off?" asked the other lab technician.

"They've got us on the run. If they keep this up they just might win this war," replied the Major. He walked to the table and grabbed a magnifying unit.

"Not my idea of a fun time," said the lab technician.

"Nor mine, but there's nothing we can do about that right now, or ever. Let's see if we can find a way in. Indications are good that this thing may still be functional."

CHAPTER
3

Damn, they're closing fast," said Captain Washington while watching the red dots move across the screen. "Must not have support ships. Can we outrun them?"

"Not likely, sir," replied Commander Mito. "We have a crippled cargo ship that can only attain one SU. I estimate they'll be in attack range in two hours."

SU stood for Solar Unit, which was equal to one trillion kilometers. The UE ships used SU as a speed reference for transiting space and Mach for atmospheric flight. SU was used to measure both distance and speed, depending on the context, although Light Year was more widely accepted for longer distances. As a speed it related to traveling one trillion kilometers, one SU, in one hour. Light traveled at a little over one billion kilometers per hour, or almost nine point four trillion kilometers per year. Traveling at one SU it would take almost nine and a half hours to travel one Light Year. No ship could travel one Light Year in one hour, although the corvette class of ship came close with a nine SU maximum speed. Carriers, and most of the other capital ships, could attain five SU but rarely did so since their support ships could not. The cargo class of ships had a maximum speed of two SU.

"Order all hands to evacuate that damaged cargo ship and get as much of their cargo onto any capital ship that has room. They have ninety minutes."

"Aye aye, sir," replied Commander Frank Mito as he reached for the communication panel in front of him.

Captain Washington did not need to hear the order being passed down. Frank was a competent and trusted officer, and the best First Officer he ever had. He pressed the call button on the communication panel in front of his command chair and waited until a picture of a tired Lieutenant Colonel Terry Nelson appeared.

"Yes? Sir?"

"Terry, we've got an incoming attack force. Report to my wardroom as soon as you can."

"Yes sir, be right up." The viewer clicked off and Captain Washington shook his head slowly. At least one of them had gotten a little bit of sleep, because he had not.

*

Terry arrived at the wardroom five minutes later. The sleep still showed in his eyes and a tired look covered his face. There was never any rest for the weary and the entire Ticonderoga Battle Group was feeling the effects of it.

"How large is this enemy force, Jeff?" asked Terry. He still felt uncomfortable calling Captain Washington by his shortened first name, but the Captain insisted upon it for informal circumstances. Captain Washington wanted some kind of reprieve from constant military protocol. Terry filled a coffee cup with the wonderfully smelling black liquid. He did not bother adding anything to it, it would have taken too much time and effort.

"We don't know yet," said Jeff as he examined a piece of paper in front of him. "We have one cargo ship that is damaged and slowing us all down so I've ordered it abandoned. That won't help us much but every bit counts nowadays."

"Most of my pilots are green, just out of the Flight Academy. Seasoned pilots are a thing of the past and it can only get worse," said Terry as he watched the steam ascend from his cup of coffee. "This battle will probably cut our fighter force in half, if we're lucky."

"Damn, I didn't want to hear that," replied Jeff as he leaned back in his chair. The chair groaned in protest but remained solid. "At this speed we are still six weeks out from Virginia Prime. Those were our last replacement pilots before our scheduled arrival, and I had to call in a few favors to get those."

"It won't be long now," said Terry quietly as he took a sip of his coffee.

"Yes, it won't be. We'll be neck deep in alien shit by early next year."

Terry nodded in silent agreement. The war would be over soon and the outcome was bleak. No one knew what the aliens did with prisoners, but the general consensus throughout the galaxy was to not find out.

The two of them sat in silence and enjoyed their cups of coffee as much as they possibly could. After fifteen minutes had gone by, Jeff slowly stood.

"Well, Terry, let's get ready."

"Yes sir, I'll get every fighter we have available spaceborne. Maybe if we can go into the battle with four to one odds we won't get our asses kicked as badly."

"One could only hope," replied Jeff. "Keep Defend Squadron close to the carrier though and have them fly cover. The Ticonderoga took a beating the last time the enemy hit our Group. Put Reserve Squadron on cover for the rest of the capital and cargo ships."

"Jeff, Reserve Squadron is only four pilots now."

"Dammit, so much for that idea. Oh well, do what you can, Terry. Just get us through this so we can make it to Virginia Prime for rearm and refuel. I heard a rumor from a friend at Fleet Headquarters that we might be able to get some more capital ships for our Group."

"Really?"

"Unfortunately, we lost the McClary two days ago, along with more than half of her Battle Group and support ships before reinforcements arrived."

"My God," said Terry in shock. "I went to school with her Flight Group Commander. She is, was, a good pilot."

"Even the good are given the chance to die in this war, my friend. Let's concentrate on getting our asses safely to Virginia Prime so we can resupply. One small step at a time."

"Yes sir. I'll see you on the bridge, I'm heading to Flight Ops to get this ball rolling."

"Good luck, Terry."

*

Major Scott Carson examined his short-range scanner and sighed in frustration. The enemy force was two thirds the size of the human force. Those odds equated to a very messy fight for the humans, since they usually traded kill for kill on a good day. They could never win the war like that, no matter how hard they tried.

"Listen up everyone," said Major Carson over the short-range frequency, which had more than enough strength to reach all the fighters in both the Alert and Attack Squadrons. Major Carson was the highest-ranking flying pilot so he was in charge of coordinating the assault. He had a total of thirty-two fighters under his extended command and expected to lose twenty of those before the end of the hour.

"The enemy is going to try and hit the capital ships and Ticonderoga. Our job is to break them up and thin them out before they get to Defend and Reserve Squadrons. Hit the gumdrops first, they are the biggest threat. Keep the chatter to a minimum and try to remain on wingcom or the short-range frequency if you need to do any talking. Remember that the enemy can translate our language. Any questions?"

No one responded. They all knew what they had to do. Alert Squadron was the most seasoned of all the pilots on the carrier. The greenest of which had only been flying actual combat missions for three weeks.

The UE intelligence personnel were certain that all Fleet communication, including the encrypted and supposedly secure channels, were being intercepted and decoded instantaneously. Their only suggestion was to keep transmissions to a minimum and never say anything important over any frequency. The Major wanted to tell all those intelligence idiots to pull their heads out of their asses and find a real job, but he was sure that would only get him sent to the worst possible section of space that they could find. Which, these days, would not be a very difficult order to fulfill.

"Let's hit them and hit them hard," said Major Carson as he eased his throttles forward. The other Stilettos followed suit and advanced toward the enemy group.

The enemy ships split into two groups as the humans approached. There were a total of twenty slugs and eight gumdrops split evenly. One group headed for the approaching Stilettos while the other went for the cargo ships.

*

The odds for the humans today were in their favor, but the gumdrops were known to reduce that lead fairly quickly. The two groups merged and the eruption of missiles and laser fire flooded the scanners with more information than it could process. The outcome of the battle could neither be predicted nor the progress watched effectively. Everyone on the bridge waited in silence as the battle commenced.

"Sir, the second group of alien ships is approaching the cargo ships. It looks like they are lining up on the damaged ship that was abandoned," said the scanner operator.

"Good," replied Captain Washington. "Have Defend Squadron intercept and protect it like we care about it."

"Aye aye, sir," replied the communication officer. He transmitted a one word message over the command frequency, "Defend."

"Acknowledged," said Captain Silvio Brannick as his voice crackled over the speaker on the bridge. He was the leader of Defend Squadron and the third highest-ranking pilot on the Ticonderoga. Defend Squadron appeared on the scanner and approached the enemy group of fourteen ships. It would be an evenly-matched battle but an uneven outcome.

"Fire forward batteries," said Captain Washington. He heard the order echo in front of him as they were passed on to the gun crews. The carrier shook with the power dispersal as energy forced the projectiles down the rails and out into space. The shells trailed sparkling residual magnetism as they streaked toward their targets. Multiple explosions lit the darkness of space as shrapnel peppered the alien ships within range of the bursts. Only one alien ship was destroyed while several others took minor damage.

Four of the gumdrops let loose with a volley of missiles that easily destroyed an equal number of fighters. The other four gumdrops fired their missiles at the damaged cargo ship. All four missiles connected with the large ship and the damage was nearly critical.

"Let's just hope that the damage looks a lot less deadly than the enemy thinks. Depressurizing that ship should buy us some time, I hope."

"I sure hope so, sir," replied Lieutenant Colonel Nelson as he watched his fighters at work.

Alert and Attack Squadrons managed to remove two gumdrops and five slugs from the area on the first pass. The gumdrops ignored the fighters and fired a volley of missiles at the nearest cargo ship. The two missiles impacted the right engine exhaust port and ruptured the outboard nacelle, sending a stream of gas and plasma into space. The gumdrops were able to launch another volley before several Stilettos teamed up and successfully destroyed them. The second missile volley entered the damaged engine section and bounced around in the corridors before detonating near the fuel cells. A violent explosion blew the upper hull wide open and spread various fragments and bodies around the area.

Four gumdrops fired another volley at the abandoned cargo ship and it buckled under the explosions and blew apart. The shock wave caused the Ticonderoga to shake and Captain Washington had to steady himself with the nearest handrail.

"Increase speed to two SU."

"Aye aye, sir," replied the helmsman and communication officers in unison. The helmsman entered the new speed into the computer while the communication officer passed the order to the rest of the Carrier Group with one word, "Go."

Defend Squadron concentrated on the gumdrops and destroyed one but lost three Stilettos in the process. The three remaining gumdrops fired a volley of missiles at the closest cargo ship and turned to engage the Stilettos. The missiles impacted the cargo ship along the starboard hull and cracked a large section of metal off into space. Oxygen escaped rapidly taking along several crew members in the process. Secondary explosions signaled the end of that cargo ship as the remaining crew struggled to abandon ship.

"Come on Colonel Nelson, get your pilots working together," shouted Captain Washington.

"Yes sir," replied Lieutenant Colonel Nelson. He pressed the communication button and transmitted over the command frequency, "Regroup." He hoped that that one word would wake them up and get them coordinated. The majority of his pilots were fresh from the Flight Academy and this was their first actual combat mission. It would also be their last as the death toll increased.

Alert Squadron broke off from the remaining slugs and turned to assist Defend Squadron. Attack Squadron had a few problems taking out the final two slugs but with five-to-one odds in their favor they were successful.

Defend Squadron was taking a beating from their group of enemy ships. Seven slugs and three gumdrops remained but they had only nine Stilettos left. Another gumdrop was destroyed and two more Stilettos were lost before Alert Squadron arrived and removed the final two gumdrops from space.

"Not very pretty," said Captain Washington, "but successful."

"Yes sir," replied Lieutenant Colonel Nelson quietly as he lowered his head slowly. What did the Captain expect? Green pilots were fighting for their lives with less than half the training they used to receive. The Flight Academy syllabus was cut in half and the new pilots were expecting on-the-job training once they arrived at the carrier. The harsh reality of the lies being told usually sent seventy-five percent of the new pilots to their graves. Terry was running out of kind words to say about the new pilots to their families in the letters that he wrote to inform them of their loss. He had to resort to a standard form letter for the grim process. He shook his head to clear his mind so he could watch the battle finish playing out on the screen in front of him.

With six-to-one odds in their favor at this point it took ten minutes to clear out the remaining slugs. There was nothing good to write home about from this sloppy success. The enemy was roughly equal in skill to the human's most seasoned pilots, but that group of pilots was dwindling rapidly. The sad realities of war left a dry taste in Terry's mouth as he sighed softly.

CHAPTER

4

C leanup and repairs after the battle took six days and the final results were the same as they usually were, grim. Captain Washington entered his room and saw that the light on his communication
unit was flashing as he closed the door. Most people talked with him on the
bridge unless it was something important, and that concerned him. He
pressed the button as he sat in his chair and a text note indicated that one
message was left for him. He touched the *Play Now* button on the screen and
waited.

The picture changed to a white room with a dark gray cylinder lying in it.
The lab technician Major appeared and his message was succinct.

"Call me, sir."

The screen went blank and it took Captain Washington a few seconds to
remember what the hell was going on. There was a long cylinder on his ship
that was somebody's coffin. It was a badly misplaced burial in space. He
spent several minutes wondering what the Major had discovered and realized
that he was becoming stupid. He was running on empty and it was wearing

away at him. He needed a good long uninterrupted sleep lasting at least a day, or maybe more. That was probably asking too much though.

Captain Washington pressed the *Return Call* button on the screen and waited. It took more seconds than normal but the screen changed colors and an office scene appeared. The Major sat behind the desk and looked as tired as he did. The marine khakis were wrinkled and he had not shaved in a couple of days. *He most likely spends every waking moment working*, thought Captain Washington, glad that he did not have to be in the same office as the Major. The air down there was probably rather ripe regardless of how well the ventilation system worked.

"Ah, Captain. I was wondering when you would call. It's been almost a week since I left you that message."

"Hmm, I think it has been that long since I've seen my room," shot Captain Washington with a struggled laugh.

"Sorry sir, I'm too tired to laugh."

"Fair enough. We are a month out from Virginia Prime. I'm going to try desperately to get us some shore leave. I think everyone could use it."

"Thank you, sir. I hope I can finish by then."

"I guess that depends on what you've found," said Captain Washington as he leaned back in his chair. "What did you find?"

"Well, right before we were attacked I was about to tell you that this coffin holds a man that died quite some time ago."

"Are we talking ten or twenty years, or a hundred?"

"More ... three hundred and twenty-eight years to be exact. The exact date of death, indicated by the plaque, is October thirteenth, two thousand and nineteen. It is extremely odd and somewhat eerie in a way at how close that date and ours are together, minus the year of course."

"Damn," replied Captain Washington.

"Not exactly the same word I used, but close enough."

"So, what are you doing with him?"

"Well, Captain, since you were busy with a battle and then ignored me for a week I took it upon myself to do the only thing that made any sense whatsoever. I cracked open the case. Surprisingly I discovered that this coffin was actually an ancient cryogenic storage cylinder. I removed his body and placed him into one of our cryogenic capsules."

Captain Washington frowned and the Major saw it, but both knew it was too late for any argument concerning his actions. The Major would not have done it if he thought any harm could come to the ship. Captain Washington was certain of that.

"It's okay, Captain. I mean, I did all sorts of tests for radioactivity, carcinogens, biological or chemicals, and anything else I could think of. I ran them three times just to be certain and had the results cross-checked by two different people. Then I sealed the case up and turned off the power unit."

"So, now what would you like to do?" asked Captain Washington as he felt like a pawn in this game. The Major was leading up to something. He knew the man to be cautious and intelligent. He was also a very dedicated scientist with a background in medicine. Why someone became a doctor just to further his own scientific studies was way beyond the reasoning of a simple Combat Group Commander. At least that was the way the Captain looked at it.

"Captain, I can fix him."

"Bullshit?" came out as a question before Captain Washington could think of a more proper response.

"No sir, I really can."

"But he's dead."

"But, from my studies, it wasn't a natural death, or a violent one either. I examined his body before placing him into our cryo-capsule. There was no sign of trauma either, blunt or puncture. A full body scan indicates that there is no degradation of any of his internal organs either. His brain scan shows very minimal activity as if his body went into some kind of hyper-hibernation sequence."

"That sounds familiar," replied Captain Washington.

"Very good memory sir, I see you do recall some history. Without going too far in depth with an explanation I'll try to summarize. The Bectolothians used a highly poisonous substance at the Orion peace talks. This had the effect of killing everyone there, including their own ambassador, or so we thought. The poison induced a total system slowdown up to the point that it appeared to kill the subject. There was very minimal brain activity that no one could explain. So everyone there was given a funeral except the Earth President, who they cryogenically froze for study."

"Oh my God," said Captain Washington. "Are you telling me that they cremated everyone there and they were still alive?"

"Well, yes, barely alive. The technology at the time indicated that they were all dead, so they did the only thing they could." The Major dug into a pile of papers on the corner of his desk. He flipped quickly until he made it to a section of yellow papers and then moved a lot slower until he found what he was looking for. He tapped at a particular line and held it up to the screen.

"Here is the report from one of the autopsies. These brain waves, indicated right here," he tapped the paper, "are identical to these ..." He put that paper down and opened a folder in front of him. He held it up so the Captain could see it. Then he held up the other one so the Captain could see the two together. "See how they map the same way?"

Captain Washington nodded blankly, not really seeing what he was supposed to see in those lines. He grasped the general idea behind what the Major was saying and knew where he was going with it. But there were still many unanswered questions. Too many puzzles and not enough answers. Lack of sleep was getting the better of him and his brain started to hurt more so than usual.

"So, what happened to the President?"

"Fifty years later some scientists analyzed the poison found in a captured Bect's luggage while he was trying to attend a very large and public dinner. The chemical matched that residing in the cells of the President so they created a cure for the poison and tried to revive him."

The Captain nodded slowly as he remembered the botched attempt at revival. It was all over the news for almost two months. The scientists cured the poison and the defrosting process was begun. Cryo-technology at that point was still being refined and water crystals formed in every cell of his body. As the temperature increased the crystals melted and the body became confused. There was much more water than there should have been so the organs began shutting down. The President died for real at that point.

"I remember that fiasco," said Captain Washington. "So, how can you fix this one?"

"I've already started the process. The poison is still in his system because I wanted to wait for your approval before administering the costly antidote. By transferring him to our cryo-capsule, along with the introduction of some common drugs, it will help to prevent the crystallization from worsening. I haven't started the revival drug process yet, once again I'm waiting for your approval."

"That's a tough call."

"That's why you're the captain, sir."

"Yes, and the way this war is going maybe this guy is better off dead."

"Then again," started the Major as he leaned closer to the screen. "Maybe this is the puzzle piece that you've been looking for."

"What do you mean?" asked Captain Washington while he absently scratched his chin. He was pretty sure he had not fallen asleep somewhere during the conversation but felt like he had missed something important along the way.

"Sir, we are losing the war, everybody knows that. Then we just happen to find a tiny coffin floating around in the vastness of space that contains a three hundred some-odd year old man that died of a poison that hadn't even been discovered for another two hundred years? It's a Bect poison! How did it get there over one hundred years before we even encountered the Bect race? And, more importantly, why him? Plus, if my history is correct, the common form of funeral in his time period was a burial in the ground after having all the blood drained from your body and some preservation chemical pumped in. How did he get himself frozen and shot into space? I'm sure that rocket travel was not a very common thing at that point in history either. There are too many bizarre coincidences for me to ignore the facts on this one. I don't particularly care to acknowledge divine intervention but this certainly sounds like it to me. If this isn't Fate screaming out to be noticed then I don't know what is."

The Major leaned back in his chair and stretched his neck. He was tired from all the long hours of studying that coffin and its dormant occupant. He kept finding more and more questions and his brain hurt from all the possibilities. But it was his project and he wanted to see it to the end. He wanted to revive this man and find out who the hell he is and was. Maybe this man had some answers.

"What would you like to do?" asked Captain Washington in a subdued voice. Yes, there were many questions to be answered and many things that probably never could be. But this was his carrier, his Group, and his responsibility.

"Sir, first off I'd want to keep him on-board when we hit Virginia Prime. That means the quarantine works both ways. Nobody there can have any access to him whatsoever. I don't want this pet project to pass into someone else's hands. I *know* I can bring him back. After that we keep him in quarantine until we are certain that he poses no risks to the crew."

"What about risks unseen? What if he's a psychopath or some bizarre Bect plot to kill us all? Not trying to sound paranoid but instead to be the voice of reason."

"There are tests for both things, sir. I will use all the tests I can find or make up and will comply with any request you have to ensure our safety, the safety of the ship, and the safety of the entire human race."

"I'll need that in writing," said Captain Washington with a blank look on his face. The Major paused and stared at the screen until the Captain began laughing. The Major joined him and they both shook their heads. "Sorry, it has been a long week and I needed a good laugh."

"Me too, sir. I'll keep you posted on my progress. I'll give you a detailed verbal report every day if you'd like and more often if something really unusual comes up. Is that okay with you, sir?"

"Yes, Major. What about his coffin?"

"Oh yes, I almost forgot about that. We don't need it anymore so feel free to eject it at the nearest sun or black hole."

"Consider it done, and thank you Major."

"Thank you, Captain. Let's find out what Fate has in store for us."

"Yes, let's."

Captain Washington closed the connection and walked to his bed, sitting on the edge to remove his boots. He did not bother undressing and just stretched out on the blanket and closed his eyes. If sleep could not find him like this then there was no amount of comfort that would help.

November
2347

CHAPTER

5

Major Bill Dorney examined the results to his latest tests and smiled. Two weeks had gone by and everything was progressing nicely. Every single test had near perfect results and he was growing nervous. This was too good, too much like the textbook best case scenario. He documented everything he was doing and made copies that he secured each night. Most of the things he did were what he had learned in school or from obscure texts that others had left behind or ignored. He consulted various sources for more information to make certain that he had not forgotten anything. A mistake now could cause a rather messy death for an already dead man. That thought boggled his mind.

He filled another syringe with a light-blue fluid called dyptotherium. It acted like a moisture magnet that traveled along with the blood, collecting ice crystals. The man currently had a pulse somewhere around one heartbeat every hour, which was still nearly impossible to detect. A body could not be kept alive with that little blood flow. Because of the nature of the poison, the body would last for a few days without assistance but after that there was not much anyone could do.

Bill needed to have six syringes ready for immediate use during the revival process. As soon as the heart reached one beat per minute he needed to inject the fluid into the aorta. The thaw-out needed to be as prolonged as feasible so that the fluid had time to remove all of the ice crystals that had formed. He would need to check the blood under a microscope to determine if it were clear enough for progression to the next step. Luckily he found a document in his personal library that was written by some radical scientist detailing the process in the manner of a personal diary. Bill racked his brain trying to figure out how and why he had saved that, and where he had ever found it in the first place. Fate had a very big hand in this, putting the pieces into place a long time ago.

Bill carefully placed the six syringes into a hard plastic box with felt-lined indentations for each. He closed and latched the box before placing it into his small floor safe. That fluid was a vital component and he would take no chances with it.

He walked to the vertical capsule full of cryogenic fluid with a suspended body in it. There were several tubes plugged into the man and various electrodes to monitor bodily functions, of which there were very few. The new cryogenic process did not use what most people considered freezing as the technique. It did not turn the body into an ice cube like the original process had. It contained a liquid that was below freezing but not overly so. The move from the ancient cryogenics to the new one actually warmed the man's body and started the thawing process.

"So, Mister Iceman, have any good stories to tell?"

*

"Sir, we're picking up an enemy contingent on the outer edge of our long-range scanners," said the female Lieutenant Junior Grade on duty. The Ticonderoga Group was on the run from an equal-sized enemy force. They had lost three support ships at the end of the past month and at least two dozen fighters in that same battle. Most of the new replacements already needed to be replaced, and they had not even been aboard for a month of deployment. Some had died before even seeing the carrier on their scanners.

"Wake up the Captain," said Commander Mito. He did not like to wake the Captain so soon after he had left the bridge but if he knew the old man, he had never fallen asleep.

"The Captain is on his way, sir," replied the Lieutenant Junior Grade.

"Thank you." He did not know why he said the nicety but it felt right. Everyone's nerves were near to being shot from all the fighting and running. Just a few kind words might make the difference some day, or at least that was what he believed.

Commander Frank Mito was a short man at one hundred and sixty-one centimeters tall. He was of Japanese descent and just another in the long line of warriors that went back over one thousand years. He was slim and muscular, from visiting the ship's gym almost daily, with dark brown hair in a crew cut.

"Whose bright idea was it to wake me up?" asked Captain Washington as he stormed onto the bridge. He glanced at all the tired faces as he stopped next to Commander Mito.

"I did sir," replied Commander Mito.

"It figures," said Captain Washington. The Commander smiled and nodded, knowing that the banter was just an attempt to lighten things up.

"We've got incoming unknown craft."

"Sound general quarters," replied Captain Washington as he examined the scanner screen. Unknown craft most likely meant Bect. Even if they were not it was always better to treat them as if they were.

The alarm for general quarters sounded as the red lights began flashing. It was still early in the morning according to the clock on the wall, although in space everything was night, or day, depending on your perspective.

"Do you have a count yet?" asked Captain Washington as he peered out the front window. Ahead was a small moon circling a green planet with long white streaks mixed in.

"Sir, I show the signatures of ten fighters, two bombers, and one cruiser-class capital ship ... all confirmed hostile," replied the scanner operator.

"Where did they come from?"

"Sir, direction of flight indicates they possibly came from the moon just to the right side of the planet."

"So, they weren't from the group following us?"

"Negative sir. Maybe a local patrol group called by the others?" asked the Ensign cautiously. Most likely the Captain was not asking a question but just voicing his thoughts, but the Ensign was young and did not know any better.

"Maybe. Maybe sent in to slow us down so the others can catch up." Captain Washington turned around and walked to his Flight Group Commander, who was yawning absently while standing near the door.

"What do you think, Colonel?"

"I think you're right, sir," replied Lieutenant Colonel Nelson while nodding. "They had our last position and knew our direction of flight, and communication has always been faster than travel."

"Can your pilots handle this?" asked Captain Washington as he cracked his knuckles.

"Yes sir," replied Lieutenant Colonel Nelson a bit quicker than he had wanted to. Thirteen alien ships would not be a walk in the park but they had no other choice but to win, somewhere and somehow. Even if by accident.

"Then do it," said Captain Washington as he turned to the view screen. The alien ships were straight ahead and closing fast. "Have the rail gun crews begin firing when the aliens are in range. Maybe we can thin them out a bit."

"Aye aye, sir," said the Ensign. He pressed a button on the panel in front of him and his voice came over the combat intercom. "Gun crews, commence firing when the enemy is in range then secure and proceed with defensive mode as our fighters engage."

Within minutes the carrier shook from the recoil of firing the high-energy rail gun. Massive amounts of power charged the magnetic fields used to accelerate the huge proximity projectiles along the energized rails and out of the fore and cheek tubes. The projectiles streaked across the distance with a single purpose. At a preprogrammed distance, estimated with laser optics, they burst apart sending shrapnel in random directions in the target area. One explosion was within three meters of an alien ship and shredded it into several large pieces. The remaining shrapnel hit the two alien bombers, but their energy shields absorbed the majority of the force.

*

"Okay boys and girls. No guts, no glory," said Major Scott Carson as Alert Squadron formed up two kilometers from the carrier.

"No guts, no blood pressure," said Second Lieutenant John Bowyer over the wingcom. It was supposed to be used for wingman specific commands during combat but usually became a bullshitting channel. During combat there was always too much going on to actually use it effectively, although there were instances where its use was essential. John and Carlos knew each other well enough after all the combat flying together, so they knew when they could bullshit and when it should be all business.

"Yeah, and no more sex," replied Carlos.

"Sex? What's that?" shot John. It was the running joke between the two of them, since John found very little free time to actually attempt chasing women. He was still trying to play catch-up with his truncated flight school. There was so much to learn about these fighters and combat tactics that he was certain the task was impossible. But he tried, a lot harder than all of the new pilots combined.

Carlos brought his fighter alongside the Alert Five crew. Their flight of eight fighters, Alert Five through Eight with one wingman each, would angle off to the right and try to flank the enemy. Hopefully they could get by the fighter escort and take on the bombers. That was the plan and all plans fell apart as soon as combat began.

"Break," said Major Carson over the command frequency. The group of sixteen fighters broke into two flights. One flight was hoping to draw off enough of the fighters that the other flight could concentrate on the bombers. But the alien force did something different this time. Their formation split into two groups and headed for each flight, ignoring the carrier and its cargo ships completely.

Carlos saw the problem immediately. Four fighters and a bomber turned toward them while the other group of aliens turned toward the First Alert Flight. The cargo ships were not the targets this time ... they were. He figured the alien strategy was now to reduce the fighter protection so the bigger ships would be easy prey.

"Um, Carlos," said John in a rather concerned voice over the wingcom. The combat strategy books that were required reading, but left untouched during the Flight Academy, were still fresh on his mind.

"Yeah, I know," replied Carlos. "Try your baby?"

"Roger that."

"Okay, shuck and duck."

Both Carlos and John pulled back their throttles. The other six fighters in their flight slowly pulled ahead of them. Carlos figured it would take just a couple of seconds before the Flight Group Commander started chewing their asses. It took less time than that.

"Alert Six, get back in formation!" yelled Lieutenant Colonel Nelson over the command frequency.

"No way sir, they're coming after *us* this time," responded Carlos. He tried to make his voice sound as scared as possible, which was not too far of a stretch. He calmly nosed his fighter over and John stayed close on his right wing as they increased their negative incline.

"I'll hang your ass for this, Lieutenant. Get back in formation immediately!"

"Now," said Carlos over the wingcom as he pushed his throttles forward to the stops. Both fighters increased speed and quickly closed the distance to the combat area. He pulled back on the control stick slightly and leveled off at a negative three incline as they watched the rest of their flight pass by above them. The six fighters had just closed within range of the four slugs as the laser firing commenced.

"Now," said Carlos, as the laser beams sprayed the space above them. They both pulled back sharply and aimed for the gumdrop. As soon as their ships changed direction the gumdrop initiated a rapid turn to the right. It figured correctly but was too late for effective evasion.

"Engage," shouted Carlos before he realized he was wrapped up in all the excitement. He never expected this to be as easy as it was. This would probably be the last time they could use this plan, either the aliens would smarten up or the Lieutenant Colonel would ground them.

Carlos depressed his weapon release button twice and his two high-speed

Devrac-Two missiles shot right into the energy shield of the gumdrop. A flash of light quickly dissipated while the gumdrop rocked violently from the shock. John's missiles were a fraction of a second behind his and they passed through the space that was a shield just moments before. They impacted the bottom side of the gumdrop and tore a giant hole in the craft. The oxygen, or whatever gas it was that the alien's breathed, shot out of the hole and into space.

Carlos and John continued their attack and fired several laser blasts into the dying ship, causing it to break up even more. As they passed the gumdrop they assessed the damage and deemed it a kill.

*

"Well, that worked," said Captain Washington as he watched the battle on the view screen.

"Insolent bastard," Lieutenant Colonel Nelson grunted under his breath.

"I am not," replied Captain Washington with a chuckle.

"Oh no, sorry sir. That Lieutenant has been a pain in my ass since he got here. He always does as little as he can get away with. I should string him up for his attitude."

"I don't recommend that, not after what he just did."

"I know," said Lieutenant Colonel Nelson with a sigh. "But without discipline ..."

"Yeah, I know ... blah blah blah."

Lieutenant Colonel Nelson laughed.

"Unfortunately we need creative thinkers and doers if we want to have any hope at all to beating these freaks," said Captain Washington as he stretched his neck and sighed.

"This war is wearing on all of us," replied Lieutenant Colonel Nelson as he nodded.

"Well, he's under your command, so it's your decision."

"But Jeff, what would you do?" whispered Lieutenant Colonel Nelson, so as not to be heard by anyone nearby.

"That's easy, Terry, promote him," replied Captain Washington quickly and without further thought.

"Promote him? Why?"

"That pilot just disobeyed orders, broke formation and jeopardized his entire squadron. He ignored a direct order with flagrant insubordination, and successfully destroyed a gumdrop before it took out any of our fighters. He was obviously aware of the enemy intercepting our command frequency so he used the ruse of running away, thus tricking the enemy into ignoring him. His wingman apparently trusted him enough to follow him. I think he might make a good leader. How long has he been a wingleader?"

"A little over a month."

"Wow. Okay, so he's rather fresh. This is war, so the rules get bent. I'd bend them all if I thought it would do any good. You don't have to decide now. He might get himself killed before this is over."

Terry nodded as he watched the view screen. There was still one more bomber out there and a cruiser that was holding back.

*

"Good plan John, let's go help our flight," said Carlos. The smile on his face was overly large. Success was very uplifting.

"Roger that, thanks."

Both ships looped over and pointed at the fight below. Their flight had lost two fighters and the enemy still had three fighters left. They would have lost a lot more if that bomber had had a chance to launch at them. Carlos picked out the nearest fighter, targeted it on his combat computer, and headed for it. An on-board laser shot a tight, one-kilobit, encrypted and scrambled beam to John's ship. His on-board computer decoded the information and displayed the target for him. All this occurred in just a fraction of a second. Instantaneous Combat Information System, ICIS, is what the manufacturer called it.

Carlos opened fire on the slug, sending a stream of laser energy into the ship. The blue light beams streaked across space toward the alien allowing the pilot to adjust his flight path for better placement. The slugs did not have energy shields like the gumdrops had, so the lasers blew several holes into the topside of the ship. Carlos kept filling the slug with energy as the distance closed until the slug blew apart when its fuel ignited. The slug never turned toward him or away from him so it probably had no idea that Carlos was there.

John saw the slug pop. He angled a bit to the right, away from Carlos, and put as many laser shots as he could into the nearest slug before reforming on Carlos' wing. John did not disable the enemy fighter but softened it up for the next guy. Sometimes that was all it took to give somebody an easy kill. John did not care about scoring kills though, nobody did. They just wanted all of the alien craft destroyed by any pilot available.

Carlos did not shout out in glee for the destroyed enemy fighter. There would be time enough for that back on the carrier. Then the stories would fly and the egos would bloat. There were at least two more slugs nearby, and he did not know how the other flight was doing.

Carlos turned his ship around and lined up for another pass. He picked a target but seconds later it disintegrated. He moved to the next one and tracked it but the slug was on the defensive. It was being followed by Major Carson and two other fighters while two more Stilettos were watching the action from nearby.

The slug tried to run but when it turned Major Carson lit it up in blue laser light and it burst open. Several pieces began spinning out of control and the following Stilettos struggled to evade the fragments. One piece impacted the left engine of Major Carson's wingman, fouling the internal workings. A blast of plasma erupted through the engine nacelle causing the fighter to veer to the left and into Major Carson's fighter. The nose of the wingman's Stiletto removed Major Carson's right engine and wing, knocking his fighter into an uncontrolled roll. Before the wingman had time to pull his throttles back and regain control, the engine vibration increased until the engine mount failed and the engine nacelle separated from his fighter. Another flash of light and the tail section burst into subdued flames.

"Get out!" shouted Carlos over the short-range frequency. He was more than one kilometer from the dying ships and hoped he was within range to be heard.

The wingman ejected, his armored and sealed cockpit ejection compartment violently being pushed away from the fuselage on rocket motors. The damaged and unmanned ship forcefully impacted the rolling Stiletto piloted by Major Carson and blew apart seconds later, sending chunks of molten metal in various directions which quickly froze. Major Carson never knew what hit him and he and the two Stilettos disintegrated in a giant ball of flaming gas that quickly extinguished in the void of space. Breaking thrusters on the top front and rear of the cockpit ejection compartment fired to halt the unit nearby.

Carlos sighed and shrugged at the loss, there was nothing he could have done. He moved his throttles slowly forward and turned to the right with John following him. They headed for the other flight, which was now down to five fighters. There was only one slug left and it did not last very long. He checked his long-range scanner and the cruiser was nowhere to be seen, but that told him very little. The damn scanner would sometimes omit a moon that filled most of his front window.

*

"Where did that cruiser go?" asked Captain Washington of no one in particular.

"Sir, about halfway through the battle the cruiser ducked behind the nearest moon and we lost track of it. It must have run off using planetary shadows for cover," replied Commander Mito as he struggled to keep track of everything happening on the battlefield. Some battles were next to impossible to follow so he delegated as much as he could.

"Tell me when all fighters and any stray pilots are recovered," replied Captain Washington.

"Aye aye, sir," replied the Ensign sitting at the flight operations station.

"Navigation, update our course for Virginia Prime."

"Aye aye, sir," replied the Lieutenant Junior Grade at the navigation computer. The woman pulled up her database of the local section of the galaxy and opened the search engine. She tapped a few of the choices on the screen and waited. A nearby star began flashing and she tapped that, which caused the view to zoom in. She selected the base on the planet and tapped the *Set Course* button. "Course set for Virginia Prime, sir."

"Sir, all fighters and pilots have been recovered," said the Ensign at flight operations.

"Helm," said Captain Washington as he turned and looked out the front window. "Take us to Virginia Prime at two SU."

"Virginia Prime at two. Aye aye, sir," responded the Ensign at the helm. He pressed the *Initiate* button on his screen and selected the number two, then pressed *Go*. At a speed of two SU it would take them one week to reach the base. This was, hopefully, more than enough time to determine if they were still being followed.

"Sir," started the communication officer, "the rest of the Group has acknowledged the order and is following."

"Very good. Colonel Nelson, damage report."

"We lost seven Stilettos sir, and six pilots, including the Alert Squadron leader, Major Carson. Three other fighters are moderately damaged and the repairs have been started. Request permission to check on things, sir," said Lieutenant Colonel Nelson as he stood.

"Permission granted."

Lieutenant Colonel Nelson nodded and turned toward the portside door.

CHAPTER
6

L ieutenant Colonel Terry Nelson stopped at the centerline tram station. The *Next Tram* sign indicated a twenty-two second wait so he glanced at the printout again. Seven more ships lost, out of sixteen. It was damn near a fifty percent attrition rate of pilots and equipment. They entered that battle with the odds slightly in their favor. At the rate that skilled pilots were dying in fights where they outnumbered the enemy it would not be long before the war was over. They were replacing equipment as fast as they were replacing pilots. The equipment stayed the same quality, but the pilots were younger and less skilled. Flight training was down to just two months now and the pilots shipped out for their first duty station expecting to receive some on-the-job training before being thrown into battle. That rarely happened anymore. They were either self-taught or dead.

Terry knew that Second Lieutenant John Bowyer had checked out several flight and combat manuals from the ship's library. He also had never seen Bowyer anywhere having a beer or gambling or playing various video games in the recreation hall. He was one of the few pilots that took learning seriously, unlike his wingleader, First Lieutenant Carlos Mendez. Even though they worked well together it might be a good idea to split them up just so Mendez's attitude did not rub off on Bowyer.

The tram pulled into the station and a few people stepped off of it. The tram had no doors and Terry climbed aboard and sat. It only took a few minutes to walk to the Flight Operations area in the lower center of the carrier but he did not feel like walking there. He needed more time to think before dealing with his flight crews without being concerned about which way to turn so he did not end up in the chow hall.

The tram did not move very fast, only as fast as a normal walk. It just made getting from one part of the ship to the other a little lazier. The tram stopped a few times and people shifted on and off of it. There was still a lot of activity and that would never end. He recognized a few of the people and they nodded in his direction but because he was sitting saluting was unnecessary. He did not really know anyone else on the carrier outside of his command circle for there was never enough time. During a war it was all work and no play. Some found time for playing but he never could.

Terry stood at the next stop, exited the tram, and headed for Flight Operations. He turned the corner and two armed guards saluted him as he approached. They wore battle dress uniforms and had laser pistols on their hips. It was not one of the more secure areas of the ship so that was all that was required. They checked his ID badge despite seeing him every single day. That was their orders and he was glad to see discipline maintained somewhere on the ship. Lack of respect was something he would never tolerate, but he was told to accept it because this was war. Maybe a promotion would straighten Mendez out, maybe it would not. It was a tough call and lives depended upon it. He had to come up with some kind of plan for that man.

The guards opened the door and Terry walked down the hallway to his office. He grabbed an item from a desk drawer and continued to the squadron bunk areas. The yelling increased slightly as he walked silently into an ass-chewing session. It was never a wise thing to chew someone's ass out while others were present, unless of course it was used as a training tool. It was at this point that Terry formulated his plan.

"Mister hot shot here tried to get us all killed by disobeying orders," yelled Captain Julie Runzik, in command of Second Alert Flight. "I'll have you scraping shit out of the latrines until hell freezes over ..."

"Flight Group Commander on deck!" shouted a Second Lieutenant that noticed Lieutenant Colonel Nelson walking into the room. This made everyone within earshot stop what he or she was doing and stand at attention. No one made a move or spoke until the officer in question allowed him or her to. It was at this point that the superior officer had control of a situation and could do what they liked.

Lieutenant Colonel Nelson walked amongst the officers in the room inspecting them without saying a word. He knew this would raise the tension in the room to extremely high levels and he felt that this bunch needed it. A good ass-chewing sometimes needed another one to even things out, but he was not in the mood today. Too many ships were lost, too many pilots were dead, and there were too many letters home to be written.

"Colonel ..." started Captain Runzik.

Lieutenant Colonel Nelson cut her off by raising his hand and shaking his head. "Quiet, I like quiet, so let's just keep it that way for a while," said Lieutenant Colonel Nelson. This raised the tension a notch further. The pilots all knew that someone was going to be reamed ten ways to Sunday. As he continued walking around the room several wondered how many of them were on his list. The list appeared to be growing and he might take the whole bunch of them apart. He stopped and sat on the corner of the table in the center of the room.

"Captain Runzik, you are now Alert Squadron leader. Any problems with that?" asked Lieutenant Colonel Nelson.

"No sir. Thank you, sir," replied Captain Runzik.

"I should rip some of you apart," said Lieutenant Colonel Nelson as he paused for effect. "I would probably enjoy it too. But there is a higher purpose here for all of us. Some of you can't see it, but I can. This war ... we are losing badly. It's just a matter of time, of attrition. Every confrontation results in close to fifty percent losses for us. Soon there will be nothing left to lose fifty percent of."

The newest members of the squadron looked a bit frightened and Lieutenant Colonel Nelson noted this. His speech was meant as a reality check, a wake up call for the living to stay alive and to keep fighting. If you thought you were doing well this speech would slap you down to reality. If you knew things were bad then it would get everything out into the open so that you could see it instead of ignoring it.

"Many of you were tricked into believing that training would be here waiting for you. The Flight Academy was accelerated and the hours required were reduced. Hell, your first day on the carrier you were probably thrown right into a cockpit and thrust into battle before you even had a chance to find your bunk, or take a piss."

Lieutenant Colonel Nelson paused once again and lowered his head with a sigh. The grim truth was painful and the looks on some of the young faces in the room attested to that.

"Today, even though losses were way too high, one good thing came out of it. Most of you probably didn't recognize this. It was something very subtle. One of their bombers didn't even get off a shot. That has never happened before. Never! Usually a bomber will get one or two, or sometimes four of us before we can take it down. Those are the cold hard facts." He looked around the room and paused briefly on various faces.

"Did anyone notice that cruiser?" He still had not released them from standing at attention so nobody answered him, but he could see the looks on their faces change.

"That's right, hard to miss that monstrosity. Where did it go? After that bomber was destroyed it ran off in a hurry. Most likely to report a new tactic that we've developed that might threaten the war for them." He paused again before changing subjects.

"Am I happy that orders were disobeyed? Not only no, but hell no. Discipline *must* be maintained. Orders *must* be followed. Do you all understand that?"

"Yes sir," yelled everyone in unison.

"Lieutenant Mendez, front and center," said Lieutenant Colonel Nelson loudly.

First Lieutenant Carlos Mendez turned sharply and marched to the Lieutenant Colonel. He snapped to attention and saluted. Lieutenant Colonel Nelson returned the salute from his casual sitting position. What he was about to do usually stayed behind closed doors but he was on a roll and felt that this would benefit everyone in the room. The pilots needed a reality check and this seemed like the perfect opportunity.

"Why did you separate from your flight against orders?"

"Sir, I wanted to try something and it worked," replied Carlos.

"Yes it did, but the results don't justify disobeying an order. Where did you come up with that idea?"

"Uh," stammered Carlos.

"Lieutenant?"

"It wasn't my idea, sir."

"And? Do I have to wait all day for a complete answer to my question?"

"My wingman, sir. Lieutenant Bowyer came up with it."

"Lieutenant Bowyer, where did you come up with that idea?" asked Lieutenant Colonel Nelson as he leaned to the side to look around Mendez and at the Lieutenant.

"Uh," replied Second Lieutenant John Bowyer.

"Not you too. Don't worry, Lieutenant, I'm saving the ass-chewing for later."

"Sir, I've been reading the tactician manuals, combat manuals, and other required reading that I never had a chance to read while in the Flight Academy."

"Are you insane?" shot Lieutenant Colonel Nelson in a half shout. "Why aren't you out there having sex, drinking beer, gambling, playing games, and whatever the hell else is going on during everyone's abundant free time?"

"I want to live, sir."

"You want to live? Well, Lieutenant, so do I. Good job and keep hitting those books as much as you want to." Lieutenant Colonel Nelson tossed him a small package.

John barely caught it because he was off guard. He opened the package slowly and saw the two sets of a single silver bar within. It was his first battlefield promotion and he looked askance at the Lieutenant Colonel.

"Congratulations, First Lieutenant Bowyer. You're also moving to act as wingleader of Alert Six."

"Thank you, sir," said John, somewhat confused but relieved. Alert Six wingleader was currently Carlos' position and John wondered how deep a hole Carlos had dug. He did not care much for being a wingleader and having to watch out for some greenie but the recognition was good. He just hoped that the added duty would not cut into his study time very much.

"Oh, one thing though. Don't you ever try out any more ideas without first clearing it with the proper chain of command. I want every single idea given careful consideration before it is used or discarded. Imagine the outcome had your idea been approved and *both* gumdrops had been taken out without firing a single missile. The only way we'll ever win this damn war is by outsmarting those freaks and we can't do that if we just sit around and take it in the ass. Is that clear?"

"Yes sir," replied everyone in unison.

"On the plus side, we are destroying enemy ships. We just need to do that without losing an equal number of our own in the process. Ships can be replaced even though they cost a lot. Pilots, well ... I don't like anyone dying for any reason, not even if it is for a good cause. Martyrdom still leaves a corpse and corpses smell. Got it!"

"Yes sir."

"Dismissed. Get some chow and relax, we're one week out from Virginia Prime for rearm and refit."

"Yes sir," the pilots dispersed and headed for the showers. It was not very often that they visited a base. That usually meant some shore leave however short it may be. Feeling real gravity even for a short while made a world of difference to most of them. This news raised their spirits some although the sadness would come when they saw the empty bunks of their fallen comrades.

"Lieutenants Mendez and Bowyer, please come with me to my office," said Lieutenant Colonel Nelson while still in his business voice. Both lieutenants snapped to attention and followed him down the hallway. They turned the corner and entered the second room on the left, which was the Flight Group Commander's office. Both men followed him in and stood at attention in front of his desk. Lieutenant Colonel Nelson slammed the door closed behind them and walked behind his desk.

"At ease. Do you have anything to say before I start chewing some ass?" asked Lieutenant Colonel Nelson with a grin on his face. He did not care if they noticed because he was serious and it was time for a wake-up call for Mendez.

"Sir," began Carlos immediately, "it was John's plan but I gave the order. I am the wingleader, so I take full responsibility."

"Wow, that's a first," said Lieutenant Colonel Nelson as he pulled out his chair and sat. He pulled a pad over and began writing on it. "What is wrong with you, Lieutenant?" He really wanted to know what had changed with this young pilot. Maybe his speech worked better than he had originally thought. Mendez had never thought about anyone but himself and had never used initiative in combat before. He was a capable pilot but never really showed much leadership ability until today. Maybe his new girlfriend had cut him off or dumped him. War was hell, and love was even worse, he could attest to that. Maybe having his wingman promoted out from under him and into his current flight position helped.

"Sir, I think I'm defective," said Carlos.

"Either that or crazy. What should I do with you? What would you do with you?"

"Uh, I don't know, sir," replied Carlos a bit worried.

"Here are some options. I could ground you, throw you in the brig, give you latrine duty, bust you down to second lieutenant, transfer you to another carrier, or I could probably think up some even nastier things." Lieutenant Colonel Nelson began tapping his pen on the pad as he leaned back in his chair. Now it was time to let that sit and gestate before he continued because sometimes things fixed themselves.

Carlos opened his mouth and took a deep breath to speak but Lieutenant Colonel Nelson cut him off.

"I've got the perfect idea," said Lieutenant Colonel Nelson as he threw the pen and pad on the desk. He stood quickly and walked to the window. He looked out at the stars for several seconds before turning back to the two junior officers that stood silently before him at parade rest, legs apart and hands crossed behind their butts.

"First, I'll ignore the fact that you disobeyed orders and all that other fun stuff that usually pisses me off. Second, I'm placing you in temporary command of Second Alert Flight, sections Five through Eight. Third, you will maintain the rank of first lieutenant until you prove to me that you are worthy of being a captain. Fourth, I want to see an attitude change, mister. No more of this insubordination and you need to start showing a good example for your fellow pilots to follow. If you're a good leader they will follow you right to the grave. If you're a bad leader, they'll be the ones digging it for you."

"Sir, won't my promotion piss someone off?"

"It pisses me off," yelled Lieutenant Colonel Nelson rather loudly, causing Carlos and John to cringe. He paused briefly to regain his composure. "No one will say anything about it. You are a good pilot and they can't deny that. It will go into your records that you are the acting leader of Second Alert Flight until a replacement can be found. Since you were not promoted to captain there won't be any questions as to your position, especially with our current pilot count. Also, I will put in my personal file a very watered-down version of your failure to follow orders. I know that can be an officer's death sentence, but you can do with it what you will upon your successful promotion to captain."

"Yes sir. Thank you, sir."

"If you screw up again then party time is over and I'll probably feel like invoking my entire list of reprimands in random order. Is that clear?"

"Very clear, sir."

"Good. I'll post the new assignments. We are getting some new pilots along with the supplies so be sure to show them the leader you can be, and not the current one. Now get the hell out of here so I can deal with all this paperwork."

"Yes sir," said Carlos and John at the same time. They both snapped to attention and saluted Lieutenant Colonel Nelson, holding it in place until he returned it. They both performed an about face and exited his office, carefully closing the door behind them.

CHAPTER
7

S o, Mister Iceman, have any good stories to tell?"

"Not any as good as the one I seem to be in at the moment."

The man wearing the white lab coat laughed at his poor attempt at a joke. He was in a white room that was devoid of windows or of any other type of trappings. The room had a bed with four chairs and a small table next to the right side of it. The chairs were padded and were a dull gray color that contrasted against the white walls. The ceiling was also white and paneled with recessed lighting that did not appear to be florescent. At least he could not discern any tubes extending across them.

The man wearing the lab coat was about his age and had not shaved in quite some time, or at all for that matter. He had a full beard that had never been trimmed and his brown hair was a disheveled mess. He also had large bags under his eyes and yawned frequently. He was intently writing on a clipboard that was balanced precariously on his right knee, stopping only to briefly flip a few pages and scribble some more.

"What is your name?" asked the man wearing the lab coat.

"Peter McCabe," he replied. Peter tried moving his fingers and toes and was relieved to see the white bed sheets move in response. He lifted his arms and removed them from beneath the sheet and rubbed his head. A terrific headache was appearing and his hair was a sticky mess. He had the start of a beard growing and both eyes seemed to be working fine. He could hear from both ears so he did not appear to be that bad off, overall.

"How about you?" asked Peter when he finished his self-assessment.

"Major Bill Dorney, you can call me Bill though."

"Okay, Bill. You can call me Peter. Where am I?"

"Sorry Peter, I'm not authorized to answer most of your questions at this time, but feel free to ask and I'll answer those that I can. Someone will be here shortly and they can help you. I do have some questions for you though, if you feel like answering them?"

"Sure. Am I in trouble with the military?"

"Oh no, nothing like that at all," replied Bill while shaking his head quickly and moving his hand from side to side. "What is the last thing you remember?"

"I vaguely remember being sick. Then I was in a waiting room of some kind which seemed to last forever. Then I woke up here. This place seems more real than the waiting room though. That place was surreal if that makes any sense."

Peter looked around a little more. He reached to the small table near his bed and tapped the tabletop. He heard his knock and it sounded and felt real enough. The pounding in his head was real enough too.

"What kind of waiting room?" asked Bill as he made some notes. Bill wondered if Peter had touched upon the afterlife being as close to death as he had been. It only made sense that something must have transpired for the past three hundred and twenty-eight years.

"It was packed full of people and ..." said Peter as he paused and looked to the ceiling. He was finding it difficult to remember very many details about it. His memory of the room and everything that transpired was quickly fading away. "I don't know. My general impression is that I had taken number fourteen billion and they were *now serving number one thousand*, if you catch my drift."

Bill guessed that that was as good as an interpretation as any. He made a few more notes as the door to the room opened. A large black man wearing a neatly pressed white military uniform with four gold bars and a star on his shoulder boards entered. His smile was wide and genuine.

"Good morning, gentlemen," said the man as he approached and stood near the bed.

"Good morning, Captain," replied Bill.

"Good morning," said Peter as he shook the Captain's extended hand.

"I'm Captain Jefferson Washington, you can call me Jeff or Captain, whichever you are more comfortable with."

"Hello Jeff. I'm Peter McCabe, just call me Peter."

"Okay, Peter. How are you feeling?"

"I'm mostly confused and I have a splitting headache, but other than that I seem all right. I think I was sick, am I better now?"

"Well son, you were dead," replied Jeff.

"Dead?" asked Peter as he looked to Bill for an explanation.

"It was a mild case of dead," replied Bill with a shrug.

"Mild case? I thought dead was dead."

"Well, in your case it was poison-induced, and not even death really," said Bill. "You are perfectly healthy now. Do you have any recollection whatsoever of how you may have been poisoned?"

"None that I recall. I can remember eating something and then having a terrible pain in my stomach. So I ran to the bathroom and then ..." Peter paused and looked to the ceiling again. "And then, well, here I am."

"Ah, tainted food," said Bill while looking at Jeff. They shared a nod between them and then looked at Peter.

"What happened to me?"

"Well, Peter, it's complicated," said Bill as he struggled to find the right words to say. "The poison induced a state of hyper-hibernation that mimicked death to the untrained eye. All of your bodily functions were slowed to the point of not being noticed except to people that were specifically trained to detect it, and even then only with specialized equipment."

"Do you remember the date?" asked Jeff.

"It's October ..." Peter paused and looked to the ceiling for help. "Hmm, October something I think. Maybe the tenth?"

"What year?" asked Jeff, looking for more general information.

"Oh, twenty nineteen of course."

"Does the information check out?" asked Jeff as he looked to Bill for confirmation.

"Yes sir," replied Bill while nodding.

"Well son, here's the real confusing part," started Jeff as he walked to the nearest chair and moved it next to the bed. He turned it around and sat. "The current year is twenty-three forty-seven."

"Oh shit," said Peter in surprise.

Jeff laughed, "I keep saying the same thing myself about something or other."

"The poison simulated death so those around you did the only thing they could. They complied with your request to be cryogenically frozen and shot into space," said Bill.

"My request? I never requested that," shot Peter.

Jeff and Bill glanced at each other quickly and Bill just shrugged. The look of shock on both of their faces was enough information to cause a chill to crawl up Peter's spine. Both men expected him to have requested the bizarre circumstances that had brought him to this place in time.

"If that's *when* I am, *where* the hell am I then?" asked a frustrated and confused Peter as he rubbed his temples.

"You are on the United Earth space carrier Ticonderoga, of which I am the commanding officer," said Jeff as he leaned back in his chair. "We are currently en route to Virginia Prime for rearming and resupplying. Then we will be heading for Vega Prime to recover some people from a planet that is about to be overrun. We are at war with an alien race called the Bectolothians. We just call them the Bect for short, because their full name is a mouthful. We came across your coffin as it floated around in space and collected it. Bill has spent the better part of a month correcting the defects of Twenty-First Century technology in order to revive you safely and intact."

Peter looked at him as if he had grown another four arms and tentacles from his skull. He waited quietly for the next burst of information to overload his brain and pop his growing headache.

"That's the short version," said Jeff as he looked to Bill and shrugged. "Would you like the long version?"

"I'm kind of hungry and could use something to kill this headache," replied Peter. "Maybe after that I'll take the refresher course in Confusion-101."

"Okay Peter," replied Jeff with a chuckle.

Jeff turned to Bill and said, "Why don't you take a much needed break, Bill. Take a shower and get presentable again before you come back. Send in the orderly with some food for our guest, two cups of coffee, and some analgesic for his headache. I'll keep him company until you return."

"All right sir, it will be nice to get rid of this smell I seem to have acquired." Bill stood and walked to the door.

"Yes Bill, it will," shot Jeff. "Oh, Bill?"

"Yes, sir?"

"Good job."

"Thank you, sir."

The orderly showed up within minutes with a tray of food and some pills. Peter popped the analgesic into his mouth and swallowed it with some water. He then sampled the orange juice, which was really good. The food tasted a lot better than he had expected from a military vessel but he was not complaining. He had not had a meal in almost three hundred and thirty years so it did not matter what they put in front of him, he was going to eat it all. He reminded himself to eat slowly so he would not get sick.

Jeff was friendly enough and sat there with a cup of coffee that the orderly had brought for him. He sipped it slowly and continued talking about the current state of affairs. The war was going rather badly and the end was coming soon, and the outlook was bleak.

The alien race began being friendly when they had first encountered them back in the Twenty-Third Century. After the Bect had spent a few decades learning about us, they started attacking our colonies without provocation. Apparently we were deemed an easy kill and then they could scoop up all of our real estate with very little work on their part. Unfortunately for the aliens, the price was becoming a lot higher than they had originally antici-pated. Humans, despite being a rather open and overly-trusting culture, were some mean sons-of-bitches when push came to shove. It was a bloody war for both sides but the aliens were making progress.

Jeff tried to touch upon a little of the happenings in the civilian world but he did not have much information, which was understandable. The military tended to be one-sided in that regard. War also changed a lot of perspective too. Peter was not completely devoid of ever experiencing war. He had left the military just months before a war had broken out but he was still involved in the gearing-up process. He was a civilian for that war, the second in his lifetime, and that was an experience for sure. He was too young to remember the first.

While Peter was eating, Jeff examined the man. Peter was in his early thirties and slightly balding in the forehead area. His brown hair was short but not within military regulations. His eyes were green and he appeared well rested, which was an odd observation for Jeff to make, considering that Peter had just spent the last three hundred and twenty-eight years in a cryogenic sleep.

Peter finished his food and was sipping the remainder of his coffee when Bill returned. Bill was wearing his dark gray uniform with gold oak leaf clus-ters on the lapels. He was neatly shaved and looked a lot better than he had earlier. Bill sat in his chair and crossed his legs so he had a platform for his clipboard.

"Welcome back, Bill," said Jeff. "You look a lot more presentable now, my friend."

"Thank you, sir. I feel a lot better too."

"Hey, that funny smell is gone too," shot Peter between sips. "I thought it was me."

Both officers laughed and relaxed a bit more. This was an awkward posi-tion for the two of them, having a civilian aboard a war vessel.

Bill glanced over his few pages of notes. "Peter, I'm sure the Captain has explained to you our current state of affairs. Please tell us something about yourself."

Peter began a synopsis of his life. It quickly turned into a full-fledged story-telling session as the two officers asked questions at various points throughout. What he thought might have been fifteen minutes worth of background soon became an hour. Peter had figured a good place to start would be high school and his learning of computers. He tried to hit the points of interest that would pertain to the current predicament and elaborated on those.

After high school he joined the Air Force and spent eight years fixing aircraft as an electrician. He made it to the rank of technical sergeant before deciding that he wanted a change from that and moved into the computer field. He found that annoying and tried various other jobs before he began learning how to fly. Then things changed drastically for him. Peter lucked into a flight school where he later became a flight instructor. After doing that for a few years he ended up at his current, well, most recent position before his elongated demise, as a pilot flying business jets.

"So, an accomplished pilot and instructor too," remarked Jeff as he nodded and glanced in Bill's direction.

Peter continued answering questions for another hour, a pot of coffee, and two trips to the small latrine nearby. It felt very good to walk although it was a bit challenging at first. Bill had mentioned something about using electro-stimulation on his muscles to accelerate their recovery.

"Peter," said Jeff when he had returned from the latrine, "we've told you our story and you've told us yours. We are going to keep you out of sight until we have left Virginia Prime in order to give you a chance to absorb everything. Plus we'd like to monitor you some more before we are comfortable that your recovery is complete. After we pick up the people and their equipment from Vega Prime we are returning to Virginia Prime to drop them off and collect our new orders. We can deposit you there if you'd like. The big question is, what would you like to do? You don't need to decide right now."

"Well Jeff, I've got a lot of catching up to do," said Peter as he leaned against the pillows.

"You sure do," replied Jeff with a nod.

"How long do I have to stay cooped up in here?"

"Maybe a week, once we have left Virginia Prime's orbit. As far as I'm concerned, after that if you are physically stable you can wander the ship if it's okay with the Captain," said Bill as he looked to the Captain.

"It's fine with me," responded Jeff.

"I really hate the idea of being a bump on the log. Is there anything I can do to help out around here until we get to where we are going?" asked Peter.

"There are no other civilians aboard, this is a military war machine," said Jeff. "You are so far out of date that I don't know what usefulness you could present to us though. You will probably only get in the way."

"True," replied Peter, "but I'm not a normal civilian. I do have some military background so I'm not unaccustomed to following orders. Until I catch up I'll be a technological idiot no matter where I go in the universe. I learn things quick and can keep out of the way easy enough. Besides, what the hell else do I have to look forward to? Everyone I knew is long dead and everything I owned is long gone. I have nothing in this time, nothing except my self and what's in my head. Do you have a training department where I could at least sit in on some classes or something?"

"Our only flight training officer died in combat a few months ago, and that was the only organized training on the ship," said Jeff as he thought about what Peter had said. It was ringing bells deep within his mind.

"Is his position still open? I'll gladly join the military again," shot Peter quickly and with a laugh. He really had nothing to lose in asking. Here he was, thrust more than three centuries into the future onto a carrier in the middle of a war. There had to have been some reason for it. Why not run with it.

Jeff laughed, "But why would you want to? This war is going badly."

"So you have said. I've been a teacher before and I'm so far behind things here that maybe the best thing for me to do is to learn all I can about your current fighter technology. And the best way to learn is to teach. Do you have any simulators on the carrier?"

"I believe we do, but you'd have to talk with our Flight Group Commander. I'm not so sure this is a good idea but I can have him stop by to chat with you if you'd like." Jeff's mental wheels and warnings were turning at high speed now. The Fate card that Bill had planted earlier was echoing loudly in his mind. Then the possibility of Peter being a spy crept in. Although it would be a rather counterproductive attempt to infiltrate the military, and for what purpose?

"But why join the military?" asked Jeff.

"Why not? Here I am three hundred plus years in the future with absolutely nothing to do while on a military vessel. I have nothing but what is in my head and that is so outdated that I'll be considered a moron by most. I could spend every waking moment studying and learning all that I can to try and get back up to speed since there's nothing else for me to do. Then maybe at that point I can be of some real use to you. I have to thank you guys somehow for reviving me and, in essence, saving my life."

After a short pause and silence from the two officers, Peter continued. "Yes, the war is going badly, I get that. Maybe a Twenty-First Century man supplanted from his life will have a different perspective on this war and assist in ways you can't begin to imagine. Either that or I do nothing constructive and you kick me off the ship with the other civilians and then you are done with me. Everything gained or nothing lost."

"Good point," said Jeff as he considered it. "I will have a conference with some of the other commanders and see what they think about this. This delay in your departure from my ship will give us some time to evaluate the possibilities. Come on Bill, let's get something going immediately."

"Yes sir," said Bill as he stood and followed Jeff to the door.

"Jeff?" asked Peter as he watched them leave.

"Yes, son."

"Could I have something to read please? I'd rather be doing something constructive other than staring at the boring white wall while you're gone. Either that or find me a window to look out of."

"Sure," replied Jeff. Peter was a likable enough person but there were still many questions to be answered. Bill closed the door behind them and the two guards snapped to attention as they left the quarantine ward. Neither of them spoke as they walked down the hallway and headed for the Captain's wardroom.

December
2347

CHAPTER

8

The UE Ticonderoga Group entered the Virginia Prime solar system almost two hours behind schedule. The primary reactor needed to be shut down unexpectedly for a valve replacement while en route. The secondary reactor had a computer malfunction that limited total power output to ten percent no matter how much convincing it was given. The Ticonderoga Group was forced to plod along at only point three SU until the mechanics could replace the important valve.

Lieutenant Colonel Nelson dispatched the entire Alert Squadron to patrol the area and had Attack Squadron ready for launch. There were only ten ships left in the usual sixteen-ship Alert Squadron after the last battle had whittled away some of their numbers. Terry wanted to take no chances that an ambush lay in wait for them. He was fairly certain that the aliens were following them and had been for some time. He had not figured out exactly why they kept their distance or for what purpose. He did not want any surprises.

Captain Washington left the bridge for his cabin to wash his face. He could not remember the last time he had a relaxing shower but made a mental note to take care of that while in orbit. He filled his coffee cup for the seventh time today and was hoping to achieve caffeine burnout. He was looking forward to the twenty-four hours of leave and hoped he could sleep through all of it.

*

First Lieutenant Carlos Mendez sat on his bunk with his back against the wall while he read the list he had been given an hour earlier. They were almost at Virginia Prime and would be there in less than an hour. The list had twenty-five names on it. Twenty-four of them were second lieutenants and one was a captain. All of them were pilots joining them to fill the open slots. The captain on the list gave him pause to think. Carlos was in a captain slot but maintained the rank of first lieutenant, so this was a very bad sign for him. But why would the Lieutenant Colonel elevate him like he did just to replace him before he had a chance to prove that he really deserved it? Did he really deserve it? Carlos studied the list and did not hear his girlfriend enter the bunkroom.

"Carlos? You awake?" she said mockingly.

"Huh? Oh, hey Del. Sorry, I'm kind of preoccupied." He returned to looking over the list of names but did not recognize a single one. The captain was from some planet he had never heard of and had actually requested transfer to a combat ship, which was another bad sign.

Delilah stood with her hands on her hips and tapped her foot impatiently on the floor. The bunkroom was three meters long by three meters wide and contained two sets of bunk beds. Four pilots shared the room that had a sliding door leading to the common area. There were four identical bunkrooms, two per side of the common area. The main doorway led to a hallway to Flight Ops. The two doors opposite the hallway were for the Squadron Leader and Second Flight Leader. Both were three meters by two meters and had enough room for a bed and a desk. Built into the walls opposite the doors in each room were storage areas containing shelves for clothing and personal items. There was not much free space available to anybody.

"Aren't you coming?" she asked in an annoyed voice. She was one hundred and sixty-five centimeters tall and weighed fifty-six kilograms. Her petite form was well-proportioned in all aspects and that made Carlos, and every other man on the carrier, very happy to look at her.

"Huh?" replied Carlos as he looked up from the list. She shook her head and crossed her arms in front of her chest as her blond hair swayed from side to side. "Oh, sorry Del. You're gonna have to go on leave without me. I've got to collect the new recruits and get them situated on the carrier. That means I have to come up with bunk assignments for six pilots and then get with the squadron leaders for the other ones. My twenty-four hours of so-called leave will be quite busy."

"So, this is your punishment for being a smart-ass?" She was not helping him any at the moment and was beginning to make him angry.

"No, this is just the beginning."

"It's gonna get worse?" She threw her hands into the air like a spoiled brat not getting her way. She grabbed her hair with both hands and wrapped it into a ball at the back of her head. Then she pulled out a clip from the hair behind her left ear and stuck the ball in place. She tested it and it held so she lowered her arms to her side. "Fine, I'll just go and have some fun without you."

She stormed out of the room before he even had a chance to say *bye* so he did not bother wasting his breath. If she were not such fun in bed he would have kicked her out a long time ago. It was then that he realized she was a lot like him in many ways. Both were arrogant and tried to do just enough to get by in life without working themselves to death. It was not going to be easy to stay away from her for a while but he needed to try. At the rate this war was progressing he had only two choices left; either fight with all that he had in him or die like the rest. He did not like the latter option and the former meant changing his current way of life drastically.

He folded the list and put it in the left breast pocket of his flight suit before zipping it closed. He turned toward the small mirror and checked to see that everything was in order before he grabbed his flight cap and exited the room.

There were a few people playing cards at the common area table and he waved to them as he headed for the hallway. They were busy complaining about having to go on duty in an hour and missing all the sun and fun on the planet. Carlos did not care about any of that. He tried to put it out of his mind as he made his way to the shuttle bay.

There was a short line when he arrived but the shuttle was boarding so it did not last very long. He took a seat near the rear door and noticed only two empty seats remaining before the hatch was closed.

"Seat belts and barf bags everyone. I don't wanna clean up after you," said the Sergeant as he walked toward the front of the shuttle. His oversized boots had magnetic soles that clunked against the metal floor as he moved away.

A few minutes later Carlos felt the gravity dissipate and the all too familiar feeling of weightlessness. Most people on the carrier only experienced that feeling when arriving or disembarking from the ship. Very rarely would the artificial gravity fail or be damaged in battle. From some stories he remembered hearing things became very interesting if that happened. Three people used the barf bags almost in unison as he turned his head to examine the rear door and its tiny window. He surmised that the window was for docking verification before opening the hatch and not for actual sightseeing.

Carlos leaned his head against the wall and looked at the ceiling. He knew the flight to the planet would be about fifteen minutes so he had some time left to think. The sound of metal footsteps brought him out of his reverie.

"You must be a seasoned pilot," said the loadmaster as he sat opposite Carlos. In one smooth motion the Sergeant buckled his belt and sighed audibly.

"I am," replied Carlos, not really feeling like talking to anyone.

"Figured as much. You pilots just stare blankly at the walls or ceiling wondering why the hell you are crammed into a tin can. She ain't got no view but some conduits and she smells like dead rats."

Carlos nodded.

"Ah, a quiet one. Most pilots don't shut up. Always have something to brag about, some kind of conquest. I usually don't get much of a chance to say anything since they won't let me get a word out most times."

"Yeah, we're usually a bunch of egotistical bastards with a stick up our asses."

The Sergeant laughed, "You said it, I didn't."

Carlos nodded and smiled. He liked being abnormal for a change. Maybe this new attitude he was having forced upon him was not so bad after all. He would give it a chance and see what happened. It may turn out to be fun messing with people's minds. That was when the bigger picture clicked for him. He had been thinking of everything from his perspective along with his peers. That was not the problem area. That was only the most visible problem. The bigger picture was humanity versus the aliens. He had to take the current situation and change it, but how? He already used one change on the battlefield and it paid off quite nicely. What else could he do?

"Sorry to bother you, sir," said the Sergeant. He had been watching him the entire time and waited before interrupting. "Looks like you got something on your mind a whole lot more important than my babbling. I'll go bother someone else."

"It's okay, Sarge," said Carlos as he held out a hand to stop the man from leaving. "This war is getting to me."

"No shit, me too," replied the Sergeant. "How much longer do ya think it'll last?"

"Well, a lot longer if I have anything to say about it."

"Sir?" asked the Sergeant with an odd look on his face.

"I'm planning on getting some payback from those alien freaks. I'm sick and tired of getting kicked in the ass just so they can piss on me and send me running back to my mommy. I think it's time we changed things and take the fight to them instead of running all the time."

"Easier said than done, Lieutenant," remarked the Sergeant as he noticed the change in the look on the Lieutenant's face. It went from passive to wild in a fraction of a second.

"Yes, it is. It may take a while, and we may need to run some more, but I will come up with a plan. Then it will be time to kick some alien ass."

"Sir, the aliens don't got asses. That's why they're full of shit."

Carlos looked at the Sergeant for a second before he burst out laughing.

The Sergeant joined him and the two kept laughing while the shuttle shook violently as it entered the atmosphere. A half dozen more people used their barf bags.

After landing there was a one-hour layover while various cargo vessels took priority handling by the dock crews. Carlos found the twenty-five pilots assembled together and waiting nearby. Most of them were young and of various ethnic backgrounds. He saw the Captain standing three meters away from the group and trying to look busy. The twin silver bars on both shoulder boards shone brightly in the sunlight. He was tall and thin and in his mid-twenties from what Carlos could gather. The man was also clean-shaven and his uniform was neatly pressed. Missing from the uniform were the gold wings of a pilot, which Carlos found very odd.

"Flight crews bound for Ticonderoga, I'm Lieutenant Mendez, your tour guide for the day. Please climb aboard the shuttle behind me when I call off your names," shouted Carlos as he pulled the list from his pocket.

"Captain Roger Cleam," said Carlos. Out of respect, he began by calling out the highest-ranking officer. The Captain walked up and Carlos raised his salute first, as was the custom of the junior officer acknowledging the senior.

"Welcome aboard, Captain. Your choice on seating, sir," said Carlos. "It's a fifteen minute flight."

"Thank you," responded Captain Cleam. Carlos watched as the Captain entered the shuttle a bit awkwardly. Something seemed out of place with that man.

Carlos held the list with his left hand and began reading off the names one at a time. For each name a man or woman grabbed their duffel bag and entered the shuttle while saluting him. He returned each salute with precision and a renewed pride in the armed forces. He made sure to say *welcome aboard* to each one of them as they passed. That was a hell of a lot more than what he had received when he first deployed.

Carlos was surprised when every single name on his list was accounted for. He folded the list and put it in his pocket as he looked around the space-port one last time. That would be the extent of his shore leave this time around. Various shuttles and ships packed the small port to overflowing.

There was an abundance of activity at the port with thousands of men, women, and in some cases children, moving about.

"Sometimes I miss the blue skies," said the Sergeant, standing a little behind him and to the right. He was looking up at the sky and the white clouds moving across it.

"Me too," said Carlos as he looked up. It was a beautiful sight and one he had not seen in quite a few months.

"I hope your plan works."

Carlos turned toward the Sergeant and looked him in the eyes. He wished he had a plan, but he could not tell the man that. All he had was the basis of an idea, of a possibility. He hoped to find the something that could fill that void and allow him to succeed where so many others had failed. Carlos could think of no witty remarks so he nodded and turned for the shuttle. The Sergeant turned with him and Carlos clapped the talkative man on the back.

"Sarge, let's get back to business."

"Back into the maw of the beast."

"Roger that."

"Is this a load of pilots?" asked the Sergeant as he started up the rear ramp.

"Yes, greenies."

"Good, no barf bags."

"You might wanna give one to the Captain."

The Sergeant laughed and nodded as the two of them walked onto the shuttle. The rear door closed as the shuttle engines started. As soon as they had clearance the shuttle lifted off and climbed for orbit.

CHAPTER
9

I t was a smooth flight to the Ticonderoga and the docking procedure was flawless. Everyone exited the shuttle cautiously, for some it was their first time weightless outside of a cockpit. The gravity introduction process began and soon everyone was back to normal. A couple of weak stomachs protested the abrupt change as the other pilots examined the nearby walls.

"Captain Cleam, my list doesn't indicate what position you are filling on the carrier," said Carlos as they walked out of the shuttle bay and into the corridor. "I'm not quite sure where to bring you."

"Training officer," replied Captain Cleam.

"Ah, okay," said Carlos as he felt a weight being removed from his shoulders. Things became a little bit brighter in his life, although the training officer would also have flight duties.

Carlos turned to address the rest of the group and spoke loudly. "Welcome aboard the UE carrier Ticonderoga. There will be an orientation briefing at thirteen hundred hours on deck three in the theater. Just ask around and people will be happy to give you directions, otherwise I'll come looking for you before then. Follow me and I'll show you to your respective bunk areas."

"Who's in charge of training on this ship?" asked Captain Cleam as they walked down the corridor.

"You are," responded Carlos without breaking stride. "Our last training officer was killed in combat."

"The training officer has combat duties?"

"Yes sir. If you can fly then you fly. Every pilot is needed badly out there. You have flown combat, haven't you?" Carlos was beginning to worry since the Captain seemed a lot greener than someone right out of the Flight Academy usually did. The lack of pilot wings on his uniform may have more ramifications than if done by accident.

"Actually, no."

"Huh? How did you get the job of Flight Training Officer on a combat vessel? Can you even fly?"

"Uh, no. I'm a teacher."

"Oh shit ... does anyone else know this?" asked Carlos as a baffled expression appeared on his face.

"Guess not. There are no schools on this ship?"

"Hell no, Captain. This is a warship and we don't even have civilians on board."

"I think there's been a screw-up somewhere," said the very concerned Captain that had no idea what he had just gotten himself into.

"Oh yeah, a big one," said Carlos as he approached the first squadron's bunk area. He stopped and called out seven names from his list. Carlos gave them a short speech and introduced them to their squadron commander so that he could give them the tour and show them to their bunks.

Carlos continued down the hall and repeated the procedure until he made it to his squadron's area. Luckily John was in the common area reading a stack of books and making notes on a white pad of paper.

"Sir," said Carlos to the slightly worried Captain, "if you could wait here a second I need to have a friend take care of the new recruits for my squadron. Then I'll be right back and we can go see my commander so he can sort out your small problem."

"Okay."

"This is your new home everyone," said Carlos as he returned to the new pilots. "I'm the acting Second Alert Flight Leader and this here is Lieutenant John Bowyer. He'll make sure to give you your bunk assignments and the brief tour in my short absence."

John looked up from his books in wonderment at having the greenies pawned off on him. He figured it was just typical of Carlos to try shrugging off his new duties so he could get some sack time with his girlfriend on the planet somewhere sunny.

Carlos walked over and whispered into his ear, "The Captain by the door is our new training officer. He's a teacher, not a pilot."

"Oh shit," replied John in shock.

"That's what I said. I'm gonna take him to the Colonel and hopefully help figure out what the hell happened. If you could just show this bunch to their bunks and have them relax a bit I shouldn't be gone too long."

"All right, Carlos."

"Here's the bunk assignments," said Carlos as he handed John a slip of paper. "Thanks, I'll owe you one."

John laughed. He was certain that he owed Carlos many more than one for all the times he had saved his life when he was new on the ship. It all evened out somewhere along the line so he never kept track of it. He stood and introduced himself to everyone as Carlos and the Captain disappeared down the hallway. John knew he had the easier job in this deal.

"Sir, let's go see if we can figure this out," said Carlos to the worried Captain.

"Where are you taking me?" asked Captain Cleam.

"I'm taking you to my commander, Lieutenant Colonel Nelson. He's the Flight Group Commander for the Ticonderoga. He's a good man and the best place to start."

It was a short walk and the Lieutenant Colonel's door was open as he was filling out paperwork. Carlos stepped up to the door, snapped to attention, and knocked once. The Lieutenant Colonel looked up from his desk and sighed heavily.

"Now what is it, Lieutenant?" asked a very tired man.

"Sir, I have a slight problem and need your assistance."

"What's her name?" Lieutenant Colonel Nelson asked quickly.

"Sir? This is Captain Roger Cleam, the new training officer that I just picked up on the planet. He's a teacher and not a pilot."

"Oh shit," said Lieutenant Colonel Nelson. He stood, quickly walked to the door, and shook the troubled man's hand.

"That's the general consensus, sir," said Carlos without laughing, even though he really wanted to.

"Please come in Captain. I'm Lieutenant Colonel Terry Nelson, Flight Group Commander for UE Ticonderoga. Please have a seat."

The troubled Captain sat and Carlos moved the man's duffel bag out of the way and stood by the door at parade rest. The Lieutenant Colonel had not dismissed him yet so he wanted to stick around in case he was needed for any reason. Then a rather odd thought came to mind.

"Can I get the both of you sirs some coffee?" He could not believe he actually asked that but his main concern was somehow comforting this misplaced Captain.

"Yes Lieutenant, good idea," said Lieutenant Colonel Nelson as he raised one of his eyebrows in surprise.

"It was my understanding," started Lieutenant Colonel Nelson as he sat at his desk, "that you were a flight instructor based at Virginia Prime wanting to transfer off-world for active combat duty."

Carlos nodded, glanced at the Colonel's empty coffee pot, and proceeded down the hall to his squadron's bunk area. There was always a pot of coffee brewing around the clock for some poor soul that had duty. John was still busy reading when Carlos walked in quickly and poured two cups of coffee. He did not need to add anything to them since the Lieutenant Colonel kept a supply of additives in his office. John wondered who possessed Carlos' body as Carlos nodded and left the area as quickly as he had arrived.

Carlos stopped at the door and the conversation ceased. He entered the office and placed both cups on the Lieutenant Colonel's desk. He stood by the door at parade rest and waited for further orders.

"Thank you for the coffee. Dismissed Lieutenant, and please close the door behind you."

"Yes sir," replied Carlos. He closed the door and slowly returned to his bunk area wondering what conversation was taking place. He knew things were becoming interesting but this was beyond what he had imagined. John looked up from his books as Carlos entered and waited patiently.

"And?"

"And it gets more and more bizarre by the minute," said Carlos as he took a seat across from his friend.

"What about some coffee for me?" shot John as he tapped his finger on the table. Much to his surprise Carlos stood and fetched two more cups of coffee. When he returned to the table he handed one to John and took a sip of the other.

"Now I'm scared," said John between sips.

"Huh?"

"When do you ever bring me coffee?"

"Oh my, I really am not myself today."

"I'd say. Who the hell are you and what are you doing in my friend's body?"

Carlos laughed and shook his head. He took a sip of coffee and looked into the cup for some answers, but did not find any.

"What kind of teacher?" asked John, breaking the silence.

"What?"

"Exactly. What does he teach?"

"Oh, I never asked."

"Well, what good are you then?"

"Not very good today. I think Del is pissed at me too. What the hell is going on all of a sudden?"

"Beats me," said John as he closed the book and stared at Carlos. The new pilots grabbed some coffee and joined them at the table. They sat silently and looked blankly at each other, not knowing what to say. The quiet was uncomfortable so John began introducing himself again while giving the welcome aboard speech. Then the conversation drifted toward their flying backgrounds and what training they were getting, or not getting, in the Flight Academy. The six new pilots were four males and two females, one of latter being assigned as John's wingman. Carlos did not say very much, he kept thinking about the teacher and how something like that could occur.

*

"Request denied," said Captain Washington tersely. "Do you know how difficult it is to get any kind of training officer these days? Damn near impossible."

"But he's not a pilot," shot Lieutenant Colonel Nelson as he struggled to reason with his tired Captain. He silently wished the ranking structure was normalized between the branches, since the Captain on his view screen far outranked the Captain sitting in his office. A captain on a ship was the equivalent to a colonel in the flight department, or marines. It was confusing sometimes, especially for the new recruits. When you were tired the confusion just made things worse and angers flared. Luckily for the both of them they were using a view screen to communicate. This way they could see just how worn out they each were and not let anything said make their tempers run away. A screw-up like this training officer's orders was becoming more common just as the new pilots were barely old enough to drink.

"What kind of teaching does he do?" asked Captain Washington as he took a deep breath to calm himself down.

"Don't know," replied Lieutenant Colonel Nelson. He turned his head to the right and Captain Cleam quickly whispered the answer to the question. He looked at the screen, "Military history, sir."

"See? This is a military vessel and we need some military history. Get him a bunk, show him to the training section, and get him busy. I want him studying, teaching, recording, or creating history as soon as possible. And that's an order."

"Yes sir."

"Colonel, report to my wardroom as soon as we leave orbit."

"Yes sir," replied Lieutenant Colonel Nelson as the screen went blank. He turned toward the Captain that was now very heartbroken and scared. His request for transfer was botched somewhere along the line and now he was stuck on a carrier headed for combat in some dark splotch of space where death had everyone's name on his list.

"Sorry Captain Cleam, it looks like you are screwed like the rest of us. Welcome to Shit Central." Lieutenant Colonel Nelson punched a button on his screen and an armed sergeant appeared.

"Yes Colonel," said the Sergeant while standing at attention.

"Please have Lieutenant Mendez report to my office immediately."

"Yes sir," replied the Sergeant before the screen went blank.

"On the plus side, you won't be flying combat missions. That should keep you alive a lot longer than most people."

"That helps some, sir," replied Captain Cleam with a light snicker. The laugh was there mostly due to the futility of his plight. He never thought things could go from bad to worse so quickly. Now he was stuck here and shipping off to war. He prayed that no one would teach him how to fly. Everyone by now had heard the stories of the estimated life expectancy of an active duty combat pilot. Those numbers were extremely bleak and listed in days, sometimes hours.

Carlos knocked on the door once and waited for the command to enter. He opened the door and saw the look on the poor Captain's face. He knew that things for him had just gone from bad to worse, if that were possible.

"It looks like Captain Cleam will be staying with us for a while. Get him situated in your bunk area and make him as comfortable as you can. Do I need to make this an order?"

"No sir, it would be my pleasure," replied Carlos as he picked up the man's duffel bag and threw it over his shoulder. "Please follow me, Captain."

Captain Cleam stood and saluted the Lieutenant Colonel and then they shook hands. Lieutenant Colonel Nelson told the Captain he was sorry, which was something that Carlos had never heard him say before. That could mean only one thing, the Lieutenant Colonel had gone to bat for the teacher and was struck down firmly.

Carlos made a mental note to stay very far away from the Lieutenant Colonel for a few days until he cooled down. That made him think of

Delilah. She was probably dancing around half-naked on some beach with an entire troop of marines chasing her around or just drooling over her. She would like that.

Carlos entered the bunk area and John was still chatting with his new wingman. She was shorter than John and had brunette hair. She was average looking but attractive. The uniform hid her form rather well, which was either a good thing or a bad thing. *Maybe the flight suit will allow a better look*, thought Carlos as his mind drifted into the gutter.

He crossed the common area and placed the Captain's duffel bag against the wall in the empty commander room. Even though Carlos was the acting commander of Second Alert Flight he took one of the regular rooms instead. He wanted to make sure that he kept a low profile for a while, which turned out to be perfect for the unfortunate Captain. He would have his own room.

"This room will be yours for the time being, sir," said Carlos as he indicated the room he just exited. The sign above the door read 'Second Alert Flight Commander' in blue letters on a white background.

"I thought that was your job," replied Captain Cleam.

"I'm just the acting commander. I'm staying in that bunkroom," said Carlos while pointing to the first room to his left. "If you have any questions or need anything at all just ask."

"I have one request, please call me Roger."

"Call me Carlos," he replied while shaking Roger's hand. "You really got the shit end of the stick, sir. But things will work out okay."

"I sure hope so, just don't teach me how to fly."

CHAPTER
10

Lieutenant Colonel Terry Nelson entered the wardroom and went straight for the fresh pot of coffee. They had left orbit the day following the meeting request but Captain Washington kept postponing it for various reasons. Four days out from Virginia Prime he finally found time for the meeting concerning the civilian on the carrier.

Captain Jeff Washington, Major Bill Dorney, and Commander Frank Mito were already seated so Lieutenant Colonel Nelson poured himself a cup and joined them.

After several minutes, Captain Washington broke the silence and began the meeting. "This meeting is informal. I need your honest input, comments, and opinions. Understood?"

"Yes sir," replied the others in unison.

"Well, the hapless man we found drifting through space has been awake for over a week now. His name is Peter McCabe and he seems nice enough." The conversation switched to a background analysis where Jeff summarized Peter's life and experiences. Most of them already knew about the man's past but Jeff wanted to reiterate before continuing.

"I'd like to know what you all think before making a decision on his future," said Jeff.

"I like him," said Frank while nodding. "He has a good sense of humor and a pleasant personality."

"He passed all the tests I could dream up, I don't think he will be a menace or cause any damage," said Bill as he flipped through his notes. "He also has an above average IQ."

"I haven't had the chance to meet him yet but the idea of having a civilian on the carrier causes me concern," said Terry as he sipped his coffee. "If he's been awake for over a week, why didn't we just drop him off while we were at Virginia Prime?"

"I still had some tests to run on him to assure that his organs were stable and his body was adjusting to a normal routine. I didn't want him deteriorating on anyone. Besides, they may have wanted to dissect and study him," said Bill as he shook his head in disgust. The scientific community could be so heartless sometimes.

"They could have run the tests there. Why should we be responsible for him? This is our war, not his. He's just a civilian," said Terry.

"It's too late to change things now. We can drop him off once we return to Virginia Prime and let Headquarters deal with him," said Jeff. That certainly seemed like the easy way out. Just make it SEP ... Somebody Else's Problem.

"We could," replied Terry. "Who's to say he would even like it here?"

Jeff nodded slowly as he sipped his coffee. It may have been wrong for him to keep Peter on the carrier when he could have easily been moved to the planet. Bill had wanted to keep him here for observation. Since it was a medical concern under a doctor's jurisdiction, Jeff felt that Bill had the final say on Peter's immediate future.

"What do we have to lose by showing him around, maybe even put him to work to see what happens?" asked Bill as he moved to the next item on his list. "Fate had to have put him there for us to find for a reason."

"There's that Fate card again," said Jeff. "Is it Fate or Desperation that deals the cards this time around?"

"Does it matter who dealt?" asked Frank. "The end result is what matters."

"I really don't know what to think. We are losing this war, can we lose any worse?" asked Terry.

"Things can always get worse," replied Jeff. "So, the big question remains, do we take a chance with this man and see what happens?"

"I say yes," replied Bill quickly. "It might prove to be interesting."

"I would like to see what happens. The real test will be to see how quickly he can adapt to a world more advanced than that which he has come from. I vote yes," said Frank.

"I'd like to meet him first, then I'll decide," said Terry.

"All right, we'll go with that then. Terry, please visit Mister McCabe as soon as possible. I'm willing to agree with Frank and Bill and give the man a chance as long as we keep a close eye on him. If you feel likewise, do what seems right to you and get the ball rolling. Otherwise, we will meet again and go from there."

"Yes sir," replied Terry as he finished his coffee and stood. As soon as possible usually meant now, so there was no point in delaying.

*

Lieutenant Colonel Terry Nelson walked casually down the corridor to the quarantine room containing the new arrival. The Captain had asked him politely, which was rather odd for him to do, to interview the temporally misplaced man. Terry spent his walk thinking about the man that was over three hundred years out of his element. The biggest concern Terry had was one of usefulness in his newfound world. As far as this man being a threat to those aboard or to society as a whole, that was something as yet to be determined, despite Bill's tests. The truly dangerous individuals were so good at deception that you could live with them for years before seeing their true colors, and by then it was too late.

Terry hoped that was not the case with this man. He had not met him yet but he certainly sounded like an interesting individual as far as Jeff, Bill, and Frank were concerned. Terry did not believe that Jeff had had enough free time to visit with Peter again. He was almost positive that Bill and Frank had. It was Bill's pet project and one in which the scientific significance was astonishing.

Terry rounded the corner and saw the two guards at the end of the hallway. They were there mostly to prevent the new arrival from wandering around without an escort. Peter was not a prisoner and, surprisingly so, had not even bothered to open the door to see where he was. He was content, or probably just very patient.

The guards snapped to attention and one opened the door at his arrival.

"Thank you, Corporal," said Terry as he walked into the room. It was a very plain room. There was not much to do or to see in it. Peter was wearing a hospital surgeon's pants and shirt, which was much more comfortable and a lot less revealing than the normal hospital gown.

"Good morning," said Terry as he approached.

Peter was sitting in a chair with both feet propped up on the bed. In his lap was a large printed manual of some kind. He put the manual on the bed carefully to keep it opened to the current page. He was halfway through it from what Terry could see. The first thing Terry noticed about Peter was his piercing bright green eyes. Peter also seemed to be the same build as him, one hundred and eighty centimeters tall and weighing about seventy-five kilograms.

"Good morning, Colonel," said Peter as he extended his hand. Terry shook his hand and took a seat next to him.

"I'm Lieutenant Colonel Terry Nelson, Flight Group Commander of the Ticonderoga. I see you are familiar with our rank insignia."

"Yes sir, I was a sergeant in the Air Force for eight years and your rank structure appears to be similar. Second lieutenant, first lieutenant, captain, major, lieutenant colonel, colonel, and then the generals."

"Correct. It's that way on the Marine and Flight sides of the carrier. The Space Corps rank structure is different. Ensign, lieutenant junior grade, lieutenant, lieutenant commander, commander, captain, and the admirals."

"Sounds just like the Navy ranks I remember. The enlisted ranks are probably similar too so I'll just figure it out when I need to. My name is Peter

McCabe, pleased to meet you."

"Hello Peter, it's very nice to meet you. I hear you are a rather interesting individual."

Peter shrugged, "More like an oddity, sir."

"True enough," laughed Terry. He pointed to the book on the bed, "A little light reading?"

Peter placed a bookmark at the page he was on and closed it so the Lieutenant Colonel could see the cover. It read *Stiletto Flight Manual* and was over one thousand pages. The binder was a thick plastic material overlaid with a hard dark-blue leather-like shell. Three pieces of metal tubing ran through the pages and held it all together quite nicely.

"Light? I was kind of surprised to see a printed book. I expected everything to have been digitized this far in the future."

"It goes both ways. New books are created in both formats. Have you been enjoying it?"

"A very interesting read," replied Peter, "although a lot of the technology within is obscure and I can find no further description of it or explanation for it. They take for granted that I know what a *particle evaporator* is."

"Looks like you're about halfway through it," said Terry as he shifted to get comfortable in the chair.

"It's my third time through."

"Third time? How long have you had it?"

"I don't know. I started counting days but without a clock, who the hell really knows. I sleep when I'm tired and read when I'm not. There's not much else to do in here and the Captain was kind enough to provide me with something to read. I guess he figured since I was a pilot that this would keep me busy, and quiet."

"Damn, I don't think any of the new pilots out of the Flight Academy have even had the chance to open one of those books."

"Wow, is training that bad?"

"Well," started Terry with caution, "the Flight Academy is now only half as long as it used to be. The students are told they will get further training when they arrive at their first duty station. When they get here they are, most likely, jammed into a fighter and thrown into battle. A lot of them die within their first week."

"Shit, that is bad."

Terry nodded grimly. "I was sent to interview you so that I can get a general impression about you. I think that will be a waste of both of our time, something that I don't have the luxury of. Since you've read our flight manual I'd be really interested to talk with you about that, if it's okay with you."

"Yes sir, I would like that," said Peter as he moved his seat to face the Lieutenant Colonel.

"Please call me Terry."

"All right, Terry."

Terry talked with Peter for over an hour. They discussed various aspects of the Stiletto and Terry asked him many general questions about it. Peter proved to be very knowledgeable about the craft so Terry threw some direct and in-depth questions. He asked about total weapons load, maximum speeds in various configurations, systems operation, special features, and several other things that he was certain that most new pilots had no clue about. Peter answered them all intelligently and without referencing the book.

Peter in turn asked questions about the Stiletto that Terry had trouble answering. He had not flown intensely in some time so a lot of the technical questions he was unsure of. Some of the system questions truly boggled his mind and would have been best answered by an actual technician or engineer.

Next they talked about how the Stiletto handled in combat and how the alien ships compared. This put the grim nature of the human's predicament in perspective for Peter. To read about such an amazing combat craft and hear how useless it was in actual combat was a travesty. What was being done wrong?

Eventually the questions turned to the physics of space and how the ships were able to turn without gravity and friction. Terry knew he had dug himself in over his head.

"I think I've had enough mental torture for one day," said Terry while he held up his hands at Peter's next round of questions. "I'll need to have you sit with some technicians for a while on those."

"Sorry Terry, I just have a lot of catching up to do."

"Yes you do, but I have one last question for you."

"Sure," said Peter, "go ahead."

"Would you like to see a Stiletto?"

Peter nearly jumped out of his seat as he sat up abruptly. "Yes sir!"

Terry laughed as he stood, "Let me just get you some proper clothing first." Terry walked to the door and talked briefly with one of the corporals. It took a few minutes before there was a knock at the door and the Corporal opened it.

"Thank you, Corporal," said Terry as he took the boots and flight suit from the soldier. Terry tossed them onto the bed and returned to the door.

"Get dressed and just open the door when you're ready. I'll wait for you outside."

"Okay."

Peter quickly stripped off the surgeon's gear and jumped into the light gray flight suit. It was a near perfect fit. The boots reminded him of his old Air Force boots although these were much more comfortable and easier to put on. He went into the latrine and checked himself in the mirror. He could have used a shave and a long hot shower but that would come eventually, he hoped. The smile on his face was the largest he had remembered ever seeing.

Peter opened the door and zipped the flight suit to a decimeter from his neck as the two guards snapped to attention. Terry turned and smiled as he examined the man. They were about the same age but Peter had less hair than Terry, and it was a lot longer than his crew cut. The flight suit fit Peter well and it was remarkable how close they were in size and build.

"Not a bad fit," remarked Terry. "Now for a tour of Flight Ops."

The two guards followed them silently and Peter glanced in their direction once or twice. Terry caught the gesture as he walked alongside Peter.

"They are here in case I need to run off all of a sudden. Then they can guide you back to your room," said Terry.

"That's okay, sir. Whether they are here to protect me, guide me, or guard me it doesn't matter. This is your ship and your world and I know that the military has rules that must be followed no matter what. I just keep looking because I couldn't help but wonder, are those laser pistols they are wearing?"

"Yes," said Terry.

"Cool," replied Peter.

"Cool?"

"Sorry Terry, that's Twenty-First Century slang for 'very nice'."

"Ah, yes, I suppose a lot of our technology is going to have that effect on you. We may have some communication problems with slang and such, but we'll adapt."

"Yes, we will."

They turned a corner and encountered two more armed guards standing on either side of two large metal doors. Both guards were armed with pistols on their belts and rifles at the ready. They also wore battle armor on their chests and the standard issue military helmets. Both were sergeants and a lieutenant sat at a desk inside a small alcove on the side of the hallway just out of view until they were close enough. The Lieutenant stood as they approached and walked into the middle of the hallway, barring their way.

"Colonel," said the Lieutenant while saluting.

"Morning Lieutenant. I'm here with a friend to give him a tour of the flight deck."

"Sir, no unauthorized personnel are allowed beyond these doors without the express permission of the ..."

"Me," finished Lieutenant Colonel Nelson as he smiled slightly. "You must be new here."

"Yes sir. I arrived at Virginia Prime, sir. I was assigned to flight deck guard duty this morning."

"Well Lieutenant, do you recognize the name on my ID card?"

The Lieutenant read the name and nodded absently.

"And?"

"Welcome to the flight deck, sir," said the Lieutenant as he saluted and then stepped aside. Both guards reached over and opened the doors for them. Terry, Peter, and their two guards walked onto the flight deck.

The hanger area was rather large and packed full of fighters and various other small craft. The flight manual had a few pictures but it did not prepare

Peter for the size or shape of the real thing. Peter stood in awe until one of the guards gently pushed him forward so they could close the door. He ambled toward one of the Stilettos.

"What do you think?" asked Terry.

"An amazing piece of machinery," said Peter as if in a trance. "Oh God, I am one lucky bastard."

"Why is that?" asked Terry as he moved to stand next to Peter.

"I've always felt that I was born either way too early or way too late. Now, thanks to Fate, I've finally found a home."

Terry was not sure what to say at that bit of information. They were all knee-deep in a war that was going badly. Personally, he would have loved to be anywhere but here. Sitting on some planet having sex and drinking beer with not a care in the world, now that was his idea of a home.

The Stiletto was the top-of-the-line UE military fighter. It contained state-of-the-art electronics, power plant, and engines. It could carry the newest munitions designed for any mission that one could dream up. The dark gray color of the ship and its sleek lines almost made him drool. In a way it reminded him of a cross between an A-10 Warthog and a Russian Hind helicopter. The fuselage extended to a point from a rather large middle section. The forward fuselage had one landing gear positioned to the front where the twin-laser phased-pulse energy weapons were housed. All of the avionics and various computers were also located before and after the cockpit area. The Stiletto could seat two fairly comfortably. It was a single seat fighter but in an attack role the rear seat could control the missiles and bombs. It could also be flown, somewhat awkwardly, from the rear seat.

The blocky main section of the Stiletto was directly behind the cockpit and contained the power plant. The main landing gear were positioned on the outside portion just below the stubby wings. The wings themselves were only a meter and a half long and mostly contained hard points for mounting ordnance. They provided absolutely no aerodynamic use whatsoever. They did contain fuel cells of various liquids or batteries depending on the model. The newest designs mentioned in the manual would be filled with a coolant for the nucleonic power plant that could provide an almost endless supply of power. Above the wings and mounted to the fuselage were two motors of a design that Peter could not yet comprehend. He needed to find some engine manuals to help fully understand how they functioned. He gathered that the power plant either fed or turned them to provide thrust.

Covering the entire fuselage were over one hundred tiny rocket motors called thrusters, which would help the ship turn in zero gravity. On the bottom were several larger ones that allowed the ship to land vertically on planets, like the Harrier jet did. The fuselage also contained a built-in storage section underneath for luggage, weapons, and environmental suits. A lot of thinking and planning went into the construction of this bird.

Peter walked around the ship with Terry following him. Terry watched him quietly and waited for questions but Peter was too busy absorbing the sight before him. He examined various panels and placards printed on the ship. He noted tie-down points and the many hard points beneath the wings.

"No hard points on top of the wings?"

"Dual purpose. The Stiletto was designed as a dual role fighter, planetary or space. Gravity caused some interesting problems," remarked Terry with a chuckle.

"Understood. But wouldn't it stand to reason that the hard points could be there, just with a limitation on them to not be used in planetary gravity conditions? That would increase your weapons load."

Terry shrugged, "In that case it could be a design defect."

"Or maybe they removed them to cut costs."

"Possibly," said Terry as he walked to a vent on the aft side of the fuselage. "What's this?"

"Emergency vent for the power plant, depending on the plant itself and the fuel used."

"Very good," replied Terry with a shocked expression on his face. "Most students don't get that one."

"Well, according to what you said earlier, most students don't read the book."

"Exactly, most don't have the time."

"Yeah, too busy dying, unfortunately," replied a sullen Peter. "War sucks."

"Yes, it does."

"The manual said that the D-model Stiletto has a maximum speed of four SU or Solar Units. How fast is that?"

"One Solar Unit equals one trillion kilometers per hour. SU is used to measure both speed and distance."

"One *trillion* kilometers?"

"Yes. To give you a frame of reference, the straight-line distance from Earth to Pluto is a little less than six billion kilometers. Not accounting for acceleration or deceleration and traveling at one SU it would take you roughly twenty-one seconds to make the trip."

"Holy shit."

"Colonel Nelson, gonna take her for a spin?" asked a man wearing dark green coveralls as he approached the two of them.

"Not today, Tim. Showing our guest the Stiletto. Peter, I'd like you to meet Master Sergeant Tim Minor, our lead mechanic and in charge of maintenance."

"Oh boy, do I have some questions for you," said Peter as he shook Tim's hand.

"This is Peter McCabe, our accidental guest," said Lieutenant Colonel Nelson. Peter noted the subtle shift in Terry's demeanor, from teacher to commander.

"Welcome aboard, Peter, nice to meet you."

"You'll have time later for the questions," said Lieutenant Colonel Nelson as he clapped Peter on the back. "First we need to find you a real room to stay in."

"Nice meeting you Tim, see you later."

"Okay," replied Tim as he watched the two of them leave the flight deck.

"After we get you settled in I want to introduce you to the simulator technicians. I'd like you to become acquainted with flying this bird, mostly out of curiosity. The Captain said you flew jet-propelled aircraft back when you were previously alive. I'd really like to know how they compare to more modern technology."

"Curiosity? Hell, call it whatever you want but I'll call it the opportunity of a lifetime," shot Peter with a huge smile on his face.

They left the flight deck with the two guards following silently behind them. They turned a few more corners and he saw the sign *Pilot Country* over the doorway. It was amazing how the pilot mentality remained even after more than three hundred years. Several pilots were walking around and Peter noticed the various nationalities represented. There were also several women wearing flight suits. The variety was pleasant in an odd sort of way. The society he had come from was so wrapped up in labeling people that it forgot they were people.

Everyone saluted the Lieutenant Colonel as they walked down the hallway until Peter came to a door with the sign *Alert Squadron* over it. They entered the common area and several people were gathered around the table, some playing cards and others examining an open book. They all turned when the Lieutenant Colonel walked in and snapped to attention as someone yelled out, "Flight Group Commander on deck."

"At ease," said Lieutenant Colonel Nelson as he walked to the table in the center of the room. "Lieutenant Mendez, I'd like you to meet Peter McCabe."

"Ah, the Iceman," said First Lieutenant Carlos Mendez as he extended his hand. Peter shook it and gave the man an odd look in return.

"Iceman? Like from *Top Gun*?"

"Huh? Aren't you that frozen guy?" asked Carlos.

"Yeah, that's me, I guess," replied Peter.

"Call me Carlos."

"Carlos is the acting leader for Second Alert Flight," said Lieutenant Colonel Nelson. "We have our squadrons split into two flights and each flight contains four groups of two ship formations."

"Isn't he a civilian, sir?" asked Carlos.

"Lieutenant, Peter has a lot of catching up to do and will be stuck on this carrier for some time. The Captain has asked that we help keep this man busy. Since he has prior military experience, we felt sending a little current knowledge his way might in turn help us somehow."

"Sir, what if he's a spy?" shot Carlos.

"For the Bect? Does he look like a Bect?"

"What the hell is a Bect?" asked Peter, dumbfounded. He had heard the name before but it was only a name.

Lieutenant Colonel Nelson turned toward him and sighed. "Sorry Peter, I don't think anyone has told you about them. The Bect are the aliens we are at war with. Bectolothian is the proper name for them. They look somewhat like a pseudopod, maybe a meter tall and very slimy. They have two short arms or truncated tentacles just under the bulbous head area. They don't have feet but sort of slither along. Disgusting looking freaks with an attitude that is filled with hate. To our knowledge not a single race of being that we've met in the galaxy had anything good to say about them."

"And now they want the human race dead," said Peter as he looked around the room. "Well, that's good enough to make them my enemy. If someone wants to kill you then you better kill them first."

"Yeah!" yelled out a pilot in earshot.

CHAPTER

11

The klaxon began as a red warning light set near the top of the wall started flashing. When the general quarters alarm went off the pilots immediately jumped up from what they were doing and ran for the door. Peter knew what the sound was. He had seen enough war movies to know that much. He quickly cleared away from the door and stood silently as the room emptied out.

Once the room was empty a lone figure stepped out from the far doorway. He stood there looking at Peter and the two guards. His glasses were hung on the tip of his nose and the captain bars shone brightly on his shoulder boards. Peter did not know what else to do so he waved to the man and smiled as the klaxon continued.

The man approached and extended his hand.

"Hi, I'm Roger Cleam, history teacher."

"Hi, I'm Peter McCabe, frozen wonder of the world. Kind of an odd place for a history teacher, isn't it?"

Roger laughed as he shook his head slowly. Peter was not sure which comment the man was laughing at but he seemed pleasant enough.

"Yeah, I'm sort of misplaced. They were looking for a flight instructor and got me instead. I was just looking for a way off the planet I was stuck on."

"Ouch, a very extreme way to get off a planet," said Peter with a slight whistle. "I'm rather misplaced myself."

"From the sounds of it you had a rather extreme way to get off of your planet too."

Peter laughed for they had a lot in common in just the uncommon nature of their ending up on this carrier. Both of them were here by accident because they had vacated their current planets rather abruptly. Peter knew a long time ago that he was in the wrong place and time. He either should have been a knight in shining armor or out amongst the stars doing anything in space. Now he was in deep space in the middle of a war and he had yet to see a single star.

"Are there any windows around here? I've always wanted to go into space and now that I'm here I'd really like to see some stars."

"Will your guards let you out of here?" asked Roger while pointing at the soldiers.

"Don't know," said Peter in reply as he turned toward his guards. "Corporal, is it okay for me to go and find a window somewhere so I can see the stars?"

Both the Corporal and the Private looked at each other blankly. It was plain to see that neither of them were prepared for that question or for general quarters to be called. They looked back at him and shrugged.

"Well Corporal, what exactly were your orders?" asked Captain Roger Cleam, shifting into military officer mode.

"Sir, we were to accompany the civilian and make sure that he didn't wander off to someplace that he shouldn't be."

"Sounds reasonable," said Captain Cleam as he straightened his uniform. "You can accompany us to the port observation deck."

"Yes sir," replied the Corporal.

Peter followed Roger out the doorway and down the hallway. The klaxon finished its screaming but the flashing red light continued. Roger slowed so he could walk alongside Peter as they turned a corner and entered another hallway.

"How long have you been aboard?" asked Roger.

"Not sure, no one has said. I think it has been several days, maybe a week. Most likely longer than that but as an ice cube."

"Oh. Have you seen much of the ship then?"

"No, mostly the quarantine room and the latrine. The Colonel took me to the flight deck and then to the bunkroom where we just met. That's all I've seen."

"Ah, this carrier houses about ten thousand people. It's part of a group of eleven ships, if I heard the rumors correctly. Can't tell you how many decks there are or where much of anything is. I know where the observation deck is, the bunkrooms, and the chow hall. Oh, I also know where the ship's library is. I was surprised to discover that they had one."

"How long have you been here?"

"Five days. They keep you very busy around here with the war going on and all," said Roger as they entered a doorway and Peter gasped in awe. All three large windows were full of stars.

"Damn," said Peter as he walked blindly into a chair on his way to the window. What appeared to be a planet sat at the lower left corner of the window while stars filled the remainder. He opened his mouth to comment on a nebula on the right side but stopped when he saw the flashes in the middle window. He focused on those and saw objects moving about within a bunch of bright flashes.

"I think that's the battle," said Peter while pointing to the flashes.

Roger walked up next to him and pushed his glasses up his nose. He studied the flashes and nodded absently. The Corporal tapped Roger's shoulder and presented him with a tubular object, which was some kind of telescope. Peter watched in curiosity as Roger took the object, thanked the Corporal, and then placed one end against his eye. Roger then looked to him and handed him the object.

"Here, try this."

Peter took the object and placed one end against his eye. He saw the ships clearly as if they were in front of him. The odd shapes of the other ships were easily separated from the Stilettos that he was familiar with. He silently watched the ensuing battle and felt as if he were a part of it. He counted about sixteen Stilettos which, according the information he just received, was a full squadron. There were at least that many alien fighters so it was a somewhat even fight. He thought about what the Lieutenant Colonel had said, an even fight being more detrimental and damaging than they should be. The best odds were four to one in their favor, which they did not find very often.

*

Captain Julie Runzik lead First Alert Flight directly at the group of enemy fighters while First Lieutenant Carlos Mendez came at them from a different angle. She was not too sure of this plan but the Lieutenant Colonel liked it and wanted to see what would happen.

Carlos led Second Alert Flight forward as the enemy ships grew in their windows. They were careful not to say much of anything on the radio as he glimpsed the cruiser in the distance monitoring the activity. He was beginning to see a lot more things on the battlefield than he had ever seen before. Between Roger and John his brain was beginning to hurt. The ideas were flowing and the conversations were becoming interesting as well as educational.

"Go," said Carlos as he pushed his throttles forward to forty percent power. Since space combat happened in a much smaller area, a smaller speed requirement was necessary. The throttle quadrants had three sections separated by stops that would not let you pass unless you lifted the latch at the base of the levers. The main thrust section filled most of the throttle travel area and had a stop at both ends. This was the combat maneuvering speed area. Lifting the latch to allow the throttles all the way back would cut the engines off. Lifting the latch to allow the throttles to the forward-most section gave access to the higher traveling speeds, as well as maximum speed.

Second Alert Flight followed Carlos as he turned slightly to the right. First Alert Flight was going in headfirst on the group of twenty enemy fighters that had jumped them. His plan was to hit the alien group from the side and cause a mess. He was not really sure what kind of mess he was about to create. The texts said that this was advantageous but not how or, more importantly, why.

Carlos angled to the left and depressed his trigger. The blue laser light shot from the cannons on his forward fuselage and strafed the enemy fighters as they passed by. The rest of his flight also fired and many scored hits but there were no kills. The enemy did not follow his flight but continued on course to intercept First Alert Flight, approaching them from head-on.

"Pass," shouted Carlos as he turned left and brought his flight around. The slugs were closing on First Alert Flight and things would get messy very soon. "Go seventy," said Carlos as he increased power to seventy percent. It would be a lot harder to hit anything at this speed but he had to make one more pass before the two groups collided. Hopefully he could thin their numbers slightly before they engaged.

First Lieutenant John Bowyer lined up on one of the slugs and, ignoring orders, fired off his only two missiles. His wingman, Second Lieutenant Diane Jensen, fired off her missiles at a separate target. Then they joined the others with laser light flashing across space. Two slugs popped almost instantly when the combined laser blasts and missiles ripped them apart. Metal strips became shrapnel, which the other slugs haphazardly flew through. The human flight claimed four kills on that pass, thinning the herd to an even fight, which still were not very good odds.

Three of the following slugs flew through the shrapnel taking minor damage. One of those slugs ended up with a piece of shrapnel lodged in the front thruster port. When it tried to fire breaking thrusters to turn and engage First Alert Flight it burst into subdued flames. The slug directly behind it impacted the disabled ship as it slowed and the two of them exploded violently. The gas cloud quickly dissipated as the vacuum of space quenched it.

The alien fighters passed First Alert Flight head-on with lasers blasting. Captain Runzik's wingman took several hits and veered off his flight path and into a slug. Both exploded and spun out of control with their living organisms killed instantly. The first pass thinned the battle even more with three Stilettos destroyed and six slugs damaged. A crippled slug wobbled away from the carrier and headed for the alien cruiser, but never made it before two Stilettos finished it off.

Carlos turned his flight around and reduced power to thirty percent before closing in on the battle. A burst from his lasers filled the passing four-ship formation of slugs before they turned to engage First Alert Flight. He paused briefly as he considered pursuit but quickly returned to the mission profile. They were supposed to keep as many of the alien fighters busy until Defend Squadron could form up and join them. Then the aliens would be outnumbered and the battle could be theirs ... in theory.

"Die Bect," yelled Captain Runzik as she fired one of her missiles into the tail of the slug she was following. The slug popped open and shrapnel showered her Stiletto as small pieces of metal clattered off her hull and cockpit window.

Laser fire from her left caused her to glance in that direction just in time to see two slugs quickly approaching. The slugs walked their laser fire across her left fuselage rupturing the power plant housing and tearing apart her flight computers and navigation systems. She shoved the control stick forward and pulled the throttles to zero percent power, watching helplessly as the slugs redirected their fire. As the lasers hit her hull she was late in shoving her throttles forward and against the stops. Both engines screamed to life as several laser blasts connected with the fuel cells. The engines pushed the Stiletto forward as the rear section of her ship blew off, causing both engines and wings to separate from the fuselage. The entire front section was propelled forward and slowly disintegrated as Captain Runzik gaped in horror out of her left cockpit window.

"Split," said Carlos over the command frequency. His eight-ship flight split into two four-ship formations and went after separate targets. He picked the enemy ship with the least amount of damage and closed the distance with the other three Stilettos following closely. Once within range he depressed the trigger and watched the line of blue strafe the alien ships. Just seconds later more blue lasers shot from his formation and joined in creating damage. A slug popped and the left side blew out causing it to turn into its nearest companion. The impact of the two slugs sent the undamaged one spinning out of control and into the oncoming fire of a Stiletto coming the other way. The burst of fire blew the slug apart and the evasive maneuvers of the Stiletto caused a near miss between the last ship following Carlos and the oncoming Stiletto.

"I just peed my pants," said Diane over the wingcom.

"That's okay," replied John as he fought to stay in formation with Carlos and his wingman, "it'll keep you warm." His ship was having problems maintaining lateral control although his caution annunciator panel was still blank. The vibration was almost unbearable.

Diane would have smacked him if she could but made a mental note to take care of that later. She returned to the formation and quickly backed off when John swerved toward her.

"I'm going on top," said Diane over the wingcom as she maneuvered her Stiletto over the tail end of John's ship.

"Ah, what every man likes to hear," shot John before regretting it.

"Shut up, I think you took some damage."

"Where?"

"Left wing root. Oh, I see it. There's a big chunk of alien ship lodged between your left engine nacelle and the wing. You need to return to the carrier before you lose that engine."

"No, not until Defend gets here," said John.

"Mendez, Wing Six," said Diane over the short-range frequency.

Carlos was a little annoyed but changed to their wingcom frequency. He was about to make a turn for another pass and this was not the time to chit-chat.

"Mendez on Six, what's up?"

"Lieutenant, John's ship has an alien chunk of metal lodged between his left engine nacelle and wing root," said Diane before John had the chance. John did not really mind because he was struggling to keep the Stiletto flying straight.

"How bad?"

"Ship is shaking, controls are a bit heavy. No warning lights yet but engine temperature is climbing," said John through gritted teeth. He knew Carlos would hear the tension in his voice and understand the struggle he was having.

"Stand by," said Carlos. He switched to his own wingcom frequency to advise his wingman.

"Dave, keep it straight ahead, I'm going to take a look at John's ship," said Carlos.

"Roger," replied his wingman, Second Lieutenant Dave Roberts.

Carlos pulled back his throttles and slowed so he could come alongside John's Stiletto. He instantly saw the offending piece of metal and wondered how to get the thing out of there and quickly.

"Incoming," shouted Dave over the short-range frequency as he turned to the left and applied power. "Four slugs are bearing down on us and fast."

"Shit. John, get the hell out of here. Cover his ass, Diane. Get back to the carrier unless you can dislodge that thing. We'll keep these guys off of you."

"Okay, good luck," said Diane.

Carlos switched off of their wingcom frequency and back to his own. It was time to get busy and in the worst possible way. Four on two against them was a death sentence, or so he had been told a multitude of times.

"Dave, here's the plan," said Carlos quickly over the wingcom. "Close in tight, target the guy on the right, I'll get the one on the left. Put both missiles into him on my command and then pull back. We'll go straight up at fifty percent power and back the way we came. Then we'll drop back to ten percent power and roll out and see if we can come down behind them. Okay?"

"Um, sure, okay, sir," said Dave. He had arrived with the new recruits from Virginia Prime and this was his first combat mission. It was a rude awakening for him and he seriously doubted that the outcome of the battle would be in their favor.

"Trust me, I'm only insane on Fridays," said Carlos.

The aliens approached quickly and Carlos targeted the alien on the left. He waited until the point of no return and then shouted, "Now!" Both of his missiles sped to the target as he saw two more missiles shoot out from his wingman's fighter. Carlos pulled back hard on the stick and pushed the throttles forward to fifty percent power as the Stiletto performed a half loop.

The missiles hit their marks and both damaged slugs popped. The resulting explosions sent fragments into the other two ships and they sustained damage but were not disabled. Carlos pulled the throttles back and rolled his ship to the left while pushing the nose forward as he saw the two remaining fighters bearing down on John and Diane. He glanced quickly to his side and saw Dave form up on his right wing.

"Nice job, Dave," remarked Carlos as he pushed his throttles forward again. "Two more to go."

Dave did not respond but pushed his throttles forward to maintain position. The plan had worked and now two of his new friends were in a seriously bad situation. He hoped that Carlos could pull this one off too.

Carlos opened fire on the tail of the left of two advancing slugs with Dave joining in firing on the right one. Both of their lasers bounced around on the slug's hard metal shell, burning holes in various places. The slugs did not seem to care, their concentration was focused on the damaged Stiletto running for the carrier with a lone escort fighter. It was the easy kill, or so they thought, or were told by that cruiser that ... was no longer there.

The slug in front of Carlos was the first to pop. It passed harmlessly below him as it careened out of the way. Soon after that Second Lieutenant Dave Roberts destroyed the other one. He was now considered a veteran combat fighter pilot with the unknown taste of battle behind him.

"John, your six is clear, and so is the battlefield, apparently. Where the hell did they all go?" asked Carlos as he checked the long-range scanner.

"Don't know, don't care," replied John.

"Guess we'll find out when we get back," said Carlos.

"Sir," said Dave over wingcom, now that he had his senses back, "today *is* Friday."

"Hmm, I guess I'm insane then."

CHAPTER

12

Peter became very busy once the battle had finished. Roger, as displaced as he was, had accepted his predicament and kept reading as many new books as he could find. On Peter's first visit to the library, Roger demonstrated how to use the computer book catalog and ebook reader. The large push to move all books into digital form was later followed by the Paperback Rebellion. After moving back and forth in popularity, the dust finally settled with both formats being equally sought after.

Peter joined Roger several times on his trips to the ship's library and actually selected a few books for him to read. No one else seemed to use the library since Peter never saw anybody else there, and the book checkouts were automated.

As the week went by, Peter and Roger, and the two guards, wandered the carrier as they learned about their new home. The guards cautioned them a couple of times when they accidentally stumbled upon restricted areas. Peter would try, unsuccessfully, to involve the guards in their conversations but the two young men did not feel comfortable doing so. They would politely

decline and remain far enough away from them that they could not understand what was being said.

Peter was not sure when but one day the guards were no longer there.
Roger asked Lieutenant Colonel Nelson about it and he replied that they
were no longer needed and had more important things to do.

"Hey Roger," said Peter as he placed a book carefully on a shelf and returned the securing lever to the upright position.

"Yeah?"

"I'm going to the flight deck to see if Sergeant Minor has some time to
chat."

"Okay, I'll be here for a while."

"Check out Sun Tzu's *The Art of War,* if you can find it."

"Check out what?"

Peter had to spell it for Roger who nodded while pushing his glasses
back up his nose. He placed the large tome he found onto his growing pile on
a nearby desk before he headed for the card catalog computer.

"See you later," said Peter as he exited the library.

"Have fun."

Peter was surprised to find his way to the flight deck without assistance.
The guards stopped him at the door and called Master Sergeant Minor in the
maintenance department. Tim showed up several minutes later and recognized Peter.

"It's Peter, right?"

"Yes, and you're Tim?"

"Yup, that's me. He's okay with an escort," said Tim to the guards. "He
was cleared by Colonel Nelson." The guards nodded and let Peter through the
doors.

The flight deck was active even though space had been quiet for the previous week. Several Stilettos were being worked on to remedy from minor
repairs to major damage. Peter followed Tim as they headed for his office.
Many curious eyes watched him walk across the flight deck. Not many people cared to have a civilian on the carrier but the Captain had authorized it, so
they reluctantly accepted the new arrival.

"I run this wonderful facility," said Tim as he spread his arms apart to indicate the busy flight deck. "The Captain thinks this entire carrier is his, but this part of it is mine."

Peter laughed as he following Tim into an office and took the opposite chair. Tim sighed audibly as he sat. He then shook his head as he stood and reached for the coffeepot.

"Can't think straight without my coffee. You want some?"

"Yes, please. I've got to get my brain cells working. Insert caffeine to continue."

Tim laughed as he poured two cups of coffee. He pointed to the cream and sugar and Peter shook his head. Tim nodded as he returned to his desk and handed one cup to Peter as he sat again. They both took a careful sip and sighed.

"Damn, that's some strong stuff," said Peter.

"Brewed it yesterday, I think. No one else drinks this engine degreaser except me."

"You clean engines with it?"

"Sometimes, but it tends to eat through the metal if you're not careful about it."

"Shit."

Tim laughed when he saw the look on Peter's face. It was difficult to accept that this man, who appeared to be in his early thirties, was actually over three hundred years old. They relaxed while drinking their coffee and Peter did not start his barrage of questions until they were working on their second cup. Not many people could live through even one cup of his coffee, let alone two. Tim figured that maybe Peter's Twenty-First Century stomach was already acclimated to the vile toxin.

The first things Peter wanted to learn about were the engines and how they worked. Tim fired up his computer, which he had to find first under all the paperwork on his desk. He then displayed a holographic image of the engine in front of the two of them. He was able to manipulate it and also remove panels to display the inner workings. To the left of the engine holo-gram was an engine start panel, so he could actually start the holographic engine image and they could examine the working parts.

"Holy shit, this is amazing," said Peter as he put his hand in the exhaust stream to see if there was any heat being created. The holographic plasma went through his fingers and he laughed.

"Anything like this where, I mean when, you came from?"

"No way. We had to use books and schematics and engine mock-ups," replied Peter.

"Sounds awkward."

"It was, but that was all we had. Something like this here would have rocked."

"Rocked?"

"Sorry, slang. Would have been awesome."

"It gets better. We can plug the Stiletto computer into the imager, start the engine, and then display actual engine data as the holographic image. We can then take apart the engine image while it is running and even replace parts to see if it fixes the problem. I've heard that the next version will actually recommend which part to replace."

"Wow. I like technology."

Tim laughed as he showed Peter some of the other more obscure things with the holographic imager. Peter asked questions as they went and Tim was pleased to see the man learning, and quickly. Peter picked up a lot of the more difficult concepts quicker than the technicians just out of school did.

When the lunch break arrived Tim was surprised that time had gone by so fast. Peter joined Tim and some of the technicians as they went to the enlisted chow hall. Peter was careful to not ask work-related questions as they ate. He did not want to mix work with their break time unless they started it, and they did not. It was interesting to discover anything about the current century other than the military, so he found plenty to talk about.

The week went by fast, between Peter's trips to the library with Roger and his impromptu lessons with Tim and several technicians. He found it easier to visit with Tim in the mornings and eat lunch with the technicians and then hang out with Roger in the afternoons. The maintenance department was more tolerable before lunch and easily aggravated the more the day went on.

Roger was always less responsive in the mornings since he usually dove right into his reading. All in all it worked out well for Peter and he learned a lot.

"Roger, did you find Sun Tzu?"

"Not in book form. I had to download it from the ship's computer onto my tablet," replied Roger absently as he blew the dust off of a book and placed it onto his pile.

"Well, what do you think about it?"

"Not much. He talks about fighting in forests and across rivers, sieging cities, and a lot of other stuff that doesn't pertain."

"Maybe not literally," said Peter as he approached Roger and stood next to him. "A lot of large corporations use, or used while I was alive, *The Art of War* to train their sales and management people."

Roger stopped what he was doing and looked into Peter's eyes. Was there more to this man than he first thought?

"Correlation, my friend," said Peter. "Take his teachings and apply it to our current predicament."

*

John yawned audibly as he stretched his arms above his head. Diane walked up behind him and began rubbing his neck and shoulders.

"Okay, I'll keep you," said John as he leaned back and wrapped his arms around her small waist.

"This wasn't a sexual advance, you moron," said Diane as she playfully smacked the right side of his head. "You've had your face in that book for the past two days. When are you going to come up for air?"

John thought about it briefly and stuck the bookmark into the gigantic book he was reading. He closed the book firmly as Diane stopped rubbing his neck and slid her arms around him. She ran her lips along his ear and whispered something that made his eyes open wide.

"Is that even possible?" he asked dumbly.

She just smiled and said, "I guess this is a sexual advance after all."

John had no reply and stood. She led him into their bunkroom and closed the door just as Roger entered the common area from the hallway.

Roger saw the book on the table and noticed the closed door. He shook his head slowly and went to his room. He picked up the tablet and pressed the *On* button. It responded quickly and he pressed the button to continue where he had left off. Sun Tzu was definitely an interesting character and Roger wanted to ask Peter how he had first found out about him, but had never gotten the chance to. It was not very often that someone knew about a book that Roger had never heard of. But, then again, this odd man had traveled across time to bring him this knowledge.

Most of the tactics in the book were situation specific, like always fighting from the high ground or allowing half of an army to cross a river before attacking them. At first he read the book just for the sake of reading it and told Peter about his dissatisfaction with the knowledge contained within. Peter responded with the most common thing Roger had ever heard: *Correlation, my friend*. Allow half of an army to cross a river before attacking them? Maybe the simplest reasoning would be to allow the enemy to commit half of his forces before attacking them. Sometimes easier said than done, but Roger took Peter's suggestion and found himself making more notes than words contained in the original text. Sun Tzu was a genius that easily transcended time.

January
2348

CHAPTER
13

Two quiet weeks passed and the pilots were becoming bored. Sporadic combat was either a good thing or a very bad thing and the votes were not quite in yet. On the one hand, without a fight they were not dying. On the other hand, without combat their skills deteriorated.

"You watched the battle?" asked a somewhat surprised Lieutenant Colonel Terry Nelson. He was not easily impressed but there was something about this strange man that intrigued him enough to give the man a chance. It had been two weeks since the battle and he had been too busy to check on Peter's progress. He knew that Carlos, John, Roger, and Tim had kept Peter busy learning something or showing him the carrier. Tim's comments were all positive and Peter had even turned a few wrenches during an engine overhaul.

"Yes sir, from the port observation deck with Captain Cleam," replied Peter.

"What did you think about it?"

"Well, my biggest question has got to be; are all battles fought two dimensionally?"

"What do you mean?" asked Lieutenant Colonel Nelson as he sat behind his desk. He motioned for Peter and First Lieutenant Carlos Mendez to have a seat opposite him. The office seemed to get smaller the more he used it.

"Everything took place on an even plane, for the most part. I saw only one group of fighters do anything different than that. The two pilots performed an Immelmann and then came in behind the two remaining enemy fighters."

"That might have been me," said Carlos. "Immelmann?"

"Yes, the first person to perform that maneuver was a German pilot in the First World War, and it is named after him. You do a half loop and then roll out flying in the opposite direction." Peter moved his hand to demonstrate the performance of the maneuver.

"You saw me take out those fighters?" asked Carlos.

"Yes I did, nice job, but that leads to my next question. Are your lasers always that ineffective against the alien ships?"

Both Lieutenant Colonel Nelson and Carlos looked at each other with concern. Neither of them had ever asked that question before. They just took it as the way things were and that was that.

"Ineffective?" asked Carlos before Lieutenant Colonel Nelson had the chance. "How so?"

"It seemed like it took an awful lot of hits in order to take one of them out. Is there any way to increase the power on the lasers or modify them, maybe by using a different frequency, so that they do more damage? I don't know too much about laser technology versus metallurgy since lasers were only used by governments and research facilities when I was last alive."

"Never thought about that before. Did you ask Tim?"

"Haven't had the chance. He has been busy handling the repairs from the battle."

"Well, I will definitely talk to him about it," said Lieutenant Colonel Nelson as he continued making notes. "What else do you have for me?"

"Looks like losses were still rather high despite an even fight," said Peter while shaking his head.

"Eleven ships lost and nine pilots dead," said Lieutenant Colonel Nelson without emotion. They were becoming just numbers to him, and that was not a good thing. Every battle was taking its toll in life and machinery a lot faster than positive results were being shown.

"I know the Stiletto can carry four of the Devrac-Two missiles, why do you only carry two?" asked Peter.

"As you saw, most pilots don't live long enough to use them," replied Carlos.

"So, change that," shot Peter.

"How?" asked Lieutenant Colonel Nelson, his pen poised to take more notes on his pad of paper.

"Take four missiles each and launch all of them as soon as you are in range. It looks like those alien ships are pigs so you might be able to thin them out before you even engage them. You'll put the odds in your favor right away," said Peter as he relaxed in his chair. Everything he said seemed like common knowledge to him. Maybe it really was not all that common in this time period. Maybe he could actually make a difference here. That thought excited him.

"Pigs? I know the word but not how you are using it," said Carlos while Lieutenant Colonel Nelson continued writing.

"Pig, meaning that they don't handle very well. They turn slowly and respond sluggishly. That kind of thing."

"They have their moments," said Lieutenant Colonel Nelson, "and when things don't go their way they leave in a hurry."

"I saw that cruiser bug out about mid-battle," remarked Carlos.

"That they did, as soon as Defend Squadron arrived they ran off. Then the other fighters broke off and ran, that's probably the only thing that kept your small group alive," said Lieutenant Colonel Nelson while nodding. "Good job, Captain."

"Thank you, sir," replied Carlos. He caught the twin silver bars that Lieutenant Colonel Nelson tossed across the desk.

"Sorry for the delay. I meant to give them to you after the battle."

"Better late than never," laughed Carlos, as his smile grew larger.

"That leads to my next subject, crews," said Lieutenant Colonel Nelson as he made some more notes. "Alert Squadron is now down to only seven pilots, the rest were killed, including Captain Runzik. Carlos, you are now in command of what remains of Alert Squadron. Your duty will be patrols and Defend Squadron will be on the hot seat if anything happens. You will join battles but in conjunction with Defend Squadron. We need to get more ships up for battle so that we stand a chance."

"What might help is quality over quantity," said Peter. Both men looked at him and waited for him to continue. "You already said that the training department is mostly non-existent, what about reactivating it? Would it be that difficult to do?"

"That's what I'm currently assessing. I do have to take you down there so you can play around with the Stiletto simulator and see what you think. Any suggestions will be appreciated. If our perspective on this war is doing us no good maybe Captain Washington is right and some Twenty-First Century ideas will help."

Peter nodded, "Sure can't hurt, although Carlos here seems to be doing a good job changing things himself."

"Yes, he has. Where did that maneuver come from? That Immelmann?" asked Lieutenant Colonel Nelson.

"Lieutenant Bowyer and I have been playing with ideas along with the help of Captain Cleam. He's turning out to be a wealth of information, sir," replied Carlos.

"Ah, Fate dealing the deck again," said Lieutenant Colonel Nelson.

"Fate is a rather strange beast," remarked Peter as he pointed to himself with both thumbs. "Without her tinkering I wouldn't be here."

"Case in point," said Lieutenant Colonel Nelson while nodding. "Let's visit the simulator room right now, before I get sidetracked again." He stood and walked out his door with Carlos and Peter following close behind.

The training section of Flight Ops was very small, consisting of only three rooms and one of which was inside the other. The main area was the simulator deck. There were eight simulators, two rows of four and only one that had the canopy open. Peter was somewhat disgusted to discover that it was the only working simulator. The other seven had various parts that had failed and were never replaced. The simulators themselves reminded him of an old Link trainer he had seen in a museum. It was a meter and a half long and a meter wide. It stood about a meter tall and even taller when the canopy was open. The inside of the canopy contained a layer of material that turned it into a view screen. It was technology he did not fully understand but reminded him of the LCD screens used in laptops, only much thinner.

The cockpit itself was cramped, just like the F-15s he used to work on. The throttle and control stick locations were the same and even some of the avionics packages were in identical locations. He was elated to discover that the heads-up displays were actually holographic projections instead of the old plate-projection methods.

The small room inside of the simulator deck room contained the controls and computers for the simulators and the world that they flew in. There were three chairs and several view screens where the operators could view various aspects of what was going on during the session. One of the standard views depicted the typical scanner fashion of dots representing ships, as was experienced when on the bridge. Another showed what the selected pilot saw through his forward window. The third was an external view of the selected ship, seen from however many meters you requested.

Seated in the room were two enlisted men that snapped to attention as Lieutenant Colonel Nelson entered.

"Good afternoon, sir," said the Sergeant, the higher-ranking of the two men. He was in his mid-twenties and had dark hair and brown eyes. His skin was darker and Peter guessed he was of Hispanic descent. His uniform was neatly pressed and he was clean-shaven. His smile was warm and friendly.

"Good afternoon and at ease, Sergeant. This is Peter McCabe, our civilian guest."

Peter shook the Sergeant's hand and also the hand of the Corporal that stood behind him. The Corporal was in his early twenties, if even that old. He had the start of a mustache growing under his nose. It had either been there for a very long time with no results or it was something the man had just started. Peter was not sure which but figured it could go either way.

"Sergeant Rodriguez and Corporal Taylor have been in charge of training since the training officer died in combat a few months ago," said Lieutenant Colonel Nelson as he looked around the small control room. It was clean and well kept, which surprised him. Most of the time, when an officer was not around to micro-manage people, things tended to slip into disrepair.

"Sergeant, I'd like it immensely if you could introduce Mister McCabe to the Stiletto simulator and give him some time at the controls. He doesn't have much else to do on this ship and he used to be a pilot and instructor before he was frozen and sent to us across time."

Neither simulator tech showed surprise at the information and readily agreed to Lieutenant Colonel Nelson's suggestion. The change would at least give them something to do for a while and they might actually have fun doing it. It was rather boring in the training department when nobody cared and when battle always took priority over lessons. All they did lately was fire up the simulator for some new pilot so they could become familiar with the flight controls and weapon systems.

"Peter, Sergeant Rodriguez will show you to your new quarters when you're ready and he knows how to reach me. If you have any questions I'm sure these two very capable men can help you. Don't have too much fun here, there is a war going on," said Lieutenant Colonel Nelson.

"Thank you, Colonel. Thanks for everything and thanks for making me feel like I'm at home, because I guess this is my home now."

"Not such a bad place, but kinda noisy at times," said Corporal Taylor with a grin.

"It was my pleasure, Peter. Hopefully we can find your reason for being here and put you to work," said Lieutenant Colonel Nelson.

"Please do," replied Peter as he shook hands with Lieutenant Colonel Nelson and the newly appointed Captain. He watched as they walked out the door and disappeared down the hallway.

"So," started Peter as he turned back to the two simulator technicians, "when do we eat?"

CHAPTER
14

The next two weeks were the most fun Peter had ever had with his clothes on. The very first time he flew the Stiletto simulator, Sergeant Miguel Rodriguez went easy on him and Peter played with the controls and weapon systems against stationary targets. It was a massive learning curve at first and Peter struggled to figure out all the buttons scattered throughout the cockpit. There was a mock-up in the classroom and both Miguel and Corporal Randy Taylor helped him with it. The three of them nearly lived together in that classroom for the entire first week whenever a pilot had not come in for training. Miguel and Randy knew what most of the buttons were since they had to perform limited maintenance on the simulators whenever something broke. Peter ended up teaching the two simtechs as they all learned from the experience. It felt like old times for Peter, except for the fact that the ultimate goal for this training was war.

Peter wanted to know everything he could about all aspects of the training department. At one point he prodded Miguel into the simulator so he could see things from the simulator control side. Peter and Randy could not stop laughing when Miguel had to open the canopy to avoid vomiting in the cockpit that he would have later needed to clean. Eventually they fixed Miguel's vertigo and Randy had his turn at the controls. The simtechs were very sloppy at first but after their sixth training mission they could control the ship as well as Peter first had.

When they felt like taking a break they would visit with Tim on the flight deck if he had the time available for them. Tim enjoyed the questions since they were more in-depth rather than the usual questions he received from pilots, whose answers were easily found in books.

Peter stood at the front of the classroom teaching the two simtechs about the weapons management control panel. He had an enlarged picture of the panel projected on the wall and was pointing at items with a penlight laser pointer. Lieutenant Colonel Nelson walked in unexpectedly and stopped both enlisted men from standing, as they were halfway to their feet. He quietly took a seat in the back of the room and begged Peter to continue, which he did. Lieutenant Colonel Nelson watched intently and even asked a few questions that Peter easily answered. After ten minutes the simtechs decided it was okay to ask questions of their own.

When the class ended, Peter performed a pre-mission briefing describing what the goals were for his simulator session. It would be his third mission flying against a Bect fighter. During Peter's first time in combat against a single slug he was destroyed easily. The second time he did better but ended up crashing into the slug, destroying them both. He hoped it went better this time around.

"I'm returning to Flight Ops, have fun and I'll see you later," said Lieutenant Colonel Nelson as he shook Peter's hand. He waved to the two simtechs as he exited the classroom.

Peter closed the canopy and started up the simulator for the mission. He checked the on-board systems via the checklist on the main multifunction display. It was not really necessary to use a checklist in a simulator but it was a good habit. All the systems were ready and Peter began the engine start procedures. It was much simpler than he expected for such an advanced piece of machinery.

"Sim One, you are cleared for launch," said Miguel as Lieutenant Colonel Nelson entered the control room.

Lieutenant Colonel Nelson quickly motioned for them to remain seated and sat in an empty chair nearby. He whispered, "I've never watched a simulator session before, can he hear us in there?"

"No sir, only if you hit this button here," replied Miguel as he pointed to the intercom button. "It comes into the sim just like over the radio. Makes these things good trainers for radio etiquette."

"Good, I don't want him to know that I'm here."

Lieutenant Colonel Nelson was amazed that the Sergeant took his previous statement, about never seeing a sim session before, and explained everything he did. The Sergeant talked effectively as he performed each action, expanding upon things as he found necessary. Lieutenant Colonel Nelson felt very comfortable asking questions as the session progressed.

"Take standard patrol around the perimeter," said Randy as he performed the functions of a traffic controller.

"Acknowledged," was Peter's reply, heard over the loudspeaker in the control room. The room was kept cool with an air conditioning unit and it struggled to keep the large computer cabinets behind them at the proper temperature.

One screen in front of Lieutenant Colonel Nelson showed Peter's white dot moving around the big carrier dot as it patrolled. Another was the view that Peter experienced while the third was an external view of his Stiletto. An alien ship's red dot appeared and headed straight for him.

"Bandit at your eleven o'clock and five kilometers, engage when able," said Randy.

"Engaging," replied Peter.

Lieutenant Colonel Nelson watched the Stiletto turn and head for the alien ship. The two objects approached each other and it felt like he was watching the real thing from the bridge. The realism was hauntingly familiar.

"Missiles locked. One away, two away," said Peter calmly as both missiles streaked toward the alien target. Lieutenant Colonel Nelson watched as the missiles jumped slightly to the right and changed direction toward the nearby sun.

"That's not very nice," shot Peter as Randy began laughing.

"What happened?" asked Lieutenant Colonel Nelson.

"I induced some missile failures so he would have to dogfight, sir. The missiles are on their way to the sun," said Randy.

"Dogfight?"

"Sorry sir, engage for close quarters combat. Dogfight is the word Peter uses for aerial combat. Have you ever seen two dogs fighting, sir?"

"Ah, okay, I understand. Nice word."

"Here comes the first pass," said Miguel as he pointed to the screens.

Peter pushed the throttles forward and kicked in hard right rudder. The Stiletto's nose moved to the right and when he removed rudder pressure the ship straightened out in its new direction. Peter loved the rudder system because it made so much sense to him. When you hit the rudder control, directional thrusters moved the nose of the fighter in that direction. The response he received from both simtechs when they first saw him do that was one of surprise. Most pilots hardly touched the damn things except to use them as a footrest.

Peter pushed everything else from his mind to concentrate on the task at hand. The alien ship turned to intercept and Peter pulled the throttles to idle and kicked in full left rudder. The Stiletto yawed to the left until the alien ship was in his sights, then he adjusted rudder pressure to keep it there. He depressed his trigger and the blue laser light flashed out to the alien ship. Peter kept slight pressure on the rudder while the ship's forward momentum caused his flight path to traverse alongside the alien. Peter did not mind going sideways, it just seemed so right to him in the oddest of ways. He kept telling himself that in space the rules were different. The only way to win was to learn those rules and live by them.

The alien ship struggled to target him but could not turn fast enough. It did not take very long for the alien ship to disintegrate in a brilliant flash of light. Peter smoothly applied power and adjusted his flight path.

"Damn!" yelled Lieutenant Colonel Nelson excitedly when he saw the slug pop. "I've never seen someone take a slug out with lasers that fast before."

"Neither have we, sir," replied Miguel while Randy nodded.

"He made that look easy."

"He's learning quick, sir," said Randy.

"That he is," said Lieutenant Colonel Nelson quietly. "Give him two."

"Two, sir?" asked a rather surprised Miguel.

"Yeah, can you do that?"

"Sure can, but he's gonna be pissed ... sir," said Miguel as he began pressing buttons on the keyboard in front of him. He watched the screen and selected the appropriate input line and modified it for two alien ships.

"Heads up, Sim One," said Randy over the simulated command frequency. "Scanner reports another inbound alien ship." He removed his finger from the radio transmit button and turned to Lieutenant Colonel Nelson. "I don't want to give him too much of a warning." They both laughed.

"Oh shit, this is gonna be funny," said Miguel.

"Roger that, scanners are hot, negative contact," was Peter's reply over the loudspeaker.

Peter scanned the area on the short-range scanner. It took a handful of seconds before the alien ship appeared. The blip was blurry and he thought the equipment was malfunctioning until he saw the dot split into two alien ships.

"Did I piss in someone's Cheerios this morning?" asked Peter over the intercom. "Shit, this ought to be fun."

Peter had just finished his very first successful simulated combat mission. He had never fought two before but remembered days long ago when he fired up the combat flight simulator on his home computer. There was one mission in particular where he and a friend had linked together to take on fifteen enemy fighters. They chose modern jets for themselves, his friend in an F-16 and Peter in a SAAB Gripen. They picked Vietnam era F-4 Phantoms as the aggressors. To make things more interesting they did it without missiles ... guns only. On the first pass he was able to splash two fighters before it became a twisting dogfight. He kept turning and would eventually get one of the sluggish fighters in his sights. The next one went down easy but, with all the bullets flying everywhere, he took a few rounds and ended up with a damaged fuel tank among other things. The fuel leak ate away at his fuel supply as he splashed two more fighters, bringing his kills to five. Then his engine stopped as his fuel tank went dry, but the fight was far from over. He kept turning as the altitude drained away just like his fuel had. He shot down three more before he punched out at a thousand feet, or roughly three hundred meters in this time period. He had shot down eight fighters, three of which while his engine was off. It was an adrenaline pumping ride.

Peter pulled back on the stick and gained some positive incline. There was no such thing as altitude in space so they referred to their current plane as zero-plane. Going up was positive and down was negative on the incline at one-kilometer increments. Before you exited the carrier your zero-plane was set and the strip on the heads-up display indicated either positive or negative figures. He increased to a positive three incline, which was three kilometers above the zero-plane, and rolled his Stiletto inverted. There was no up or down in space, it was all relative.

He pushed the throttles forward to fifty percent power and watched the two slugs heading toward him as he shot past. He pulled back on the stick and reduced power to idle as he came down almost on top of them. Their lasers did not have the angle on him but he filled the one on his left with several laser blasts before passing by.

Peter watched the slugs pitch forward to pursue him so he pushed his throttles forward to forty percent power and rolled over to begin another loop. He pulled the throttles back to idle and pulled back hard on the stick. After traveling through a negative two incline he began increasing his incline and returned to forty percent power. He looked up through his top view screen and saw the two ships coming toward him. It was going to be close.

Peter reduced the throttles to idle power and pulled into the two ships. They continued to struggle to get him into their sights and he was lucky again. He put a few dozen well-placed laser rounds into the fresh alien fight-er and it burst apart. He then leveled off at a positive one incline and turned to the right. The alien continued to decrease its incline before turning toward him yet again. Peter had a two incline advantage on the enemy, if that mattered in space, he was not really sure. He guessed that he was about to find out.

Peter did not like head-on combat, there was no advantage to be gained that way. Only the lucky or the first to fire or the better shot usually won, or you both died. He turned the ship to the left and began increasing his incline even more. The alien followed dutifully and was soon two kilometers behind him. Now Peter would find out just how much maneuverability those alien ships really had.

With the throttles at idle, Peter kicked in full left rudder and the nose moved ninety degrees. Then he advanced his throttles to one hundred percent power and changed direction in a heartbeat. Before his ship fully recovered he pulled the throttles to idle and performed the same maneuver again. The alien continued turning to intercept but clearly the blast of power had it off guard. The problem with computer controlled enemy ships was that they could only do what you programmed them to do. It became a matter of time before you understood their limitations and how to use them to your advantage. Peter turned toward the alien ship by performing another quick direction change and fired a few laser blasts while the two ships quickly passed. It was the alien ship he had damaged on the first pass so the extra damage he dealt this time around was more than enough to finish it off.

"Now I'm tired," said Peter as he brought the Stiletto to a full stop.

"All right, initiating shutdown. Standby for canopy opening," said Randy as he began pressing buttons to return the simulator to a safe state. They were not full motion simulators and they did not need to be since space had no gravity to act upon the ship or pilot. The biggest problem with the simulators was popping the canopy open while the view through the front window was rolling. The sudden conflict of visual input tended to cause people to vomit immediately. None of them wanted to test that theory.

"That was actually fun," said Peter as he exited the simulator. "But what a workout ... my arms hurt."

"Impressive display," said Lieutenant Colonel Nelson as he approached Peter and extended his hand. Peter shook the proffered hand with a big smile on his face.

"I didn't think I still had an audience. I thought you went back to Flight Ops," shot Peter as he glanced at the two simtechs. Both of them shrugged in unison.

"That's what I wanted you to think and I didn't let them tell you otherwise. Who do you think gave them the idea of putting you up against two?"

"Oh, I have you to thank for that?" laughed Peter as the two simtechs approached.

"Good job, Peter, gonna have to increase the difficulty level next time," said Miguel.

"Difficulty level?" asked Lieutenant Colonel Nelson as he looked at the Sergeant.

"The simulator has five difficulty levels for the alien ships," said Miguel as he smoothly switched into teaching mode. "We always use just the first one, level one. The factory named the levels *Easy, Normal, Difficult, Challenging,* and *Impossible.* To my knowledge no one has ever moved it from the *Easy* setting."

"Our next mission is to get comfortable and consistent on the *Easy* setting, then we'll evaluate the other ones out of curiosity," said Peter.

"How do most pilots do against *Easy*?"

"It's usually a fifty-fifty mix, depending upon the training they received before they arrived. The pilots who have already seen battle tend to do a little bit better, but not by much," answered Randy as he secured the simulator that Peter had just exited. Peter joined in and opened the rear panel, making sure to close all of the power switches to protect the unit.

"But if pilots can't beat the first level why even bother testing the other ones?" asked Lieutenant Colonel Nelson as he watched the men work.

"We need to change that first," said Miguel.

"We?" asked Lieutenant Colonel Nelson with a raised eyebrow.

Miguel did not know what to do, or how to respond, so he looked to Peter for help. Peter shrugged as if to say, *You're on your own, buddy.*

Lieutenant Colonel Nelson saw the exchange and quickly continued. "Sergeant, how would you feel about having Peter as your boss?"

"Fine with me, sir," replied Miguel.

"That does of course depend on Peter," said Lieutenant Colonel Nelson as he turned to Peter next. "You would have to enlist in the military."

"Not a problem, sir," shot Peter with a big smile on his face. "I don't have much else to do and nowhere else to go so I might as well join up and help out here as much as I can. I now know that I can really help you guys out."

"That's good to hear. I can't get you a commission as an officer but I can get you in as a warrant officer. In fact, I don't recall the last time I have ever seen a warrant officer. I guess they are rare but the circumstances seem rather ripe in this situation."

"Count me in, sir," said Peter as he shook Lieutenant Colonel Nelson's hand.

"I'll start the paperwork and have some uniforms issued to you. Then we'll need to have you swear in and sign some things. In the meantime, do you have something to keep you busy here?"

"Yes sir, after every session we review the video and evaluate and critique all aspects of the mission. That way we learn and can better ourselves and our teaching and combat flying methods," said Peter. He did not know whose flight suit he had been wearing these past weeks but it was beginning to smell despite frequent washing. He hoped he would get more than one uniform at least, then he could wash it without having to walk around naked for an hour.

"I get the impression that all three of you are flying," said Lieutenant Colonel Nelson as he walked to the door. He stopped before he exited and waited for a response.

"Yes sir, the best way to learn is to teach and with them knowing one side of the simulator it was only logical for them to learn the other side. So, we all learn together. Plus, it's more fun this way for all of us," said Peter.

"Well, keep it up then. If you can figure out how to make it fun for all the other pilots on this ship and actually motivate them to want to live in the simulator, improving our combat statistics, then maybe I can get you flying one of the real things."

"I'll take that challenge. Consider it done."

Lieutenant Colonel Nelson smiled as he left the room to return to his office. He had a lot to do and think about now. Fate was shining down on the human race this day. Hopefully he could get things rolling along so that this war would turn in their favor. Maybe the first group to be ordered to go for training should be Mendez's crew. They were doing the best with some of their new tactics. Captain Cleam was not a pilot but he might also benefit from sitting in on some classes. This also presented an interesting opportunity for the new pilots they would pick up once they returned to Virginia Prime ... if they returned.

CHAPTER
15

H ow is our new friend doing?" asked Captain Washington as he stood on the bridge next to Lieutenant Colonel Nelson. The scene out of the front window was of the planet Vega Prime and its two moons. The Ticonderoga was entering orbit around the planet as several support ships readied themselves for passenger pickup. He hoped the colonists were ready.

"Quite well, Captain. He has the training department humming along and is turning into quite the combat pilot, at least as far as simulators go." Lieutenant Colonel Nelson stood with both hands behind his back as he watched a large cargo ship descend into the atmosphere.

"Really?" asked a shocked and tired Captain.

"Yes sir. He's down there every waking moment. I went to lunch with him and the two simtechs a couple of days ago and they kept talking about their latest project. So even when they are supposed to be relaxing they are hard at work."

"Have you watched any of his sessions?"

"Yes sir. I saw him take out a slug so quick that if I had blinked I would've missed it. Then I had the simtechs put him up against two ... and he won without taking a hit."

"Damn."

"That's what I said, and that's why he's now a warrant officer," remarked Lieutenant Colonel Nelson.

"I was going to ask you about that. Now I know."

The large cargo ship shrank in the distance and was soon followed by a second one. There were one hundred and twenty-two colonists on the planet to pick up, along with their things. They were told to travel light and to be ready for immediate extraction.

"Yesterday I watched the simtech Corporal take on a slug and win."

"A corporal? What the hell was he doing flying the sim?"

"Well sir, Peter felt that it was in their best interest to train the two sim-techs to fly the Stiletto. He's been learning while he teaches them and they are all doing quite well at it. The Sergeant is a better pilot than the Corporal but the Corporal tends to try new and interesting things, quite effectively too I might add."

Captain Washington nodded, not really convinced that it was such a good idea. Training enlisted people to fly a fighter could only be asking for trouble. Officers had the discipline needed to handle that responsibility. But, then again, he allowed a civilian to do just that, so how could he complain.

"I was against it at first," said Lieutenant Colonel Nelson, "but they all seem happy so I let them continue. The Sergeant is a good and patient instructor too. Peter's reasoning is that if he can teach non-pilots to become combat pilots then he can make current combat pilots even more effective. I'd like to let Peter continue on this path and see what he can do with them."

Captain Washington grunted and Lieutenant Colonel Nelson took that as an affirmation. It could have been interpreted either way but if the words were not there then it was up for grabs.

"When does Peter begin training real pilots?" asked Captain Washington while he examined the small screen in front of him.

"As soon as we finish collecting these colonists. Monday morning will be his first class on basic fighter tactics. I'll ask for volunteers to attend and will order those that don't volunteer."

Captain Washington laughed out loud. "Ah, one of the benefits of command. Fill the class with the Reserve pilots first, since they spend the most time sitting around with nothing to do. We'll see how that goes and then fill the ranks with them. The new pilots we get will go into the Reserve Squadron. If it all works out it may be good for everyone."

"Yes sir, if my duties allow I will also attend the class. That way I'll keep everyone in line and hopefully learn something in the process."

"That's fine."

"Peter has requested the videos on our previous battles to study the enemy tactics. Is that okay with you?"

"Might as well let him. What does he plan to do with that knowledge?"

"Update the simulator's alien artificial intelligence to their current tactics and tailor classes to exploit their weaknesses and such." Lieutenant Colonel Nelson pointed to a screen nearby and shook his head. "Looks like we have company, sir."

"We were expecting them, weren't we?" asked Captain Washington as he looked at Lieutenant Colonel Nelson.

"Incoming enemy fighters at three o'clock," shouted the scanner operator.

"General quarters," said Captain Washington while waiting for Lieutenant Colonel Nelson to respond.

"Alert Squadron is already on station and all of Defend Squadron was on the flight deck awaiting launch orders." The klaxon for general quarters sounded and the red lights began flashing. "Attack Squadron was told to scramble if we went to general quarters so we should be able to counter with thirty fighters."

"How many incoming, Commander?" asked Captain Washington as he turned to his First Officer.

"I count roughly three dozen sir, coming in hot at three SU," replied Commander Mito.

"Launch Defend and have Attack launch as soon as ready," yelled Captain Washington. They were at a bad angle for using the rail guns so he did not even bother mentioning them.

"Aye aye, sir," replied Commander Mito. He pressed the button on his belt and gave the man on the other end the orders. Soon the screens lit up with a bunch of Stilettos forming up to greet the enemy.

"Sir, you're about to see one of Peter's ideas put to use," said Lieutenant Colonel Nelson as he pointed to the view screen showing the battle.

"Which idea is that?" asked Captain Washington as he pressed the button a few times to zoom in on the battle.

"The Alert and Defend Stilettos are each equipped with four Devrac-Two missiles. They were instructed to fire them all before engaging the enemy, to try and thin out the herd. Attack will also have a full complement of missiles and will use them liberally to see if that helps."

"Doesn't sound like you are too confident in this plan," remarked Captain Washington as he watched the Stilettos close the distance with the slugs.

"Sir, I count at least three bombers in that mess," said Commander Mito.

"Well sir, we've never done this before and Peter seems to think that that is the important part. The enemy knows all of our current tactics and expects them. If we can surprise the enemy then we can control the battle."

Captain Washington grunted, "We'll soon find out."

*

Captain Carlos Mendez smiled when he pressed his communication button and spoke the one word, "Spread." His squadron and Defend Squadron moved into a 'V' formation so that everyone could target the enemy without having a Stiletto in front of them.

"Target," was Carlos' next command spoken over the short-range frequency. Everyone's combat computer picked a target and locked it up for them. ICIS communicated between all of the Stilettos and no alien craft was targeted twice. The distance shrank considerably but Carlos waited until they were at optimal range. He wanted to have enough time to launch this salvo and then target the next row of fighters and bombers.

"Salvo," yelled Carlos as he depressed his weapon release button twice in succession. Both missiles leapt from his stubby wings and streaked toward the fighter he had targeted. Everyone else in the formation fired two missiles on his command. All twenty-one ships sent a total of forty-two missiles heading for the enemy. Two missiles failed en route and another one lost its target.

"Target," yelled Carlos for the second time. ICIS struggled to sort out the mess of incoming enemy fighters and the missiles that tracked them. It calculated which slugs had no missiles still locked on, or only one missile, and put them back in the lineup for the second volley. ICIS also noted four bombers amongst the alien craft and decided it was best to have two Stilettos target each of them before targeting the slugs.

The first volley of missiles impacted one second before Carlos yelled out, "Salvo", to put the second volley of missiles on the way. Of the nineteen enemy fighters hit by the first volley of missiles, ten of them disintegrated instantly while the other nine took various degrees of damage. Some of those nine slugs were hit by two missiles and lived while some took only a single hit before popping. One of the missiles was a dud and impacted its slug, hitting hard enough to crack the alien ship's front window.

The second volley had no mechanical failures but four of the missiles lost their lock and streaked past the slugs and bombers. Thirty-eight Devrac-Two missiles at short-range were a deadly wall of explosives. Two of the alien bombers were the first to disappear from the screens as eight more fighters followed suit. Of the eight fighters destroyed, a few of them had received damage from the first volley. Three additional fighters took damage but continued coming.

Carlos looked on in awe as he realized that the frozen man that had joined them truly was on their side. This one idea of his had just changed the war for everyone. What looked like a futile war of waste and death had just shifted in their favor. Was the frozen man a spy? Well, if he were, he was the worst spy in history.

"Break and engage," said Carlos over the command frequency as he picked the nearest bomber and turned for it. Eight enemy fighters and two bombers continued toward them. ICIS showed that all of the alien craft remaining on the battlefield had been damaged in the onslaught that had just occurred.

The bombers were the most dangerous targets even if they were damaged so they remained a high priority and everyone went for them first. Four Stilettos disintegrated when the Bect bombers launched their own missiles at close range and the Stilettos could do nothing about them. Defend Squadron broke to the left while Alert Squadron went to the right. Unfortunately this allowed the alien fighters to get in behind them and two more Stilettos were lost.

"John," yelled Carlos over the short-range frequency. "Get these fighters off of me."

"Roger," replied John as he and Diane turned away from the fighter they were trying to line up on. They turned to track the ships following Carlos but the alien fighters were not there. John quickly checked his six o'clock position but they were not there either. He spent valuable seconds checking ICIS but it came up blank as well. He pushed his throttles forward and found Carlos and his wingman chasing a bomber. Before John could say anything the three alien fighters on their tails took out Carlos' wingman.

Carlos broke off his attack on the bomber after his laser cannons left scorch marks on its aft end. Having lasers blasting at him from both the front and rear was a very bad place to be. He lowered his nose and increased power as the fighters followed him. The bomber angled toward the other group of fighters and fired off three missiles, which blew apart a Stiletto after all three impacted its tail section. The pilot never knew what happened and neither did any of the other Stilettos nearby.

Carlos banked to the left and struggled to evade the three slugs on his tail. He increased speed and they did the same, his every move being matched.

John and Diane engaged the fighters chasing Carlos. The two of them sprayed laser fire over the trailing slug and its lower right side blew out, sending it spinning out of their way. The other two fighters opened fire on Carlos and raked his left wing and engine with laser blasts. Carlos' left engine blew apart with enough force that it sent him spinning out of control to the right. The left fighter popped as John's lasers split it in half. Diane finished off the other fighter and ran into the wreckage before she could maneuver out of the way. It tore her right fuselage open and severed the right wing

and engine clean off. Her Master Caution light came on and the caution annunciator panel lit up with multiple flashing warning lights. She tried to eject
but the damage to her fuselage prevented the cockpit from detaching.

John struggled to evade the bomber that came in behind him. The lasers
peppered his tail section and ruptured the containment section of his power
plant. His Master Caution light came on as his caution annunciator panel
displayed multiple engine system failures. His computer began telling him to
eject so he reached for the lever as the bomber put two missiles into the tail
of his ship. The force of the blast sent him head first into the instrument
panel as his ship folded in half. The five-point harness held him tightly in the
wreckage as the fuel cells ignited and his ship burst brilliantly in the darkness
of space. The bomber clipped his wreckage and turned to search for the other
disabled Stiletto.

Diane reset various circuit breakers and tried once again to eject with no
luck. She looked up to see an alien bomber bearing down on her and she
screamed for help over the command frequency. The bomber launched its last
missile at the disabled fighter and turned away before the missile destroyed
the target. Diane's ship split apart and disintegrated in a truncated fiery mess
of metal.

Carlos came up from below the bomber in time to see it finish off Diane,
John's wingman and lover. Carlos was too angry to cry for the loss of his
friends. He closed the distance and held the trigger down as the blue lasers
raked the bottom of the gumdrop. Its shields were long gone and it only took
a couple of dozen blasts to pop the bomber. There was no reason for him to
be happy so he checked his scanner for another target, but there were none
left.

*

Captain Washington grunted as he watched the battle come to a conclu-
sion. He did not know what to say and the entire bridge remained silent after
that young woman screamed over the command frequency. What was first
just a bunch of dots moving around on the screen, and sometimes disappearing as if in a video game, became the harsh reality of lives being lost as the
blips went dark. It was easy to send people off to fight a battle when you

could distance the battle from reality by not having to see or hear them. Command was a difficult thing and one in which he would never truly love.

"Recover the fighters and look for survivors," said Captain Washington. Somebody had to break the silence and it might as well have been him.

"Aye aye, sir," said Commander Mito as he issued the orders down the chain of command. Thirty minutes later he would have the bad news that there were no survivors. Fifteen crafts and lives were lost. As good as the battle started the reality of their situation came quickly crashing down on them all.

"Colonel, come with me," said Captain Washington as he headed for the door. "Commander, you have the con, I'll be in my quarters."

"Aye aye, sir," replied Commander Mito as he took position on the higher deck. Another officer moved to take his position as he continued the recovery operation and dispatched some remaining Stilettos to fly patrol.

*

"Well Terry, that missile plan worked very well. At first I thought we were going to win without taking any losses and I damn near wet myself," started Jeff as he pulled a pot of coffee from the wall and poured two cups.

"I'll have to review the video myself to see exactly what the outcome of that plan was. It looked like we nailed more than half before the actual dogfight began," said Terry as he sat and took a sip of coffee.

Jeff paced across the room, stopping briefly to sip at his coffee. He looked through the window at the small section of space where the recent battle had taken place and wondered where all the souls went. Were they all still floating around out there, waiting to be laid to rest? So many souls released every time they met the enemy. So many lives lost and they could never replace them fast enough.

"Dogfight?" asked Jeff as he continued to watch the stars.

"That was Peter's term for close-in ship-to-ship combat. If you've ever seen two dogs fighting you'll get the picture."

"Hmm, that I have."

CHAPTER
16

The attitude of everyone on the ship was rather somber. People grieved in their own way and pilots tended to stay amongst themselves and share a knowing nod. Life was not fair and those aliens were the biggest assholes in the universe as far as everyone on the carrier was concerned.

Peter sat opposite Major Bill Dorney in the quarantine room that he knew all too well. Bill continued writing notes on his clipboard as Peter sat silently watching him.

"Well? Am I human?" asked Peter.

Bill laughed and looked up at him, "Yes you are. You are physically fit and I see absolutely no reason for you to return for your weekly checkups. All the pre-revival drugs and post-revival therapy has held solid. There is no cellular breakdown whatsoever and no regression on any of your internal organs."

"That's good news," said Peter with a nod.

"How have you been doing? I hear you're starting a class on Monday."

"Yes sir, not sure how many will be showing up but if the Colonel has anything to say about it there will be quite a few."

"Rumor has it that you took out two Bect slugs by yourself in the simulator while the Colonel was watching."

"That's floating around the carrier?"

"Yeah, I heard it was an impressive display."

Peter shrugged. There really was not much he could add to that. It had been a lot of fun and had it been real there was the possibility that things would have been different. He needed to make the sim sessions more difficult than the real thing. Then reality would be a much safer place to be in. It was always safer to take risks and push yourself when death was not a possible outcome.

"Well, since I don't have to run any more tests on you, don't be a stranger. Stop by if you ever get the chance. Maybe, if you don't mind, I'll stop in to visit once in a while. The Captain doesn't let me leave the dungeon very often."

Peter laughed, "Sure, to both. Thanks for everything, Bill. I owe you more than anything I can imagine so if you ever need my help just ask."

"I'll remember that," replied Bill as he stood and extended his hand. They shook hands and bid each other farewell.

Peter returned to the simulator room and found Miguel and Randy hard at work on simulator number eight. It was the most promising of the broken simulators and Peter had given them the mission of seeing if they could resurrect it. There were various black boxes and circuit cards spread out on the floor. They still had another hour before anyone was supposed to show up for training.

Motivation had fallen through the deck after the last battle. Too many pilots died although the missile volley had been devastating to the enemy.

The three of them had reviewed the seven-minute video for an entire day critiquing every confrontation, every laser blast, every missile, and every fraction of a second. They evaluated the battle from both the human and the Bect perspective. When they had finished they were all better men for it. They understood a lot more about combat and about the enemy, and even more about themselves.

The final assessment was information that would never be revealed to anyone, unless they were ordered to. Military discipline was absent and the battles were nothing more than a free-for-all. Peter did not have to say the obvious because Randy beat him to it. It was at this point that Peter wanted to fix all of the simulators. They needed to work on group tactics to ensure pilot survival. You could have one really good pilot out there but he would never be able to protect everyone. Eight mediocre pilots fighting together and working together would be more effective in the long run. Things needed to change badly and soon.

"This bitch should work," yelled Miguel. He grunted madly in frustration.

"I think that card is bad," said Randy. He pointed at the power supply card that had a light on to indicate that it was functioning.

Miguel pulled it out and examined it for a minute. He saw no reason for the card to be bad so he handed it to Randy. Randy turned it over a few times and shrugged.

"Shit," said Randy. "It's the only thing that makes sense, the only card in common with the entire sim."

Peter held out his hand and Randy passed him the board. Peter scrutinized it with eyes that had not seen an electronic component in over three hundred years. Most of the components were just smaller versions of what he remembered. The general designs of most were similar and he found many items that he had never seen before. After two minutes he held the board out and pointed to a component that he did not recognize.

"What is this thing?"

"Uh, a signal dampener, I think," said Randy.

"I think that thing is bad," said Peter with a shrug.

"How can you tell?" asked Miguel.

"See the board under the component? It's discolored as if the component has overheated. At least that's my best guess."

Miguel and Randy nodded as they both examined the component in question. Randy shrugged as he slid the board into a static-sensitive bag.

"I'll take it down to the shop and see what the circuit weenies can find," said Randy. He stood and exited the simulator room.

"Did you make a list of components we need in order to get all these things running?" asked Peter.

"Yes sir," said Miguel.

"Miguel, drop the *sir* crap with me when it's just us. Just call me Peter."

"Okay Peter. Are you sure you're an officer?"

"Not at heart. I used to repair aircraft as a sergeant way back when."

"Hey, no wonder you're cool," said Miguel.

Peter noticed that the word *cool* was catching on throughout the carrier. He could revive the best phrases and the best words and they would all be to his credit. Tapping knowledge from the past was interesting and it was fun spreading some old-fashioned Twenty-First Century slang around.

The door opened and Lieutenant Colonel Nelson walked in with a sour look on his face. Peter knew something was not good so he stood abruptly and approached him.

"Yes sir," asked Peter.

"How did you know I was going to ask you something?" asked Lieutenant Colonel Nelson as the sour look turned to one of confusion.

"Because you look pissed off and ready to tear someone a new asshole. I hope it's not me," said Peter as he extended his hand in greeting. Lieutenant Colonel Nelson shook it readily and his demeanor changed instantly.

"It's not you, my friend, it's this damn war. Have you reviewed the last video?"

"Yes sir."

"Brief me," commanded Lieutenant Colonel Nelson as he entered the classroom. Peter followed him and shot an odd look in Miguel's direction, who nodded in response. The look told Miguel to keep busy and stay clear. If anyone showed up for training Miguel was to handle it.

Peter entered the classroom and closed the door. Lieutenant Colonel Nelson took the first seat at the front of the classroom and waited for Peter to begin.

"Would you like the watered down and happy version or the cold hard reality, non-bullshit version?" asked Peter. He popped the memory cartridge into the viewer and grabbed his notebook.

"Non-bullshit version please. I need to hear it straight," said Lieutenant Colonel Nelson. He clasped his hands on the table in front of himself and waited.

Peter started the video and went through the entire battle step by step. He showed various sections and analyzed them. Some sections he reviewed several times giving feedback about both human and Bect tactics and results. Every single action and reaction was broken down into its basic form. Lieutenant Colonel Nelson sat and listened, not saying a word until Peter had finished almost two hours later.

The results were rather grim. The Ticonderoga had lost fifteen fighters and pilots while destroying twenty-eight alien fighters and four bombers. Alert Squadron was down to two pilots and Defend Squadron was down to four pilots. Attack Squadron still had a full compliment of sixteen pilots and there were twenty-four Reserve pilots on board to help recover from the battle.

"Let's go over it again and I will have some questions for you this time," said Lieutenant Colonel Nelson.

Peter restarted the video and the question and answer session began. Another forty-five minutes went by while reviewing that same seven-minute video. Every success, every failure, and every single death was discussed and possible alternatives to each were examined. The opening missile volleys were devastating for the enemy. A total of twenty alien fighters and two bombers were destroyed outright while those remaining had all sustained various amounts of damage. That was two-thirds of the enemy's strength lost right there and their remaining ships were reduced in effectiveness. That was a massive amount of destruction dealt to the enemy. But they kept coming and inflicted massive damage of their own. Overall, and the saddest part of the entire battle, the humans did better this time around than they had before, despite the amount of losses.

"Peter, that was the best debrief I've ever had the pleasure of attending."

"Thank you, sir. I did have help."

"The Corporal and Sergeant?" Lieutenant Colonel Nelson asked with a tinge of annoyance in his voice.

"Yes sir, I couldn't have done it without them. We broke this battle apart so we could update the simulator's alien artificial intelligence to improve training."

"How long did you spend dissecting it?"

"A day," shot Peter. "At least sixteen hours."

"Shit, they are dedicated men."

"Yes sir, they are, and I couldn't do this job without them."

"Are you trying to turn them into officers?"

"I think their knowledge, attitude, and dedication will eventually get them there on their own. I'm just allowing them to shine by pushing them to their limits."

"Hell, Peter," said Lieutenant Colonel Nelson as he leaned back in his chair, "you've got two enlisted men flying simulated combat missions, performing debriefs, running sim sessions, and even teaching officers things about their craft that they never knew."

"I've got them repairing one of the simulators right now too," said Peter with a near chuckle.

"It's repairable?"

"We think so. The biggest problem seems to be the power supply circuit cards. At least that's the most common card that we've found that has failed. Corporal Taylor ran the card down to electronics to see if they can fix it. If they can, maybe they can fix the others. I hope we can motivate some of them to help us out."

"It would give them something else to do in their free time. Can you get me a list of the other parts you need?"

"Yes sir, we were working on that before you showed up. I also have some other radical ideas you might not like."

Lieutenant Colonel Nelson laughed and shook his head. He pushed the chair out and stood from the table. He walked to Peter and clapped his hand on the man's back.

"I bet you do but keep them to yourself at the moment. I need to pass the information you just gave me to the Captain. You might want to make sure your two simtechs keep that info to themselves."

"We already had that talk, sir. They understand the importance of and the delicate nature of the material in question. None of the post-battle briefings we analyze will ever go anywhere other than your ears unless you want us to use this for teaching purposes."

"Not quite yet. You have a class starting on Monday. The Captain wants all the Reserve pilots and not the line pilots to attend. He's not sure how effective your teaching will be and would rather not take the active combat pilot's minds off of their job," said Lieutenant Colonel Nelson as he opened the classroom door.

"Understood sir, but that presents an interesting dilemma. Once these Reserve pilots are trained how will they be tested in the real world? I mean, who will command them on the battlefield?"

"Hmm," said Lieutenant Colonel Nelson as he stopped to think about it for a few seconds. "I guess the only person that makes real sense would have to be you. So, get busy trying to get yourself commissioned as a second lieutenant."

"Yes sir!" said Peter as he snapped to attention and saluted with a large smile on his face.

Lieutenant Colonel Nelson returned the salute with a laugh. The way things were progressing with this ambitious and talented man he had no doubt that Peter would find a way to get his commission. The only one on the ship that could give Peter that was the Captain and he was a man tougher to impress than Terry was.

Miguel ran up and snapped to attention while presenting a piece of paper to Peter. Peter took it and examined it briefly before handing it to Lieutenant Colonel Nelson. It was a list of parts necessary to fix all of the simulators.

"Damn, that was quick," said Lieutenant Colonel Nelson.

"Like I said, sir, we were already working on that before you arrived."

Lieutenant Colonel Nelson nodded to Miguel, "Good job, Sergeant."

"Thank you, sir," replied Miguel.

"Why do you want all these simulators running?" asked Lieutenant Colonel Nelson. He read through the list of bizarre parts that made no sense to him.

"The biggest failing we have found is in crew training. The crews need to train together in order to function as a cohesive unit. Hopefully we'll have a second sim online today and can start training wingleaders to work with their wingmen. That alone will make a huge difference."

"I certainly hope so." Lieutenant Colonel Nelson turned and walked to the door. He opened it slowly and turned back to the two men standing by the simulators. "Make sure to tell Corporal Taylor that I stopped by. All three of you are doing a great job so keep up the good work, for on Monday the real fun begins."

"Thank you, sir," said Peter and Miguel in unison as Lieutenant Colonel Nelson entered the hallway and headed for the bridge. The two of them stood there watching the empty doorway for a while, not wanting to break the silence. It had been a long few days and that would not end anytime soon.

"Things are going to get interesting real quick," said Peter.

Miguel nodded slowly in agreement with his boss as he thought about how interesting things had already become since Peter took over the training department. Sure the work was a lot more intense and there was much more to do now than ever before, but he liked the extra duties. He did not think of them as work because it was too much like being a real person and not some nameless grunt. The officers that came down for unscheduled training treated the two simtechs a lot better now than most of the officers ever did. Miguel could feel the respect whenever a pilot asked him a question, actually listening to the response, and he liked that feeling. At first the officers were reluctant and even antagonistic at being trained by enlisted men. It was bad enough that they had to learn from a warrant officer that had never flown combat missions before. Those attitudes changed quickly when the pilots coming in for training realized the depth of the knowledge that these men had to pass on to them. It was the first time Miguel actually enjoyed his job since the war began.

February
2348

CHAPTER
17

The electronic technicians were successful in fixing the power supply so Randy took the remaining ones to see if they were also salvageable. Peter needed to visit the shop to work out a deal with them, otherwise they were 'too busy' to help. Peter spent an hour discussing some options with the supervisor. They finally agreed to provide as much electronic support as they could in exchange for as much simulator time as was possible. Peter's only requirement before he agreed was that all of the simulator use was in strict accordance with current training policy. This meant that all those technicians that wanted to fly the simulator needed to first attend a ground school on the Stiletto and its systems. They needed to be trained as pilots because the simulators were delicate tools that needed to be treated with care and respect. And, as always, active pilots took priority.

The man in charge of the electronics shop was a short man in his late thirties and balding a lot more than Peter. He had at least two missing teeth and the man's breath stank of bad coffee. Master Sergeant Chuck Vallance was his name and the smile on his face after they shook hands was overly large, matching the stomach that hung over his belt. He was friendly enough and probably thought he was getting the better end of the deal.

Peter saw this as a win-win situation with himself coming out on top. By allowing the electronic technicians to fly the simulators he was conscripting their shop to support them, to keep them flying. In turn he would have to spend more time teaching, which was good in a way. He could have Miguel and Randy teaching classes by themselves at night since enlisted personnel would not balk as much with enlisted teachers unlike the officers were apt to. For Miguel and Randy, starting from the beginning with people that had never seen a fighter up close would be the most educational experience they could ever get. Peter would need to sit in with them for a while until they were comfortable teaching, then they could go it alone.

This was the perfect setup for his next idea to dump on Lieutenant Colonel Nelson. *That poor man is going to kill me for this*, thought Peter. Lieutenant Colonel Nelson was sure to find out soon enough, especially when the *new students* began showing up. Peter also had a few more ideas that needed to be worked out before his master plan could begin. He would need some help for those. It was time to have another long talk with Lieutenant Colonel Nelson, if he was available.

Three weeks had passed since the post-battle debriefs with Lieutenant Colonel Nelson. His first class was only seven pilots, Peter had expected more. Eight of the Reserve pilots had moved up to Defend Squadron. Nine moved to Alert Squadron. The other seven could have been used to fill the ranks of missing pilots a little bit more but this was the bare minimum that Captain Washington wanted available for training. With Peter as the acting flight leader they at least had a full flight to work with. He could do a lot with that.

The class was going quite well. Peter supervised Miguel as he taught the ground school on Stiletto systems. Miguel and Randy ran the simulators for two pilots as Peter coordinated the observation with the rest of the students. Peter swapped the pilot's roles and partners as he learned each of their strengths and weaknesses. Each simulator session lasted thirty minutes, with each crew flying four sessions a day, and allowed for them to perform various functions as a team. During that time they went up against four or five fighters, one at a time, depending upon how long it took them to win or to lose. After three weeks of working in the simulators the pilots were showing their true colors. Peter needed a good starting point for training purposes, so he assigned three of the best natural leaders as wingleaders and the others became wingmen. Peter told them all that these roles were not set in stone and could be changed at any moment. In fact, he changed them every week so that the different roles could be learned by everyone.

Peter would trade out the final wingleader position with himself, Miguel, or Randy. The wingmen would rotate between wingleaders so that no one grew comfortable flying with any particular person. The most important point that he stressed was that discipline and structure were to be maintained. They had a set way to do things and it was designed this way so that any pilot could fill any position and knew not only what was expected of them but what to expect from the others as well.

Morale in the Reserve Flight increased dramatically, as they were able to destroy alien fighters more consistently. Miguel began everyone at level one for the first day and moved to level two the next. As they become comfortable he stepped them up even more and by the end of the week they were slaughtering level five enemy craft easily.

Then the real fun began for everyone. Randy programmed the alien bombers into the simulator, which had never been confronted before until in actual combat. He also took all of their data for the operation of the slugs and updated the simulator database for accuracy. At first this threw everyone for a loop because the artificial intelligence proved rather difficult to confront using the previously learned tactics. Peter was pleased that his students were able to refine new battle tactics to deal with the change in the alien threat.

Peter was amazed to discover the pilots sitting around during break time discussing tactics and comparing notes of previous sim sessions. They loved the debriefings and found them more informative than the classes. Peter's first change to the curriculum was in having the non-flying pilots run the post-flight debriefings for the two pilots that had exited the simulator. Several new tactics were derived from these briefings and were tried in the simulators with mixed results. Peter would even let them try the bad ideas since failure was the best way to learn from your mistakes. It was much better to fail in the simulator than to fail out in space and die from it.

The rumors spread fast of the flight of pilots being trained intensely for an as yet unknown purpose. Many suspected that the Captain had a secret plan to launch an offensive against the alien home world. Those that expressed that thought were laughed at. What could a single flight of pilots do against the enemy? The Reserve pilots were soon called *elite warriors* or various other terms that were meant to be derogatory.

Peter spent a lot of his free time, which was not very much anymore, talking with Roger about Sun Tzu and other pieces of work. After much discussion and a few heated arguments, Peter convinced Roger to come to the sim classroom to teach a little military history and pass on the knowledge that he had gained. Soon the seven pilots treated Roger like a long lost friend as they spent some of their break time picking his brain about history. That made Roger more eager to dig deeper into the books.

Class let out for the day so the pilots could relax and do any studying or whatever else they wanted to do. Peter climbed into the simulator with Miguel and Randy running the session and a few of the students remained to watch. There was always something new for the students to see and to learn from Peter.

Peter's plan for the day was to play with the missiles. He wanted to see how effective they were and to determine their limitations. He hoped that they were programmed correctly to begin with since he had no frame of reference.

*

Two of Peter's students entered the chow hall and began having dinner when two other pilots joined them. The two pilots were friends of theirs when they were all in Reserve Squadron together but now flew in Defend Squadron. They sat and ate quietly before one of them spoke.

"So, I hear you guys are elite now. Better than the rest of us," said the First Lieutenant from Defend Squadron between bites of food. He continued eating as he waited for a response.

"We are kicking ass," said the Reserve wingleader. He was still a second lieutenant but rank did not matter that much in the lower ranks of the chain of command.

"Kicking sim ass. You couldn't shoot down a slug if it stopped in flight for you," shot the Second Lieutenant from Defend Squadron as he began looking for a fight.

"Maybe so, but have you flown the sim?" asked the Reserve wingman.

"Once, I took out the slug," said the Defend Squadron First Lieutenant proudly.

"What level?" shot the Reserve wingleader.

"Level?" asked the stunned Defend Squadron First Lieutenant as he stopped his fork mid-travel.

The Reserve wingleader laughed. "There are five levels on that thing. The machine had been set on level one since it was installed."

"So," replied the Defend Squadron Second Lieutenant defiantly.

"So, we've been kicking the asses of multiple level five targets consistently," said the Reserve wingleader as he stood and picked up his tray. "Mister McCabe is playing in there right now if you wanna go down there and learn something for a change."

"That is ..." added the Reserve wingman as he followed the lead of his wingleader, "if you think you can find the sim room."

Both lieutenants from Defend Squadron looked across the table at each other and grunted. "So, that damn civilian thinks he can play pilot. There's no way those two Reserve holdovers could do multiple slugs in there. I had trouble with one."

"Me too, I had three attempts and got wasted each time," said the Defend Squadron Second Lieutenant as he paused to think about things. Was it actually possible that this frozen man was teaching people effectively? The last instructor died in combat because he was worthless. No one learned a damn thing from that man except where the ejection handle was ... and there were placards for that.

"Should we check it out?" asked the Defend Squadron First Lieutenant.

"Hell ya," shot the Defend Squadron Second Lieutenant. "Maybe we can watch him get splattered on the big screen. That should be worth a few laughs."

"Roger that. Let's go."

They picked up their trays and deposited the contents into the waste bin. They stacked the trays on the shelf and left the chow hall while talking about the frozen simulator guy showing off. Several people sitting near the doorway stopped eating at that point and listened. They knew where the sim room was too and had nothing better to do. So they deposited their trays, told a few friends, and headed for the sim room to check it out.

*

Captain Jeff Washington paused while reviewing the latest requests from Peter to cross his desk. Peter was asking for two more simulator technicians to help out with the overload of simulator training sessions. From what Lieutenant Colonel Terry Nelson had told him, Peter had the Corporal and Sergeant teaching classes for the electronics department and they could use a hand running the simulators.

As far as Jeff was concerned, Peter was breaking a handful of regulations with nothing positive to show for it. Peter's flight had been training for three weeks now and had not even touched a real fighter in that time. Luckily the Bect had not shown up so far on their return trip. After the last battle it had been a quiet flight.

Jeff did not know what the hell had gotten into Terry for him to allow Peter to get away with so many things at once. It was as if Peter were now running the ship, *his* ship. Jeff finally worked himself into a furor and stood quickly as he tossed the latest request onto his desk. It was time to have a face-to-face chat with Peter.

Jeff stormed out of his office and several ensigns jumped out of his way while saluting wildly. He returned the salutes quickly as he proceeded down the hallway at a very fast walk. He avoided the tram since he did not want to wait for it. Plus, all this fast walking was certain to expend some of his anger.

He turned the corner and was confronted by a large group of officers and enlisted crew gathered around the simulator room door. They were all concentrating on looking into the room and never saw him approach. He grunted loudly, clearing his throat, until one of the enlisted women turned and saw him.

"Captain on deck, attention!" yelled the Private First Class as she snapped to attention before anyone else had the chance.

"Make a hole!" yelled Captain Washington to the gathered crowd. The crowd parted quickly while everyone stood at attention. He made his way to the control room where the two technicians were occupied with running the session. Corporal Randy Taylor saw the Captain approach and stood quickly. Sergeant Miguel Rodriguez saw the movement out of the corner of his eye and followed his friend's lead, not knowing whom it was coming up behind him but figuring he would play it safe.

"What the hell is going on here?" asked Captain Washington loudly.

"Sir," started Sergeant Rodriguez while pointing to the three view screens, "Mister McCabe is in the simulator flying a mission against several alien fighters."

"Really? As you were, and give me more detail," said Captain Washington. The steam behind his anger diminished as he realized he may finally find out Peter's worth firsthand.

The two simtechs returned to their work, both grateful that the Captain's anger was not unleashed upon them. Everyone aboard had heard the stories.

"Sir," said Miguel as he pointed to the view screens once again. "Mister McCabe is up against two fighters right now. He is evaluating our missiles to learn their limitations and effectiveness."

"How far into combat is he?" asked Captain Washington as he watched one of the red dots disappear from the screen. Another screen displayed the explosion from the pilot's perspective.

"He just destroyed one of the fighters and is almost done ... he destroyed the other one, sir," said Randy.

"That quick? Colonel Nelson said there is a level selector in this thing."

"Yes sir, there is, right here."

Captain Washington looked at the switch on the control panel and saw the five levels indicated by numbers next to the selector knob. The point of the dial was all the way to the right at the *five*. He sat slowly and cautiously in the chair between the two simtechs.

"Okay, boss," said Randy while talking into the boom microphone attached to his left ear. "What now?"

"Give me five at five," said Peter, "and rearm me but put the fuel at twenty-five percent. I want to see if weight makes a difference."

"Acknowledged, standby," said Randy as Miguel began pressing buttons on the keyboard in front of him. He entered the required information and hit the red *Reset* button on the upper panel.

"Dialed in," said Randy. "Incoming bandits at five o'clock low, coming in hot."

Peter adjusted his short-range scanner and turned sharply to the right by kicking in full right rudder. He pushed the throttles forward to thirty percent power and selected the first target. He depressed the weapon release button to fire a missile at the first target while switching to the second one. He repeated this for all four missiles before turning thirty degrees to the left and increasing to a positive three incline.

"What did he just do?" asked Captain Washington while pointing. "Is he running away from them?"

"Sir, he just released his four missiles and turned off-angle from the incoming fighters," said Miguel. He paused briefly and felt it was time to do some very careful teaching. "Mister McCabe says that the aliens are not *honoring the threat* of an incoming missile. When you have a missile fired at you, the first thing you are supposed to do is concentrate on losing it or somehow getting rid of the damn thing before it kills you. By firing his missiles the aliens should, if they were reacting normally, turn away from them and try to lose them. The aliens currently just fly right into them like carefree blind automatons."

"The Bect don't avoid missiles?" asked Captain Washington as he remembered the Bect's lack of reaction to the missile volley from the last battle. All four of Peter's missiles impacted the approaching Bect fighters but all five dots remained on the screen.

Peter turned to engage the fighters. Captain Washington watched as Peter's Stiletto destroyed two of the damaged Bect fighters in rapid succession. Peter turned quickly in a maneuver that made Captain Washington gasp in awe when it positioned him right behind an alien fighter and another easy kill.

"No sir, they don't. From the video of the last battle they flew right to their deaths."

"Ah, that's right, you've seen the video," said Captain Washington in a voice more neutral than he was expecting. He watched another Bect fighter burst apart as the Sergeant hit a button and zoomed in on the view screen just in time to see Peter line up and destroy the fifth one. The group of gathered pilots, officers, and enlisted men cheered quietly despite still being at attention. The attitude in the room and the hallway was reserved but very energetic. Had the Captain not been there it would have been quite enthusiastic.

"How many pilots can beat the Bect at level five?" asked Captain Washington. He watched the Sergeant flip a few switches and type some data with the keyboard.

"Well sir, before Mister McCabe showed up this machine never left level one. Most pilots couldn't even do that," said Miguel while resetting the options.

"Five at five again with a reload please," said Peter over the speaker. "Fuel load made no difference."

"Roger that," responded Randy.

"How are the seven reserve pilots doing?" asked Captain Washington. He watched the two enlisted men setup for another simulator run.

"Doing great, sir," replied Miguel. "They can't do five at a time yet but we've been training two pilot crews. Most teams can do two at a time at level five."

"Standby," said Randy over the microphone.

Miguel hit the reset button and five enemy fighters appeared on the screen. Peter had already anticipated it so his short-range scanner was waiting for them. He turned his Stiletto toward the enemy and began his run.

"Sir, we'd like to be able to put all eight pilots of a flight into the sims at the same time in order to train them to work more effectively together. That is our biggest weakness. But some of the sims are still broken. We do have two up and running though, so that helps tremendously," added Miguel. It would be nice to have the Captain's pull behind them. *Dropping a few hints never hurt*, thought Miguel.

"Can you add more Bect to a session in progress?" asked Captain Washington as he watched Peter launch his missiles.

"Yes sir," said Miguel with an odd look on his face. He glanced at Randy and both men shrugged. "How many do you want to add, sir?"

"Does he know I'm here?" asked Captain Washington.

"No sir, we haven't told him and he's currently in his own little world," replied Randy.

"Put ten more in then," shot Captain Washington with a grin. He watched Peter remove two Bect fighters from the screen.

Randy laughed, "Mister McCabe is gonna think the Colonel stopped by again."

"Incoming, at your four o'clock high," said Randy into the microphone.

"Oh boy, thought you'd just liven it up a bit, huh?" asked Peter as he destroyed another fighter.

"It gets kind of boring just sitting here watching you slaughter these guys all the time," shot Miguel into his microphone. Peter took another fighter out and quickly finished off the fifth before he turned to engage the ten newcomers.

"Well, bring it on!" yelled Peter with a laugh. "I'm feeling real good tonight."

"All right, you asked for it, sir," shot Miguel as he dialed in another five enemy craft, but he made them bombers. "You've got bombers incoming." Randy chuckled softly.

"Captain, I added five bombers to your ten fighters just to make it more interesting," said Miguel.

"There are bombers in that thing too?" asked Captain Washington as he nodded absently.

"Yes sir, we programmed them in last week."

"Shit, I'd ask for a cruiser but you haven't programmed that yet," said Peter. He shouted rude comments about the alien's mothers over the simulated command frequency while routinely destroying them. The bombers presented a major threat to him so he wasted through a few more fighters before engaging them. He found that keeping some fighters in the mix made things more interesting for the bombers to try and single him out. He came real close to tricking a couple of them into ramming each other. Had they been real ships they may have impacted.

"My God," said Captain Washington. He watched in awed reverence as this one-man squadron wasted through a total of twenty enemy craft, five of which were bombers, on the highest setting the simulators were programmed for. Miguel was ready to add some more to the battle when Captain Washington reluctantly stopped him.

"I've seen enough. More than I imagined possible," said Captain Washington quietly. "Thank you Sergeant, and thank you Corporal." He shook both of their hands as he stood and turned toward the quiet simulators. The cheering in the room was muted and silenced as soon as the Captain stood.

"You're welcome, sir," said the simtechs in unison.

Miguel brought the simulator to a safe spot and shut it down so Peter could exit. The canopy popped open and Peter climbed out to see a large gathering of people in the simulator room. He wondered why they were unusually quiet until he saw Captain Washington standing in the simulator control room.

"Well done, Lieutenant," said Captain Washington loudly. He walked down the few steps and approached Peter.

"But I'm a warrant officer, sir," said Peter with a confused look on his face.

"Not anymore, you just earned your commission, son," said Captain Washington as he saluted Peter. Peter returned it with a big smile on his face.

"Thank you, sir."

"I have a few more things to talk with you about," started Captain Washington as he headed for the classroom. "Come with me, son. The rest of you are dismissed. I'm sure there's somewhere else you all need to be right now."

"Yes sir," was the combined response as the crowd dispersed quickly and quietly from the simulator room and hallway. Peter followed the Captain into the classroom and closed the door behind them. Captain Washington took a seat in the front row. Peter stood nearby until Captain Washington motioned for him to have a seat too.

"We need to get your flight outfitted and give you some real Stilettos. I want to see what your flight can do out in the real world, with you commanding them, of course. I will also approve your request for simulator parts to repair all the broken simulators. Since your duties are going to be changing we will need to make some small changes in the training department. I do have some questions though," said Captain Washington as he reclined as much as his chair would allow.

"Yes sir?"

"What is the purpose of training enlisted people in the electronics department?"

Peter took a deep breath and exhaled slowly. He knew this talk was coming and already had his speech planned. He expected a more in-depth questioning from Lieutenant Colonel Nelson and not the Captain. Oh well, it did not really matter who he pitched the plan to, he would need to get the Captain's approval anyway.

"Well sir, the purpose is two-fold. The most obvious and immediate is the barter of simulator time in exchange for them repairing our simulators. The hidden purpose is to evaluate potential pilot candidates from the enlisted ranks of the ship, since finding replacement pilots seems like quite the adventure by using normal channels. A somewhat similar thing was done during World War Two with the enlisted ranks and some exceptional pilots were found by accident; probably the most well-known being Chuck Yeager."

"Not familiar with that name or that war but it sounds like a decent plan on both counts. Now, how about explaining those two simtechs of yours flying and teaching?"

"They are both very good pilots and teachers, sir. As odd as this may sound, I think they would make very good officers and combat pilots."

Captain Washington sat silently and nodded as he absorbed the information. Peter wondered where this was all going and what question would come next. He was not prepared for the next words out of the Captain's mouth.

"Let's find out. I'll make them both warrant officers until such time as they complete the written portion of the flight exam. That has been waved in your case. Then they can become officers and continue as instructors until they pass their flight test. I'll also assign two more simtechs to your training department to help you all. You are still in charge of this beast so I'll let you have the pleasure of informing them."

"Thank you, sir," said Peter.

"Thank me? Oh no, Lieutenant, you've got a lot of work ahead of you. You'll probably be cursing me in the end with all the shit I'm going to pile on you." Captain Washington laughed as he stood and shook hands with Peter. "That was an amazing display in the simulator. I hope you can do that for real."

"Me too, sir," said Peter as he walked with Captain Washington to the door. He opened it and found the two simtechs performing maintenance on the recently shut down sim. They both looked at the opening door and snapped to attention as the Captain walked in.

"As you were, men. Good job today and thanks for the impromptu lesson."

"Thank you, sir," responded the two simtechs as Captain Washington left the room and proceeded down the hallway.

Peter patiently waited a minute to make sure the Captain was out of ear-shot. "What the hell happened out here while I was flying?"

"A bunch of enlisted and officers stopped by to see the Amazing Randy," said Miguel while pointing to his friend.

Randy smacked Miguel in the arm. "I thought the Captain was gonna tear our heads off when he showed up."

"And you couldn't tell me he was here?" shot Peter.

"Nope, he didn't want us to, sir."

"After you added those extra fighters I thought for sure that the Colonel had stopped by to say hi again. Then the bombers showed up and I figured you were just screwing with me, trying to watch me crash and burn."

"If we did that then we'd look bad too. I knew you could handle it," said Miguel. "Besides, with the audience we had it was standing room only. We should've sold tickets, sir."

"Quit calling me sir, dammit!"

"Sorry, sir," said Randy. The smirk on his face showed just how sorry he was.

"Okay, that's it, I've had it with you two. I'm gonna make you both warrant officers so people can *sir* you for a change."

"Yeah, right," said Miguel with a snicker, "I'd like to see you pull that one off ... sir."

They received the orders the next day.

CHAPTER
18

The name stenciled on the side of the Stiletto, just under the canopy, was *Lt. Col. Terry Nelson*. The ship was immaculate, showing no signs of battle damage anywhere. The first thing Peter noticed were the pylon mounts located on the top of the stubby wings, right where he had suggested them. This Stiletto had eight Devrac-Two missiles loaded on it as the technicians were preparing it for launch.

"This bird is modified," said Peter to no one in particular.

"That's right, Lieutenant," replied Master Sergeant Tim Minor.

"Please, Tim, still call me Peter, unless someone higher ranking is around."

"Okay Peter, it's good seeing you again."

"Likewise." The two shook hands.

"Well, this bird started life as a top-of-the-line D-model Stiletto. Manu-factured just six months ago with the latest and greatest technology all of United Earth could provide. We added the upper wing pylons per a request from Colonel Nelson, something to try out."

"Looks good," replied Peter as he examined the pylons more closely.

"We completed modifications a week ago, but haven't found anyone crazy enough to try it out." Tim laughed as he went back to his clipboard and checked off a few more items.

"Any other modifications, Tim?"

"Another as yet untested modification to the laser generators. We lucked into a piece of alien metal and used that for testing. We were able to determine that a slight frequency change and boost of power increased damage exponentially."

"He listened," said Peter under his breath and with a smile. The sharp technician heard him and examined him with renewed interest.

"You came up with these ideas," said Tim. It was a statement and not a question.

"Yes I did. I passed them along to Colonel Nelson because I figured he had the best chance of actually getting them implemented, although I didn't expect him to succeed in doing so."

"They were very good ideas and rather easy to do," said Tim as he went back to filling out the form on his clipboard. "Next time just present the ideas to me and I'll take care of it if I like them."

"Sure, Tim. I thought I'd bother the Colonel since you're usually up to your neck in work," said Peter as he examined the forward fuselage.

"I do have some free time available," replied Tim, "in October." He laughed and Peter joined him. "I think I'm going to like having a pilot with a technical background around."

Peter continued his inspection and paused when he got to the laser cannon ports. "How much has the laser damage increased?"

"Ten percent," shot Tim absently as he continued writing.

"Only ten percent?"

"Huh? What?" asked Tim while looking up from the clipboard. He looked around and tried to orient himself before continuing. "Sorry Peter, my mind was elsewhere. I meant that these new lasers can do in ten percent what the others were able to do at one hundred percent."

"Meaning," prodded Peter as he tried to figure out what Tim meant. "If it took twenty laser blasts to kill a slug before it will now take only two?"

"Something like that. It hasn't been tested on an actual enemy craft though. The only testing we did was in the lab on a piece of their ship. Not even sure if the upgraded cannons will overheat in the fuselage."

"How did you manage to get that piece?"

"One of the fighters came in after a battle a while ago with a large chunk of an alien ship stuck between the left engine nacelle and wing. From it we determined that the strange metal was absorbing most of the laser energy. That pissed us all off and we got very busy after that, to the point of being obsessed."

"When are the new lasers going to be tested?" asked Peter.

"As soon as you're ready," said Tim as he motioned for a few other technicians to come over. "The Colonel suggested, and rather forcefully I might add, that you should take his ship for a spin since he doesn't get much of a chance to actually fly it anymore. Looks like you are the crazy pilot for today."

"Awesome! How long to get all the other lasers modified if this test works out?"

"We figure we can modify the ships that are left on the carrier within a week. Probably a day for the lasers and the rest to do the pylon mounts."

Several technicians walked over and began prepping the Stiletto for launch. Peter quickly found himself in a discussion concerning the electronic technicians and their simulator deal. He made a similar offer to the hanger maintenance technicians and they readily accepted. If these modifications worked out he could probably come up with a few more ideas to increase the effectiveness of the Stiletto in combat. Then a lot of simulator modifications and programming were going to become necessary.

Peter put on the orange environmental suit and helmet with the assistance of a few technicians. He wondered how this suit would affect his flying ability. The more he thought about it the more he realized that the Stiletto was designed with the environmental suit in mind. Even in the simulator, which was identical to the real cockpit, the switches were placed in such a way that the extra bulk from the suit's gloves would not interfere with their proper operation.

It did not take him very long to suit up and climb the ladder to the cockpit. The motion was somewhat awkward since he had never done it before. Once he was seated he familiarized himself with operating the controls with the gloves as the technicians fastened his five-point harness.

"We'll have the recorders on you. We also put several monitoring devices on the wings and elsewhere to analyze the stress and things like that for those added pylons," said Tim as he patted Peter on the helmet. "Have a good flight, Peter."

"Thanks Tim," replied Peter as he turned on the computers and began the preflight checklist. The technicians vacated the launch platform as the canopy sealed Peter into his first real Stiletto.

"Stiletto Test One is ready for launch," said Peter over the command frequency. He thanked protocol in the simulator for preparing him to make all the necessary communications. It felt just like another flight in the sim.

"Test One you are cleared for launch. Proceed to a positive five incline for your test flight," said the controller.

"Acknowledged," replied Peter as the outer doors opened and the platform angled downward forty-five degrees. A green light came on and he eased the throttles forward slightly to leave the hanger far behind. With a slight backward pressure on the control stick he was increasing inclines. Being weightless for the first time in his life felt exhilarating.

The control movements felt similar to the sim but he had much more control in the real thing. The simulator tended to be sloppy in its flight dynamics. He wondered if that were possible to correct. Maybe Randy could figure it out. The closer they could get the simulator to the real thing the better it would be for everyone involved.

Peter turned on the short-range scanner and, for the very first time, saw the entire Carrier Group below him. He rolled the Stiletto inverted so he could look up at the Group. He imagined that he was actually below them and found that relative position in space was just that, relative. With no frame of reference, space was just one giant sea of blackness in every direction and for as far as you could see. He played with the navigation computer to figure out his bearings and to locate the carrier if he became disoriented. The computers on the actual Stiletto were identical to the simulator.

His first order of business was to play with the physics of space. He needed to find out if he could do the crazy things that he found in the sim. He kicked both rudder pedals a few times to feel the nose displace as the thrusters fired. He also jerked the control stick around and played with advancing and retarding the throttles, both together and one at a time. The ship responded nicely and the differences between the real thing and the simulator were very subtle.

After ten minutes of performing various maneuvers and changing directions he pushed the throttles forward and tried some high speed maneuvering. The simulator was very close in those respects too, which brought him a lot of comfort. The Stiletto was a very responsive fighter and an outright pleasure to fly.

Peter turned on his weapon systems and heard the rush of air leaving the cockpit. The cockpit pressure gauge soon read zero, which was standard operating procedure for combat. If the cockpit took damage or a fire erupted, and there was a vacuum in the cockpit, it would prevent extensive damage to the pilot and equipment. He fired several blasts of lasers at an empty section of space and ran diagnostics on the systems. Everything performed as expected.

As Peter approached the Group to call it a day his short-range scanner went blank for a second. Nothing else changed on his display and he thought it very odd so he looked out of his top window to examine the Group. His eyes were not perfect, unfortunately, but they were good enough for most things. He immediately spotted a few Bect fighters swarming around one of the support craft at the trailing edge of the Group.

"Ticonderoga, Test One," said Peter over the command frequency. "I see several enemy fighters attacking the rear support ship but show nothing on my short-range scanner."

"Negative, Test One, there is nothing on our scanners."

"Well, you might want to send First Alert Flight to check it out."

"Negative contact, Test One," was the response. "First Alert Flight has been delayed."

"Well, shit," said Peter to himself as he angled his ship toward the support craft. He had ample fuel, missiles, and was otherwise comfortable in the craft. He might as well go in for a closer look, just in case.

He turned on his combat computer and it lit up like a Christmas tree. There was intense static on the screen that he figured was some sort of jamming. He pushed the throttles forward and closed the gap rapidly, as the enemy fighters grew larger in his window.

"Mayday!" said a worried female voice over the command frequency. "Cargo Three is under attack, please send help."

"Cargo Three, Ticonderoga. We show no enemy activity on our scanners. We'll send First Alert Flight when they have launched."

"Ticonderoga, Test One. I have a visual on multiple enemy targets in the vicinity of Cargo Three," said Peter calmly over the command frequency. "I count at least ten Bect fighters and suspect one specialized ship with jamming capability. Send out the troops while I go and say hi."

"Test One, you are not authorized for combat."

"Looks like I am now, by default."

"Test One, negative. Return for landing."

"Listen up, Ticonderoga," shot Peter as he damn near yelled it over the frequency. "Scramble the fighters, the enemy is jamming your damn scanners."

"Test One, do not engage. You are not authorized for combat. Return for landing."

"Screw that, Cargo Three is taking damage and can't wait all day for you to pull your head out of your ass. I'll keep those fighters busy, just get First Alert Flight out here immediately."

"I'm not taking that kind of verbal abuse from a second lieutenant," shot the controller.

"I'm sure you will soon find someone higher in the chain of command that will gladly verbally abuse you."

"I'll have you court-martialed for this."

"You can court-martial my boot when it's up your ass, you idiot. I'm going in," said Peter as he readied himself for his first combat encounter.

The controller kept warning him to back off and to let the Alert fighters, who were still on the carrier, handle the enemy. Peter ignored the idiot and was thankful when the command frequency quieted down.

Peter lined up on the closest fighter and depressed his trigger. The laser blasts were just a slight bit slower than the simulator and the slug popped well before it should have. He turned to the next one and pulled the trigger four times and the slug burst wide open. He found two other slugs close to each other and sprayed laser blasts while turning and both of them disintegrated. The new laser upgrade was absolutely amazing.

A few of the slugs acknowledged his being there and took to following him, which was risky business but helped keep the heat off of the cargo ship. He kept them on his tail as he searched the area for a possible bomber and a few laser blasts impacted his rear hull causing minor damage. He found a large bulbous bomber under the cargo ship lining up for a missile shot. Peter pushed his throttles forward and sprayed the bomber with laser blasts. A missile exited the gumdrop's launch tube and plowed into the bottom of the cargo ship causing a huge explosion. The gumdrop's shields did not last very long under the new lasers and soon the bomber popped in a large and bright explosion.

Immediately upon its demise, Peter's short-range scanner came to life and indicated fourteen more fighters and that same cruiser that kept following the Group.

"Okay, you slimy bastards," said Peter over the command frequency. "I can see you now and I'm one unhappy camper."

Peter pulled his throttles to idle and kicked in full right rudder to whip his ship around in a smooth one hundred and eighty-degree flat spin. He depressed his trigger and the three slugs following him disintegrated in rapid succession. He pushed his throttles forward and quickly changed direction to engage another two slugs that were concentrating on the engine compartment of the cargo ship. They disappeared in a shower of laser blasts and he moved to the next nearest target. A quick check of his combat computer showed that three more fighters were playing with the cargo ship so he went after those.

His main concern was protecting the cargo ship and then keeping the fighters busy.

"Damn, you guys are like bees," said Peter over the command frequency. "Ticonderoga, do you have an ETA on Alert?"

"Thirty seconds," said a new voice over the frequency. It sounded like Captain Washington's voice.

"Roger that," said Peter as he removed the remaining direct threats to the cargo ship. The alien fighters were concentrating on him now and he counted five of them on his tail so he led them away. A few blasts came close to his Stiletto so he advanced his throttles, but the alien ships matched him. He waited until he was a sufficient distance away from the cargo ship before he tried a new maneuver, that he created on the spot, from knowledge derived from the Stiletto Flight Manual. Peter pulled back on his control stick and began increasing inclines. He quickly reduced the power to idle and pressed the button for vertical engine control and advanced the throttles. Large thrusters along the bottom of the Stiletto came to life. They were used mostly for landing vertically on planets but Peter surmised another useful purpose for them. The thrusters caused his ship to create a quick loop in a very small distance.

"Party time, you dumb bastards," said Peter over the command frequency. He pulled the throttles to idle, released the vertical control button, advanced the throttles, and depressed his trigger in one smooth motion. Two of the fighters popped immediately while one spun out of control and the other two struggled to stay clear of the wreckage.

"First Alert Flight is on the way," said the voice.

First Alert Flight was caught with their pants down. Someone screwed up big time and, if that actually was the Captain's voice, somebody was going to get reamed for it. But Peter could not think about that right now, he had three alien fighters left to dispatch. The spinning one took only one laser shot before it popped and the last two finally gave up and ran for the cruiser.

Peter advanced the throttles and placed a few laser blasts into the backsides of the two retreating slugs. They both disintegrated and Peter avoided the resulting junk easily. He brought the cruiser up on his combat computer and targeted it as he moved the throttles over the stops. He pushed them full forward to achieve a speed of four SU as the distance to the cruiser diminished rapidly.

"What are you doing, son?" asked Captain Washington. Peter was certain that it was the Captain now. Only the Captain addressed him like that and the Colonel's voice was quite different.

"Collecting data, sir," replied Peter.

"Looks to me like you might be doing something crazy."

"Oh, crazy is probably not the right word for it, sir."

The cruiser turned when it saw the lone fighter approaching and began moving in the opposite direction. It would still take it a few seconds to achieve enough speed to leave the small fighter far behind. The rear laser cannons began firing and Peter found it somewhat easy to evade the incoming blasts. When he was within range of his missiles he launched all eight of them as fast as the weapons computer would allow.

One of his missiles, the third one to leave his pylons, took a direct laser hit halfway to the target and detonated. The other seven missiles flew into the cruiser's two engine exhaust ports, creating quite a display of light with several secondary explosions. The cruiser's laser cannons ceased operation when their power plant was silenced. Peter slowed to one SU and approached cautiously while his scanners took as many readings as possible.

"Does anybody know where the fuel compartment is located on this thing?" asked Peter over the command frequency. There was no response so he shot various places on its hull while maintaining what he felt was a comfortable distance. He reduced to fifty percent power and continued peppering the cruiser with laser blasts while his recorders were working overtime.

Peter eventually found a 'soft spot' beneath the cruiser and just forward of the engines. A few well-placed laser blasts and the subsequent explosions were enough of a warning for him to vacate the area. He turned toward the Group and pushed his throttles to four SU as he watched the cruiser through his rear camera. The resulting explosion almost looked nuclear in nature as the flash nearly blinded him. Luckily, according to the flight manual, the rear optics were shielded from the extreme light of the sun.

"I think I'll call this test flight a success," said Peter over the command frequency.

"Did you just take out that cruiser?" asked a voice he did not recognize.

"Yes, it made the mistake of sticking around too long," shot Peter. "Who are you?"

"Captain Mendez, Alert Squadron leader."

"Hey Captain, you're a little late for the party."

"Communication error. Forming up on your right wing."

"Roger."

"Hey Peter," said Carlos Mendez over the wingcom. "Amazing job."

"Thanks Carlos. I'm sorry about John, he was a good guy."

"Thanks."

"Do you think I can get you and your men to come to training now?" shot Peter.

"I think if we don't volunteer we will be ordered to attend," replied Carlos, and they both laughed. "I think the Captain is going to have fun abusing that controller."

"What a moron that guy is," said Peter.

"Yeah, and the funniest thing about it was that everyone in the Carrier Group heard you rip him apart too. I think your display of spacemanship was broadcast to the entire Group. You're a hero."

"Well Carlos, the only difference between being a hero or just plain crazy is the amount of paperwork they give you afterward."

The nine Stilettos returned to the Group and Peter headed for the damaged cargo ship while First Alert Flight went on patrol. Several repair vessels were already busy trying to fix the damage as he inspected the ship from a safe distance.

"Test One, Ticonderoga. Report to the Captain upon recovery," said the new voice over the command frequency.

"Ticonderoga, Test One. Acknowledged," replied Peter as he continued to assess the cargo ship.

"Are you the one they call the Iceman?" asked a female voice over his short-range frequency.

"Yes ma'am, Second Lieutenant Peter McCabe is the name."

"I'm Lieutenant Commander Emily Conrad, commander of Cargo Three. Thank you for the save."

"My pleasure."

"I owe you a beer."

"Damn, haven't had one of those in over three hundred years. I'll take you up on that."

"Stop by whenever you get the chance, you're always welcome on my ship."

"Thank you Commander, take care. Out."

"You too. Out."

Peter turned toward the carrier and accelerated. Now it was time to see the Captain and probably discuss his actions. He was too happy about the way the Stiletto handled and how things compared to the simulator to even come close to dreading the meeting. The Captain was a very fair man, despite his reputation, and a man that he respected tremendously. Peter would bend over backward to help him out and gladly die in the process of doing so. There were not that many people he knew in this current time that he could say that about. Actually, there were not that many people here that he knew.

Upon returning to the carrier he was greeted by a large quantity of technicians who quickly began removing video memory cartridges. Another group of technicians climbed onto the wings to examine the newly added pylons with various pieces of test equipment. The technicians that helped him out of the Stiletto opened the forward avionics compartment and began unfastening the panel for access to the lasers.

"How did it go?" asked Tim.

"Better than expected. The lasers were just as you had said, two or three good hits and they are goners. The missiles had no problems or errors coming off those extra pylons and you'll most likely get better information about those from your technicians."

"We saw your entire flight via video feed and most of the battle was broadcast over the ship-wide view screens."

"Shit, everyone in the Group saw that?" asked Peter in surprise.

"Damn right, Peter. You can seriously kick some alien ass."

"All thanks to you, my friend."

"Looks like I'll need to change the name on this fighter."

"But won't Colonel Nelson still need it?"

"He doesn't fly much and I think you pretty much made this bird your own with that flight. There's no way the Colonel will want you in another one. You've earned it."

"Thanks. After my talk with the Captain I'm sure you and your crew will be very busy upgrading all the Stilettos. Maybe you can get some recognition with the manufacturer when you submit *your* ideas for modifications."

"Yeah, right. Like they'd listen to a line tech."

"Sometimes people can surprise you. Especially once you show them the video of the fight I just got into. They'll shit Twinkies."

"What's a Twinkie?" asked Tim.

"Never mind, not important. Give it a shot though. It will definitely help the war effort. I think we'll be kicking lots of ass soon. Good job with the modifications, Tim. Thank the rest of your crew for me."

"Thank you, sir."

Peter left the flight deck and headed for the bridge. He heard Tim passing along the praise from the man everyone seemed to be calling the Iceman. It was odd how the other pilots did not use call signs like in the old days but that he was quickly given one.

CHAPTER
19

The Captain was not a man to be left waiting for very long, so Peter skipped the tram ride and walked quickly to the front of the ship. It was really difficult for him to see this monstrosity as a ship. It never sank in until he saw it from the outside. Several people congratulated him as they passed by while others saluted.

Both guards outside the door to the bridge snapped to attention and saluted him crisply. They were sergeants and their uniforms were the sharpest and neatest he had seen.

"Great job, sir," said the guard on the left. "The Captain is expecting you."

"Thank you, Sergeant."

The guards opened the door for him and he walked onto the bridge. Everyone stood as he entered and began cheering and clapping, even the Captain. Captain Washington walked up to Peter and saluted him. Peter returned the salute and then shook the man's proffered hand.

"That was outright amazing, although a bit daring and very crazy. At first

I thought you were a dead man, again, until you started cleaning up the area. I was planning a good ass-chewing for overextending your orders but after that display I figured the point was moot."

"Thank you, sir. What happened to First Alert Flight?" asked Peter as he looked around the bridge. The cheering had subsided and everyone returned to work.

"Miscommunication on a new lieutenant junior grade's part. Second Alert Flight was recovered before the others had been dispatched. The Lieutenant has found himself unexpectedly reassigned to the janitorial command with a sergeant as his commander. I have a feeling that that sergeant loves his current position right about now. Come with me."

Captain Washington led him to his cabin and closed the door behind them. He grabbed the freshly brewed pot of coffee and poured a cup for both of them. He sat behind his desk and beckoned Peter to sit as well. They sat quietly for a few minutes just sipping coffee and relaxing after an interesting morning.

"So, what do you think?" asked Captain Washington, breaking the silence. It was a rather open-ended question that Peter was unsure of where to begin.

"Sir, I could answer that with a lot of different things concerning a lot of different subjects. Where do you want me to start?"

"Just start at the beginning and go from there."

Peter did just that. He told the Captain about the Stiletto upgrades and the tech responsible for accomplishing them. He described them in detail and how they affected his rescue of the cargo ship. With the new jamming bomber, which was something Captain Washington and the intelligence section never thought possible, Peter decided against using his missiles. It was a good thing he kept them in reserve to take out that cruiser afterward.

Captain Washington wanted to be angry about that stunt but found himself congratulating the man on removing the alien pest from his section of space. That cruiser had been following them for some odd reason for a very long time, constantly becoming a thorn in their side.

"Why all the chatter on the radio? You do know they can translate it."

"Yes sir, communication is essential in battle and they have crippled us in that regard. So, I figured, why not try and inundate them with some useful information along with a lot of useless crap. By the time they have it figured out it will be too late for them to use."

"Makes sense to me, start training the pilots to do that."

"Yes sir."

"You seem to like the word *bastard* very much."

"Yes sir. I use it to get myself mad."

"Mad?"

"Yes sir, mad enough to kill. It's a kill-or-be-killed war out there and I'd rather be on the side doing the killing."

Captain Washington nodded absently as he brought the coffee cup to his mouth to take a sip. "We'll be arriving at Virginia Prime in just over two weeks. Once there we are picking up replacement crew and Stilettos. I have requested a two-week layover with a special purpose in mind. First off, we could use the rest. Secondly, I want you to teach a special class and I'm requesting that the Admiral order every instructor and Flight Group Commander nearby to attend. I sent him various videos of your training sessions, debriefings, and missions. He seemed impressed by them and after he sees your recent display I think he will quickly issue the order."

"Sounds like a perfect opportunity, sir," said Peter as he smiled and sipped at his coffee. It was a good blend and better than any other cup of coffee he had on the ship so far, including Tim's engine degreaser.

"In the meantime you are to train every single pilot on this ship. I'm having one of the nearby bunk areas remodeled to contain classrooms, four total. So, if you find any new teachers in the mix feel free to put them to use."

"Thank you, sir."

Captain Washington slid a pair of silver captain bars across the desk. Peter picked them up slowly as his eyebrows furled.

"I know it's a jump in rank but it is more fitting for a Squadron Commander. You and your pilots will be a full squadron when we refit."

"Thank you, sir."

"Don't thank me, you've earned it. Tonight we're having a meeting of all

non-essential personnel in the auditorium. Wear your full dress uniform because you're giving a speech."

"A speech?"

"Yes, and you better be ready for it too."

"Oh shit."

Captain Jeff Washington laughed. The conversation and atmosphere
shifted from professional to personal as Jeff asked him about the Twenty-
First Century. The two time periods were vastly different and the enemy was
external now as opposed to over three hundred years ago. Peter liked things
better this way and was happy to learn that the Earth was united. Jeff was a
very likable fellow but Peter would never tell anyone that. It would not be
good for people to think anything other than that the Captain was a hard-ass
with an attitude you had to watch out for.

*

The time for the meeting came too quickly and Peter was nervous. It was
a struggle to get his uniform on correctly but, with the help of a passing med-
ic, he straightened it out. The Reserve officers met him in the hallway and the
eight of them, and the two newly promoted warrant officers, made their way
to the auditorium. They were told to sit in the front row, which they all
balked at. They talked for a few minutes before things began when a guard
called the room to attention. Captain Washington walked onstage and to the
waiting podium.

Captain Washington cleared his throat and said, "Good evening everyone. At ease and please be seated." All those present, which was close to two
thousand people, sat and remained quiet.

"I think by this time most everyone aboard has seen the video of today's
rescue of Cargo Three. When we brought this man's cryo-cylinder onto the
ship I thought we were just picking up some space junk. I never expected it
to change the course of this war, but that it has. If anybody hasn't realized
that then you are blind.

"Today I promoted that man, Peter McCabe, to captain. Skipping a rank
is an unprecedented thing, but so is dying and being revived three hundred
and twenty-eight years later."

Most of those in the auditorium laughed. Then the hall returned to absolute quiet as Captain Washington shifted a bit and continued.

"He has been a great asset to this ship and to our Group. There are modifications to the Stiletto taking place as we speak to greatly enhance our firepower. Soon the training department will be running around the clock to prepare our pilots for their new mission. We will no longer be on the defensive, running from fights. We will soon be on the offensive taking the battle to the enemy, wherever we can find them."

This brought a cheer from the crowd until the Captain raised his hands to silence them.

"Captain Peter McCabe, front and center." Peter stood rapidly and marched onto the stage. He marched to the Captain and stopped, saluting crisply. Captain Washington saluted and returned to the microphone.

"Under adverse conditions in the service of protecting a sister ship of the Group, Captain McCabe entered combat alone against eighteen enemy fighters and one bomber. His actions saved numerous lives on Cargo Three and of the Group by removing the alien ships from existence. He then proceeded to destroy the enemy cruiser that had been shadowing us for the past six months. For his bravery and his skill on this day, I proudly present Captain Peter McCabe with the Distinguished Flying Cross."

Captain Washington removed the medal from the blue velvet-covered case and pinned it to Peter's left breast pocket. Once it was in place he took a step back and saluted him. Peter returned the salute and the Captain ushered him to the podium as the crowd cheered and clapped. Peter waited patiently for the din to subside.

"Thank you everyone. Success is a team effort. Yes, I have done quite a bit since my revival and very few people knew about it until today. From what I have seen a lot of this turnaround was started before I was revived. Captain Mendez and the late Lieutenant Bowyer began changing things with the assistance of Captain Cleam. Luckily the foresight of Colonel Nelson and Captain Washington allowed them to continue.

"Then something odd happened. A strange frozen man joined in with crazy ideas and a bizarre notion to help out as much as he could. That was my main purpose. I was displaced from the only home I ever knew and thrust into a war with aliens that I still don't know what the hell they are."

"And neither do we," yelled out someone in the audience. This caused a few laughs as someone nearby smacked the man in the shoulder.

"Exactly. What they are doesn't matter, but they are trying to kill us. So, our team effort has begun in earnest. I can already see the change in morale so let's continue it. With everyone doing their part, whether flying Stilettos or cooking the burgers that we all love to eat, we will make this war a win for us. Everyone is important. If you can't see that just take a look around the next time you are cleaning the hallways or fixing that broken engine part. Without your job, would this carrier be able to perform its function? Hell no! This war machine needs every part working at peak efficiency in order to perform its mission successfully. So, let's get busy and kick some alien ass!"

The cheer was near deafening. Captain Washington figured that if there were more to Peter's speech then there was no way to quiet this bunch for him to finish. He shook Peter's hand and saluted him again before Peter walked off the stage and took a seat amidst claps on his back. It took the Captain almost five minutes to calm things down enough to continue.

"All right, people. Virginia Prime in two weeks and then two weeks for refit and a little shore leave. Let's get this war machine cranked up to full power," said Captain Washington into the microphone. A near deafening *aye aye sir* filled the auditorium as Lieutenant Colonel Nelson called the room to attention. The Captain left the stage and Lieutenant Colonel Nelson called out *dismissed* before following him.

Peter and his flight of Reserve pilots left the room as every person nearby patted them on the back and shook their hands. The camaraderie and morale were through the roof and Peter hoped it would stay that way for a long time. There was still a lot of work to do and it was at this point that he saw the camera crew nearby. He guessed that the meeting and his speech was being played throughout the Group and eventually would make it to the Admiral's desk.

So much for Peter keeping a low profile in this time period. He smiled because he would not have it any other way. In his previous life he was just a jack-of-all-trades-and-master-of-none. He figured that that very trait is what made him adapt and excel here. He had always been a follower and never had the chance to be a leader, so it was new territory for him. He had the chance to be the man he had always wanted to be and he grabbed it with both hands. Peter was quite proud of himself and of the men around him.

For Miguel and Randy, enlisted life had been just a job for them and being a simtech was not a very glamorous job either. They did not think it contributed much at all to the war effort, and the way the training department was run previously it really could not. Everything had changed for them, and for the better. They smiled at each other and shared a knowing nod.

March
2348

CHAPTER
20

Virginia Prime was a hotbed of activity as the UE Ticonderoga pulled into orbit. Two other carriers, the Stanwix and the Stark, were already in orbit around the planet. Hundreds of support craft and cargo vessels circled the area transferring people and equipment on and off planet. Several squadrons of fighters actively patrolled while the new carrier joined the crowd. A space station sat in a high orbit with twice the normal staff of controllers on duty to coordinate the action.

Ticonderoga's cargo vessels entered the atmosphere and descended to the overflowing spaceport to offload their goods. The usually crowded dock area was almost impossible to walk through as thousands of people tried to make their way into town for shore leave. Most of the ships in orbit were there for a high-level meeting of the command staff that was planned for the same time. The Stark, the Stanwix, and the Ticonderoga also needed to refit and collect new fighters and pilots, along with other requested personnel.

Peter was on the first shuttle heading to the planet along with Miguel, Randy, and Roger. Miguel and Randy were going to the military administration building to take their pilot written tests. Roger had seriously considered putting in for a transfer but Peter was able to convince him that he was needed on the Ticonderoga. Fate had placed both of them there so they had to stick together and attempt to figure out what Fate's purpose was for them. Roger wanted to find the military library on the base, to see what new books he could find. Peter had a lot of classes to teach and eventually the rest of his friends, his inner circle of the training department, were going to join him.

When they landed on the planet it looked like Earth to Peter. The sky was a similar blue and the dirt on the ground was just brown like any other dirt. He mentioned this to his friends and they just shrugged. It all looked the same to them too and the gravity was real enough. Peter wondered what Earth of the future looked like. Was there ever going to be an end to this war? What would he do then? The questions flowed too fast for him so he ignored them and thought about the class he had to teach in three hours.

The last ship in the line at the spaceport was Cargo Three. He bid farewell to his friends and stopped at the bottom of the ramp. The ship was a lot bigger from this angle and he stood staring at it for a few minutes. He could see the scorch marks from where he was and watched as several crews with equipment and metal began working on the damage. They were all ants with a purpose in comparison against the size of the cargo ship.

Peter walked up the ramp and was stopped at the top by one of the two guards on duty. The guard's uniform bore two blue stripes on the green sleeve, signifying corporal, and a laser pistol hung in the holster at his waist.

"Sorry sir," said the Corporal, "only crew, maintenance, or cargo handlers are allowed aboard and only with special authorization."

"Sorry Corporal, I'm new here and didn't know. Would there be any way I could see Lieutenant Commander Conrad?" asked Peter as he moved out of the way of a forklift-looking device. It entered the hold and extracted a large container that was easily three times its size. The forklift device lifted it smoothly and moved off of the ship.

"I'm sorry sir, she is busy at the moment."

"Oh, okay. Could you let her know that Captain McCabe is on planet and will be at the training facility for a couple of weeks?"

"Captain McCabe? The Iceman?"

Peter nodded, "Yeah, that's me."

"Oh hell," said the Corporal as both guards snapped to attention and saluted him proudly. "She'd have me shot if she knew I didn't let you aboard. Come with me, sir." Peter shook the other Corporal's hand and had to shake the hand of every single enlisted person and officer as he made his way through the ship. They were a very friendly bunch and extremely grateful for his help.

The bridge was a lot smaller than the carrier's was and a lot more crowded too. Fifteen people were actively repairing things or handling various day-to-day operations. Lieutenant Commander Emily Conrad sat in a chair overlooking all the subordinates while filling out a stack of paperwork three centimeters thick. She appeared to be the same age as him, or so it seemed from his angle. She had shoulder-length brown hair that was tied up neatly at the lower back of her head.

"Excuse me, Commander, there's someone here to see you," said the Corporal.

"Oh, this had better be important, Corporal," said Lieutenant Commander Conrad without looking up. She signed one sheet of paper and moved it to a pile being held carefully by a young male ensign.

"Ma'am, this is Captain McCabe."

She stopped what she was doing and quickly turned. Her skin was smooth and only marred by the tired look under her eyes. As soon as she saw him her eyes lit up and a big smile crossed her face. Peter's heart skipped a beat for she was beautiful. She took the remaining stack of papers she was working on and stood, depositing them on her empty seat along with the pen. She was slim, maybe sixty kilograms or so on a good day, and one hundred and sixty-eight centimeters tall.

"My knight in shining armor," said Lieutenant Commander Conrad as she approached him. She looked him up and down and nodded with a smile. "You don't look three hundred and fifty years old to me."

"Technically speaking I'm three hundred and sixty-one years old. But physically speaking I'm only thirty-three," said Peter as he shook her hand.

Her grip was firm and friendly and she nodded at his response.

"Thank you, Corporal, you may return to your post."

"Thank you, ma'am," the Corporal saluted and she returned it quickly.

"Welcome to my ship, Captain. Would you like the grand tour?"

"Yes Commander, as long as it doesn't interfere with the repair process."

"I think we can manage that," said Lieutenant Commander Conrad as she led him off the bridge. "It's a small ship but she does a good job."

"How many people were lost in the attack?" asked Peter as he tried to word it carefully. It came out just above a whisper and a little bit broken. As a pilot you rarely saw death firsthand. It was always pilot against machine. You did not kill people you killed the machines of war. It just so happened that people, or aliens, were in them. That made him wonder how many aliens were on that cruiser he destroyed.

"Twenty-two dead and sixteen wounded, two are in critical condition," replied Lieutenant Commander Conrad as they walked aft. "It could have been all of us so I can't thank you enough."

"You're welcome, ma'am."

"Please, call me Emily."

"Okay Emily, call me Peter. You got lucky that I was in the area." He shook a few more hands as everyone wanted to thank him personally. News of his being on board was traveling fast.

"Very lucky. Well, Peter, you really made a mess of those aliens in a hurry. I thought our success rate against the Bect was a lot worse."

"It is, or was. It will be changing soon. In fact, that was my first mission and it was an unofficial one too."

"First mission? What do you mean?" asked Emily.

"That's the first time I ever flew a Stiletto. I was on a test mission to experiment with some upgrades," said Peter as they turned a corner. They entered a large open space and he could feel the breeze coming in. A large portion of the floor was twisted metal as the maintenance crews used laser cutters to clean it up.

"Holy shit," said Emily. "I'm sorry Peter, I try not to use profanity."

"That's okay, I break that rule all the time."

She laughed before she pointed to the damaged area. "This is the area hit the hardest. We had to seal the compartment after we were hit." The walls were scorched and metal twisted to abnormal angles. The entire room was blackened and nothing that was not securely fastened to the structure remained. It looked as if a bomb had gone off, and for all intents and purposes it had. The only indication that it was an external explosion were the upturned pieces of twisted and charred metal around the gigantic hole in the floor.

"How did you do so well against the enemy if it was only your first mission and first time in a fighter?" asked Emily as they watched the crews work.

"I spent a lot of time in the simulator and teaching others combat tactics. Plus, the Stiletto I was flying has some new modifications."

"Impressive. The way you were clearing those alien ships away I figured you for a seasoned combat veteran."

"Well, I'm one now."

"You got a DFC too, for saving us," she said while tapping the Distinguished Flying Cross ribbon above the left breast pocket of his white undress uniform. Above his only ribbon were the gold wings of a pilot. The wings had a crest in the middle that displayed the Earth with the Moon in orbit around it.

"My only ribbon," said Peter.

"You'll have to work on that," replied Emily with a chuckle. She led him away from the work area and to another section of the ship. It was a storage room off of the engine compartment. It had blackened walls and a puncture in the far wall from the room they recently viewed. *The explosion must have ignited material in this room as well*, thought Peter as he surveyed the damage.

"Luckily the fire was contained and sucked into space before reaching our engine room." Emily looked around the engine area and several people watched the two of them with interest.

"Attention everyone, this is the pilot that cleared those fighters off of us," said Emily while putting her right hand on his left shoulder as she stood next to him. All the mechanics on duty stopped what they were doing and came over to shake his hand and thank him. He stunned most of them by ignoring the fact that their hands were covered in oil and grease. He stood with a smile on his face in a clean white undress uniform and his right hand black with engine remnants.

"Let's go to my cabin and see if we can get that grease off your hand before you make a mess of your uniform," said Emily.

Peter looked at his hand and shrugged, "What grease?"

Emily laughed and shook her head. "Most officers would have refused to shake hands with the workers unless they cleaned up first. You're not a normal officer."

"I used to be an enlisted man until I died and came back as an officer," shot Peter with a grin and Emily laughed. Several people wanted to shake hands with him so he used his left hand instead while holding up his right hand to show them the reason. The officers cringed while the enlisted people laughed in curiosity. Officers rarely soiled their hands doing anything, or so they thought.

Emily opened her cabin door, they entered, and she closed it behind them. There was not much room for even changing your mind. There was a simple bed along one wall, a desk on the other, and a door to a small bathroom on the wall opposite the hallway. If this was the most spacious cabin on the ship Peter did not want to see where the enlisted people slept.

Emily carefully wrapped his greasy hand with a disposable towel as she helped him remove his long sleeve uniform shirt. He was then able to wash up at the sink without accidentally messing up his shirt. It took a lot of soap and hard work to eventually clean his hand. He dried his hands and turned to find Emily watching him quietly from the chair at her desk.

"So," started Peter with a slight pause, "what's your story?"

"What do you mean?"

"How did you end up commanding a cargo ship?" Peter exited the bathroom and, not finding another chair anywhere, sat on the bed. He leaned against the wall next to the bathroom door and rubbed his hands together to work the remaining dampness off.

"Just lucky, I guess. I started out as a communication officer on a space station until the war broke out. Then I transferred to a destroyer and made my way up the chain of command until I received command of this ship."

"The only good thing about this war is that we aren't fighting ourselves," said Peter as he leaned his head against the wall. "The Twenty-First Century was full of constant antagonism and warfare between one race or another, one country or another. It kept happening and was getting worse. I'm glad to see the human race didn't cause its own extinction."

"That's a grim look on humanity," said Emily.

"Well, that was then and this is now. It's all different now."

Emily was unsure of what to say so she nodded. After a few quiet minutes the conversation turned to something other than war and death. They both had seen enough of that in the past few months. They shared information about their growing up and the towns they knew. Emily had never even seen Earth from a distance, let alone stand on it. Opportunity had never gotten her out that way and now war was preventing her from visiting.

Time went by quickly and they both enjoyed the company of the other. Peter finally saw that time for his first class was quickly approaching. He did not really want to leave because that meant the war was something real. Part of him still felt that this was just a dream and he would somehow wake up to find himself back on Earth doing some mundane job for a paycheck to pay his bills so that he could live. That thought depressed him. The vicious circle of life with no end in sight, except death. And in his case, not even that could stop the circle.

But this was different. This had a purpose, a cause, something that was greater than a stupid paycheck. And this time around he felt like he was an integral part of it instead of just being a bystander. The more he thought about it the more dreamlike it seemed.

Emily saw the strange look in his eyes. It was the look of confusion and sadness all rolled into one. "Are you okay?" she asked cautiously.

"I've been working sixteen to twenty hour days, teaching almost non-stop, and flying the simulator like it was permanently attached to my ass," said Peter. "I just realized that I do indeed receive a paycheck and, for the first time in my life, I don't give a damn about it."

"Oh, you looked sad for a minute."

"Just remembering my past life and how depressing it all was. You work all day to get paid so you can pay your bills so you can go to work to get paid. It's a vicious cycle."

"That does sound depressing."

"Sorry, it's all in the past now. It was a pleasure talking with you, Emily. I have to go and teach a class for a while," said Peter as he stood and picked up his shirt. She stood slowly and absently helped him put his shirt on. He thought it a bit odd but did not mind the attention of a beautiful woman.

"When do you finish?" she asked.

"Three hours, I think. So about twenty-one hundred hours."

"Stop by afterward and I'll buy you that beer I owe you."

"Sounds good, then we can continue our conversation in an inebriated state," replied Peter.

"Deal," said Emily. She opened her door and walked Peter to the loading ramp. The ship's cargo bay was almost empty and as the loader approached Peter realized that it was now tasked with filling it up. He shook Emily's hand again as the two guards watched and then they saluted each other.

"Take care, corporals," said Peter as he shook their hands again before walking down the ramp.

Emily and the two guards watched silently as Peter entered the crowd and disappeared onto the base.

"Are you sure he's a pilot, ma'am?" asked one Corporal.

"Yes, why do you ask?"

"Nicest pilot I've ever met."

"Me too."

CHAPTER
21

P eter found the classroom with the assistance of one of the instructors from the Stanwix. The instructor complained the entire walk to the building about being forced to take some bullshit course where he doubted that he could learn anything from some freak that used to be frozen. Peter laughed because the Major was complaining so much that he never even bothered to introduce himself. Peter kept his mouth shut just like he was always told to do when he was enlisted. You should never give information away freely.

The classroom was almost full with only a few open seats in the front row. It was not a very big classroom but could hold thirty people comfortably. As Peter walked through the door he saw Lieutenant Colonel Nelson sitting quietly in the back row. They nodded to each other and Peter took a seat in the front row. He still had five minutes before class started and he wanted to collect some data from the talkative bunch first. The Major that walked to the classroom with him moved to the far side of the room and started talking with several of his pilot friends.

Miguel, Randy, and Roger walked in and Peter put his right finger across his lips so that they would not say anything to him as they walked in and took seats next to him. The general consensus was that no one was happy to be here. They were all ordered to be here and so they were and it was going to be a fun ride for Peter and his crew.

At exactly eighteen hundred hours Peter saw the Admiral walking down the hallway toward the classroom. He waited patiently until the Admiral opened the door wider to enter the room.

"Room, attention!" yelled Peter as he stood and snapped to attention. The classroom was just a bunch of padded seats on raised steps. Without desks of any sort the protocol was to stand, which everyone did quickly.

"At ease," said the Admiral as he stood by the door.

Peter approached the Admiral while he extended his hand, "Admiral, it's a pleasure to meet you. I'm Captain Peter McCabe."

"Ah yes, the man everyone is talking about that is going to change this war for us." He shook Peter's hand firmly and expressed a large and warm smile. His gray hair was cut neatly and short and his sharp blue eyes looked him over.

"Well sir, I'm just helping to point everyone in the right direction," said Peter as he heard the muffled talking behind him. Everyone had just realized that this was their instructor for the next two weeks.

"I'm Admiral Polk and this is my First Officer, Commander Kelly Ryan."

"Pleased to meet you," said Peter as he shook her small hand. Her dark brown hair was short, just barely above her collar. She was average looking, what some would call plainly beautiful. He stared at her longer than he should have because she reminded him of a gal that he used to fly with.

"Likewise," said Commander Ryan with a nod.

"Well Captain, don't let us hold up your class. We'll just have a seat and watch for a while." The Admiral sat in the front row and crossed his right leg over his left while the Commander sat beside him.

"Thank you, sir," said Peter. He walked to the door, closed it, and then stood behind the front podium.

"Good evening everyone, I'm Captain Peter McCabe. I know most of you think this course is bullshit and what can you learn from a three hundred and sixty year old frozen freak, but I'm not going to answer that question. We are all here for the same reason ... we were ordered to be here."

Several muffled laughs went around the room including a grunt from the Admiral. Commander Ryan laughed and that brought a smile to Peter's face.

"Well, that got us here and now we must all forget that fact. Just because we are ordered to do this doesn't mean that you won't like it. Training is supposed to be hard work. It is supposed to be educational. It is supposed to be rewarding and above all, it is supposed to be beneficial. If you can truly enjoy yourselves while doing it then that's all the better. Ask yourselves, why do you teach?"

Peter looked around the room at the faces of the officers in the classroom. The ages of those present ran from the early twenties to the low-thirties. The exceptions were Admiral Polk, Lieutenant Colonel Nelson, and several other lieutenant colonels that were probably the Flight Group Commanders from the other carriers in the Fleet.

"Is it because you enjoy bringing your knowledge to others? Odds are it is not because you were forced to do it, those teachers don't last very long. Why do I teach? I enjoy seeing the look on a student's face when they finally figure something out on their own through correlation. I like seeing a student progress to being a master.

"How many of the simulators on your ships have been past the setting of level one? Do you even use the simulators? How many simulators are in use at one time?" asked Peter, not expecting a response.

"The simulators are a waste of time and manpower," said a lieutenant colonel loudly from the back of the room. Several nods and a few laughs ensued.

"So is a toaster if you don't use it correctly. Right now there are two fully operational simulators on Ticonderoga and the other six are being fitted with replacement parts as we speak. In fact, during this class I will be doing the first known training of an entire flight at one time. Squad-based training with squad-based tactics."

Murmurs of disbelief and wonderment passed around the classroom and the Admiral turned to look at the group of instructors and Flight Group Commanders gasping in awe.

"Yes, you heard that right, and that is the key to winning this war. And here's the really amazing part; Ticonderoga's simulators have been at level five for over a month now. I have one flight fully trained and ready and they can consistently take out level five slugs and level five gumdrops."

"Gumdrops aren't even in the sim," shot a captain in the third row.

"Not in your sims, but on the Ticonderoga's they are. We programmed them in ourselves and also updated the AI for the slugs too. Our next feat will be to upgrade the levels with real-time data and eventually program in capital ships. All these updates are being transmitted to your ships this evening along with updated flight models. There are also two Stiletto modifications you'll want to have."

"Sounds like a load of crap to me," shot the Colonel from the Stark. He was probably the only one in the room besides the Admiral that could get away with that statement.

"Possibly, but let's analyze the facts and come to our own conclusions about a lot of things that others tell us to believe without seeing it for ourselves."

Peter dimmed the lights and started the projector with all the videos he wanted to use at his ready. He played the video of the walk-around of the new wing pylons and explained what they were and why they were there. Several positive comments came from that information. Others complained about the limited use and effectiveness of the missiles and why bother carrying them.

"Yes, these missiles are worthless," said Peter while nodding in agreement. "So worthless in fact, that this next video will fully demonstrate their ineffectiveness in combat."

Peter played the video taken from the battle when the Ticonderoga fighters launched two volleys of missiles at almost three dozen oncoming fighters and bombers. He stopped it after the volleys were completed and before the mission became sloppy. He played it twice and then a third time, explaining what had happened, how they targeted the ships and what the outcome was.

Stunned silence filled the room at that point and Peter even noticed the shocked look on the Admiral's face.

"Worthless? Yes, worthless if they are not used and that's why I want double the standard load on my Stiletto. The next modification that was performed was a laser system upgrade. We lucked into a chunk of the Bect metal while some of the Ticonderoga's pilots were in a battle. Our technicians were able to analyze the metal and determine the best frequency for our lasers, and they also boosted the power output. There has been only one test of this in battle, so far. These two modifications are also being passed throughout the Fleet."

Peter started the video of his first combat mission and paused it for some explanation before continuing.

"You have probably already seen the area video for my first mission against the Bect. I was performing an evaluation flight of the new pylons and laser system when I discovered a Bect attack on one of our cargo ships. My Stiletto was heavily modified with sensors as well as the two modifications that I previously talked about. The technicians wanted to analyze the stress on the wings and spars for the addition of upper wing pylons. They also wanted to test the laser bay for heat and any other negative effects of the upgrade. There was a camera mounted in the cockpit that pointed out the front window so that we could analyze the missile paths and laser output from the ship. This video is from the cockpit of my Stiletto."

Peter played the video for several seconds and pressed *Pause* once more when it showed his scanner screen in the lower right corner displaying the effects of jamming. He explained what he knew of how jamming worked since most people in the room had never heard of that nor thought it possible, but the Bect were now doing it.

He pressed *Play* and let the video continue to the first fighter kill and the second one, then the third and fourth. He showed them in slow motion and went over it twice. There was awed silence in the room and a few expletives when they saw how few blasts it took to take a slug out.

"Makes me look like I can kick some ass, huh?" asked Peter. All he saw as he looked around the room were nods. "Well, you'll all have this capability and by the end of this two week class you will be different pilots. I want to impart this new way of thinking about things to you so that you can better train your pilots. My primary goal is to help you all so that we can win this war."

Peter pressed *Play* again. "What can this new laser do against a shielded bomber? Let's find out." The action moved along to where he came upon the bomber and destroyed it. He showed it first at normal speed and then played it over again a few times in slow motion. He counted the laser blasts out loud as they impacted to determine exactly how many shots it took to take the shield out, then how many to pop the bomber.

"My only failing at this point was that I found the bomber too late and it got a missile off. Twenty-two people died on that cargo ship because I was late. That bomber had the jamming device and once it was out of the picture I could see on the scanner what I had left to deal with. Now I changed my tactics and targeted fighters that directly threatened the cargo ship. I should have gone for that bomber first but, thanks to their jamming, I didn't know it was out there. So now, not only are they tougher and have shields, plus more weaponry, plus missiles, they can also carry a jammer."

Peter went through the rest of the video, up to but not including the cruiser, and analyzed every aspect of every shot that he took. He critically evaluated his mistakes and things that he could have done better. He explained every maneuver he did and the benefits or detriments for each. Someone yelled out *holy shit* when he performed the quick turn and everyone else readily agreed. No one realized that a maneuver like that was even possible in a Stiletto.

"I call that maneuver a *snap reversal*. You must know what your Stiletto is capable of and use it to the best of your abilities. Know your tools.

"Have any of you ever gone up against a capital ship? Have you ever seen one up close? Well, what I did here was blatantly stupid and I'll gladly admit that to other pilots. By now I was in the heat of battle and felt that I had the edge necessary for such an insane act. What sat at the back of my mind was that no fighter had ever taken out a capital ship before and there was absolutely no data available on any of them. I wanted and needed that data."

Peter played the video with his attack on the cruiser in normal motion. Then he went over it in slow motion several times. He glanced around the classroom and saw the shocked looks on everyone's face. He thought the Admiral was going to flip out. Every single frame of that video was analyzed by the time he was done. Ninety minutes later he had finished his debrief and every single man and woman in that room wanted to stay right there for the entire two week class.

"And that, ladies and gentlemen, is a standard debriefing after a combat mission. I do the same thing for every single mission. The only difference is that the students are a little more active and responsive than you are right now."

"Holy shit, man, you've got balls as big as the moons of Mars."

Everyone laughed and the attitude in the classroom was changed for the better.

"You just witnessed what a single Stiletto fighter could accomplish when pitted against eighteen Bect fighters, one bomber, *and* a capital ship. Imagine what an entire fleet of fully trained pilots with modified Stilettos could do. Do you all still think the simulators are a waste of time?" asked Peter. Some mumbling between groups began but Peter cut them off. "Well, let me tell you something else before you answer that question. That mission, ladies and gentlemen, was my *first* combat mission. The first time, in fact, that I had ever even sat in a real Stiletto."

The silence was almost deafening. After several seconds people began talking and the main course of discussion was the alien forces and how best to beat them. Peter did not want to get ahead of himself and he really needed to find a bathroom so he called for a ten-minute break. Most of the instructors and Flight Group Commanders stayed right where they were and kept talking about the debriefing. This one session was more information than they were ever given before.

Admiral Polk and Commander Ryan stood and joined Peter as he exited the classroom into the hallway. The Admiral shook his hand again and congratulated him.

"I thought this class was going to turn into a slugging match at first," started the Admiral. "You are one hell of a smart officer. That was the finest piece of manipulation I've ever seen."

"Thank you, sir. It's that kind of thing I want to see happening on the battlefield. Sun Tzu said that warfare is based on deception. Make the enemy see what you want him to see and he will do what you want him to do."

"Sun Tzu? Never heard of him."

"He lived almost three thousand years ago, sir. Stop by tomorrow morning if you're not busy and Captain Roger Cleam will be teaching a class on military history."

"Sounds like you have this entire two weeks planned out."

"Not really, sir, but don't tell anyone. I've got the basic idea and a rough outline but I'll modify it depending upon circumstances and reactions."

"I'll see what I can do about attending some more. I learned more in the last ninety minutes than I have from all of the information received from military intelligence for the past two years combined. Good luck with your class, Captain McCabe. It was a pleasure meeting you."

"Thank you, Admiral. It was good to meet you as well."

They shook hands once again and Peter took off down the hall to find a bathroom. Luckily, in the future, they were marked almost identically as in the past. He was not gone very long and returned to a full classroom that quickly silenced as he closed the door.

Peter continued by giving everyone a breakdown of what the two weeks would entail. They were expected to be in class from oh-eight hundred hours to eighteen hundred hours. Half of the day would be in the classroom, the first part and last part of the day. The remainder would be in the simulators. All the techniques that were in place on the Ticonderoga would be used here and Peter told them it would be enjoyable as well as educational. On Saturday and Sunday they would have free days to do whatever they wanted. He would be available for any simulator work they wanted to do but no scheduled classes would run.

Peter introduced his training staff and explained what they would be doing and how they would be helping him out. Most of the class had never even heard of a warrant officer and those that did had never seen one. A lot of them thought promoting enlisted people to be pilots was a bad idea but Peter told them to set aside all their views on that for the next two weeks. He had earned their respect in that first ninety minutes so they would give him and the warrant officers the benefit of the doubt. There was an abundance of knowledge in the classroom and they wanted to tap it no matter what the cost, no matter what the sacrifice might be.

Peter talked for another hour and ended class early. They had an early morning ahead of them and then a very busy two weeks.

Peter told his friends that he was heading back to Cargo Three to have a beer with the ship's commander and that he would see them in the morning. The rest of them went to the officer quarters and relaxed in their rooms. It had been a long day and they needed some sleep foremost.

CHAPTER

22

Peter found Cargo Three easy enough. It was the first ship on the right once you entered the spaceport. Different guards were on duty and the cargo bay was full. He told them who he was and they had been expecting him. A guard called the Commander and soon an Ensign arrived to escort him to the bridge. He followed dutifully and noticed the ship was quite different on this trip than from earlier in the day. He passed only one person in the hall on the way to the bridge and the Lieutenant only smiled and saluted. The bridge was also quiet and Emily waved briefly as he appeared in the doorway. The Ensign left him there and returned to her post.

"System check," said Lieutenant Commander Emily Conrad as she looked away from Peter and to the other officers on the deck.

"All green," responded the Lieutenant in the front row.

"Pressurization systems?"

"Ready," replied another Lieutenant that sat in the second row.

Emily turned to Peter and asked, "Do you mind spending the night aboard? The major structural hull repairs were completed a half hour ago and we are going to pressure test it overnight."

"They fixed it that fast?"

"Replacing the entire damaged hull section was easier than attempting a repair. So, do you want to spend the night?"

"That's fine with me, Commander," replied Peter. He made sure to add the respectful officer title at the end so that a talkative crew would not get any bright ideas. He already had enough ideas of his own from earlier in the day. Rumors were sure to start anyway but he did not want to fuel any of them.

She gave him an odd look as her eyebrows scrunched up a little. She smiled at him and turned back to the work at hand.

"All right Lieutenant Mason, have the loadmaster seal the cargo door," said Emily as she pressed a button on her chair and spoke into the boom microphone attached to the left side of her head. "Control, Cargo Three."

"Cargo Three, Control, go ahead," said a voice over the loud speaker.

"Cargo Three is ready for overnight pressurization check. Request caution tag and authorization for testing."

"Standby Cargo Three."

"Cargo door is sealed, Commander," reported an Ensign in the second row.

The pause from Spaceport Control lasted nearly five minutes before the male voice returned. "Cargo Three, Control."

"Control, Cargo Three, go ahead," said Emily in quick response.

"Cargo Three is cleared for pressurization check, you are tagged and authorized for overnight testing. Good luck and sleep tight. Out."

"Thank you, Control. Out." Emily relaxed and stretched her legs. "Okay people, let's bring her up slowly."

Several technicians at the leftmost station began pressing buttons and Peter could feel the pressure growing. His ears began popping as he remembered times long past. Peter had sat in on a C-5 pressurization check while in the Air Force and the same process was being employed here. The biggest difference was that this ship could not leak no matter what. A small leak could be a death sentence for all of them.

"Two atmospheres," called out the technician. "We will hold here for an hour and look for leaks before going any higher."

"All right, let me know immediately if something goes wrong. Lieutenant Mason, you have the con," said Emily as she stood and approached Peter.

"I have the con, aye aye Commander," replied Lieutenant Mason.

"Now we wait," she said quietly as she passed him and exited the bridge. He followed her once again to her cabin where she jumped on the bed and stretched out with a big sigh. He closed the door and removed his tie, placing it carefully on the desk. He unbuttoned the top two buttons of his shirt and sat on the chair while putting his feet on the desk. He sighed audibly and let his head tilt all the way back.

Emily removed her boots and tossed them against the door and they fell out of the way. "Ah, much better."

"Long day?" asked Peter as he lifted his head and looked at her.

"Oh yeah, got a lot accomplished though. The ship is repaired, hopefully completely, which we will find out by morning. We're all loaded and ready to go if the repairs hold."

"When do you ship out?"

"Oh-seven hundred or so tomorrow morning."

"Where are you headed?"

"Omega Prime to deliver supplies."

Peter nodded. He had no clue where that was or what kind of place it could be. It figured that he was just growing to like her and now she was running off soon after. He had hoped to spend more time with her on the planet while he was here teaching. Maybe fall in love and all that crap too. He barely remembered what that was like. Even though not much physical time had passed, his love life still seemed centuries away.

"There's beer in the cooler on the right side of the desk and you can grab me one too," said Emily while pointing. Peter took his feet off the desk and opened the door to see a twelve-pack of beer stuffed into the small space.

"Looks like you're planning for quite some party," shot Peter as he extracted two bottles from the cooler. He opened both and handed her one as he took a long pull from the other one.

"Well, one can never tell," she replied with a mischievous smile. She moved over on the small bed and left him some room. "Take off your boots and sit next to me. It's much more comfortable here and I can't offer you any better in my spacious accommodations. Besides, that chair gets old quick."

Peter removed his boots and left them where they landed as he sat next to Emily on the bed. She was tucked into the corner leaning against both walls. Peter leaned against the wall and took another swig of beer.

"Not bad stuff," said Peter while lifting the bottle and reading the label. Emily took a drink and smiled. "Wow, made on some planet I never heard of."

"So, what would you like to talk about tonight?" asked Emily as she wondered what he would come up with.

"Good question. One I don't readily have an answer for."

She took another sip and watched him quietly. He turned toward her and noticed that her hair was down and resting on her shoulders. She had undone the top button of her uniform shirt and looked rather comfortable tucked into the corner. She had one of her pillows behind her back and when she lowered her head her hair covered part of her face.

"Did you have any particular subject in mind?" asked Peter. "Or do you just want to hang out and stare at a blank wall for a while?"

Emily laughed. "We could, but that doesn't seem like very much fun. How about a little music," she emphasized the last word with her head tilted back, like she was talking to the ceiling. Light music entered the room upon her command. "Lights, fifty percent." The lights dimmed. "There we go, a little easier on the eyes too."

"Sounds good to me," replied Peter. He took another sip of beer and nodded absently as he tried to place the taste. It was a light-bodied pale ale that had a slight yellow-brown color to it. It was not very smooth and left an aftertaste that reminded him of the common American beers from his time. On a scale from one to five he would give this beer a two.

"What kind of music do you like?"

"Hey, that's a good subject to start with," said Peter. "I listen to almost anything and enjoy the weirdest combination sometimes."

"Anything in particular you'd like to hear?"

"Since I'm new to this time, anything you play less than three centuries old will be new to me. How about playing your favorite?"

"My favorite?" asked Emily.

"Yeah, that's as good a start as any. I seriously doubt your database would have my favorite."

"Try it."

"All right. Music, The Proletariat, Piecework." There was a short pause and then a short beep.

"Guess not," said Emily. "Okay, it's my turn. Music, Leslie Darling, Lazy Saturday Moon." A light piece of music began with a peaceful flute and the sound of rain. Soon a violin joined in and maybe a sporadic cello in the distance. A female voice began singing hypnotically and Peter leaned his head against the wall and closed his eyes. It was extremely peaceful and relaxed him almost instantly. By the time the song finished he had completed his beer and this surprised him.

"Whoa, that was too cool," said Peter as he shook his empty bottle, "and my beer is dead."

Emily laughed, "Leslie does that to you sometimes."

She had finished her beer as well so Peter jumped off the bed to grab a couple more while he explained the term *cool*. He found himself telling her a bunch of other phrases from the Twenty-First Century and had her laughing soon after.

"Your turn to try again," she said while pointing to the ceiling. "Introduce me to something you like from your time that you think we might have."

"Tough one. Let me come up with something classical, that's probably my best bet." He struggled to remember a piece he really enjoyed and finally settled on one.

"Music, Wagner, Siegfried's Funeral March."

He was surprised when it actually started. "Hey, it's in there."

"A funeral march?" asked Emily with one eyebrow raised.

"It's a powerful song and the first one to come to mind. I wonder if they played it at my funeral." Peter laughed lightly and raised his beer in Emily's direction. "A toast. To life, the second time around."

"All right," said Emily as she duplicated his action, "and to my hero." Their bottles clinked and they both took a big swig. Then they became quiet and listened to the music.

"Were you actually dead?" asked Emily after almost three minutes of quiet music appreciation.

"The doctor that revived me said I had been poisoned and was hibernating. It was a Bect poison, which he found rather puzzling."

Time passed as they talked on various subjects and traded music selections until Emily asked him a question and there was no response. She looked at Peter's face and he had fallen asleep and was snoring lightly. She took his almost-empty beer bottle and climbed carefully over him. She dumped the remnants into her sink and disposed of the bottles in a bin underneath. She carefully moved him to a more comfortable position on the bed and climbed over to lie beside him.

Peter awoke abruptly when a constant beeping echoed in the room. He was not sure where he was but memory returned when he heard a female voice next to him grunt and then speak.

"Lights, fifty percent. Alarm, off." The lights came on and the annoying sound stopped.

Peter was aware that Emily was tucked in close to his left side with her left arm draped across his chest. His left arm was wrapped around her and her warm body felt comforting. He was still clothed as was she, and he was glad things had not gone any further but in many ways he wished that they had.

"Did I fall asleep?" he asked in a whisper.

"Yeah, at some point," she replied, not wanting to open her eyes.

"What time is it?"

"Time," she said without moving. It was rather muffled but the computer could still understand it. A voice responded with oh-six-oh-three.

"Another busy day in store for the both of us. I sure could use one day of relaxation. You know, since I've been revived I have been working non-stop with no time off."

"War tends to keep things at that pace," replied Emily with her face still tucked in his shoulder.

"I really enjoyed last night. It was very relaxing, as you could probably tell."

She propped herself on her right elbow while rubbing her hand on his chest. She brought her left knee over his and brushed the hair hanging across her face out of the way and behind her shoulder.

"We still have some time left," she said with a playful grin on her face.

"For what?" Peter mentally kicked himself. He knew what she meant before she even said the words.

"For sex."

Peter rolled onto his side and wrapped his arms around her while embracing and kissing her firmly. They spent a few minutes kissing before she began removing his shirt. He broke the kiss and backed away.

"I'd like that more than you could imagine but ..."

"But?" asked Emily.

"Yeah, but I'd rather it be something more than just a reward for saving you. For being *the hero*, if you know what I mean."

"Well, it would be."

"No, not right now it can't. I still feel like it would be some kind of reward instead of sharing love with each other. I'm not like that, never was and never will be. It's who I am, the core of my being."

"The knight."

"Yes. I'm not saying that I don't want to make love to you, because I do. I just don't want to under these circumstances. I'd rather it be on even ground. As two people that are equals instead of one being elevated by an act that could have been performed by anyone."

"But this is war and we could die tomorrow never having shared that love."

"True, but doing that would destroy who I am inside, and that could never be repaired."

He reluctantly moved from her and sat at the edge of her bed while he put on his boots. She sat behind him and laid her head on his back while her arms wrapped around his chest.

"I've never met a man like you before."

"What? Someone that died, was revived almost three and a half centuries later, and turned down sex with a beautiful woman because he's a moron and is trying to live by a code of honor that died over a thousand years ago?"

Emily laughed, which lightened the suddenly thick atmosphere of tension in her room. "Yeah, something like that."

Peter stood and pulled her from the bed to her feet in front of him. He embraced her tightly and kissed her. The kiss was warm and he wanted more, as much as he could get. But time was limited and he needed to get to his room so he could shower and change before class.

"I'd really like to get to know you better, as difficult as that may be in this war," said Peter. He kissed her again because he wanted to and remained doing so because she let him. The longer he kissed her the more he thought about ripping her clothes off and just going for it, damn the results and damn those that got in the way.

She pulled back a little and said, "You want me now, don't you?"

"Hell, woman. I wanted you when I first saw you."

"Really? That soon?"

"You are an incredibly beautiful woman and I've been alone for so long. I just don't want to rush in and screw things up, which is what I usually do. I'd like it to work with us, and you're very quiet on the subject."

"Well, I am disappointed. I think most men would have jumped me a long time ago. I am glad that you actually respect me, which is also rather odd. But I do understand and I would like to see what happens between us. So I'd say yes, Peter, let's see what we can do about it."

"I'll be here for two weeks, then you can track me down on the Ticonderoga."

"All right, I'll see what my orders are after Omega Prime and send you a message letting you know. Then we can figure things out from there."

The speaker issued a two tone note and a voice came over it, "Commander, are you awake?"

"I am now," replied Emily.

"Commander, pressure checks passed and the ship has returned to normal levels. The cargo door is open and we are taking on passengers for Omega Prime. We will be ready for departure in thirty minutes."

"Thank you, Lieutenant," replied Emily with a sigh as a beep signaled the end of the transmission.

"Emily, it's time for me to depart." Peter kissed her and then broke the embrace. He tied his boots quickly, and collected his tie, putting it on haphazardly. He stopped at the door and turned. She approached slowly and kissed him one last time.

"Be safe, Peter."

"You too, Emily," he replied. He stroked her cheek lightly with his hand and moved her hair behind her ear. He opened the door and exited into the hallway. She leaned against the doorframe while looking out of her room and watched him go. He strode down the hallway before turning the corner and walking out of her life.

Emily hoped it was not the last time she would see him as a tear rolled out of her left eye and down her cheek. She closed her door and entered the bathroom to get ready for another day in the life of a ship's commander. There was never enough time for romance. Never enough time for companionship. Never enough time for much of anything she so longed for. She just had an opportunity but played it wrong. He was not like a normal Twenty-Fourth Century man and his careful rejection made her want him even more. She did not really know what love was, never had the time to find out. It was a sad day for her but she needed to push that thought from her mind for now, she had an important job to do and lives that counted on her doing it.

Peter made his way across the base and arrived at the officer quarters at oh-seven-fifteen. It left him very little time to get ready but last night made the morning rush well worth it. He heard a loud roar as the ground shook and looked to the spaceport to see Cargo Three lift off to perform its mission. Seeing the ship rise into the atmosphere saddened him as he opened the door to his room. Roger looked up from his book and smiled.

"Have a fun night?"

"Yes I did. It could've been even better but ..." Peter let the sentence hang in the air as he removed his shirt and tie and tossed them carelessly onto the bed. He headed for the shower with a pained look of sadness on his face.

"But what?"

"She wanted to sleep with a hero, and I didn't want her to."

"Well, that just confused the hell out of me," said Roger as he loudly closed his book and scratched the back of his head.

"She wanted to thank me for saving her and her crew by giving me sex as a reward. I wanted to sleep with her but not under those circumstances. I'm an idiot," said Peter as he disappeared into the bathroom.

Roger stared at the bathroom door not knowing what else to say. Over the past few months he had grown to like this odd man and as strange as Peter's statement sounded it made perfect sense to him. He decided to drop the subject and see what happened next. It was almost time for class to start and it was going to be a very busy two weeks.

CHAPTER

23

Roger was growing tired of looking at the star charts and trying to teach Peter where they were and where they had been. He knew from the brief conversation they had earlier that Emily was delivering supplies somewhere just over sixty-three Light Years away. Roger also tried to explain inter-space communication but did not know as much about the subject as Peter had hoped. From what Roger could gather, the two of them had made quite an impression on each other and had been communicating ever since.

The classes were nearing the end of week two and had been progressing quite rapidly. Active duty pilots were picking things up quicker, and with less work on their part, than with the new recruits. After seeing Peter's rescue display they were all bound and determined to outshine someone they still viewed as being out of his element. Peter never disputed the fact and challenged them to perform better without getting themselves killed in the process.

Modifications to the other carrier's simulators were near complete. A huge box of simulator parts appeared on Friday afternoon and the technicians busily collected what they needed to repair all of the simulators. The base's simulators were the first to come online so that training could use them for Peter's class. The simulators on the Ticonderoga were fixed next, since their parts had been on order the longest.

The largest tasks and most time consuming were the actual modification of every Stiletto on three carriers and one land base. Two crews of technicians were working around the clock to finish as much as possible. The priority mission was to upgrade the lasers, then next came the pylons.

"I give up," said Roger. "You'll have to find a navigator to help you out because I don't even recognize half of these symbols."

"Thanks for trying, Roger. I think the most confusing thing is that space is not a flat surface." Peter continued to look at the mind-boggling chart when Miguel and Randy arrived. They had large smiles on their faces and did not say a word once they stopped near their friends.

Peter looked up from the chart and asked, "Can either of you butter bars read a star chart?"

"Butter bars?" asked Roger as he looked at the two newcomers and then figured it out. "Ah, more Twenty-First Century slang. Congratulations, Second Lieutenants." He stood quickly and snapped to attention as he saluted them. They both laughed as they returned the salute.

"Looks like you passed. How did you both do?" asked Peter with interest.

"Ninety-two percent," said Miguel.

"I only got a ninety-five," remarked Randy with a frown.

"Only? Great job guys," said Roger as he shook both of their hands.

"Captain Washington yelled at us this morning," started Randy as he took a seat. "He showed up in the officer quarters screaming like a psychopath and told us to get our asses down to administration in a hurry. Scared the living shit out of us. We ran down there in our undress uniforms expecting the end of the world and there was the Captain again, laughing his ass off. He seemed extremely proud of us and pinned these bars on himself."

"Wow, most captains wouldn't have taken the time to do something like that. He must be watching you guys closely," said Roger.

"Once he heard the test results, the Captain scheduled our flight tests," said Randy, sounding a bit nervous.

"When?" asked Peter.

"This afternoon," replied Miguel. "The examiner will meet us on the Ticonderoga and test us in our simulators."

"Good, you'll have the home field advantage. You'll both do great, just remember your training."

Miguel and Randy nodded absently. There was a lot riding on those flight tests, both of their futures. They had to pass because neither wanted to return to the lives they were previously living. The path they were now on was too enjoyable in comparison.

Peter folded the star chart slowly as he sat quietly on the table. He was preoccupied with thoughts of Emily as he looked up at the sky. There were a few mid-level clouds and he noticed no difference between those and the ones on Earth. The trees looked the same as ones in the northeast region of North America, some pines and oaks. The weather here was a lot warmer though.

Peter's three friends stopped talking and stared at him with concern. He was sitting and quietly looking around as life moved about them. It was a peaceful place, except for the engine noises of landing and departing space-craft. Peter could not tell the difference between this planet and Earth, no matter how hard he tried to find just one thing different. If someone told him this was Earth he would not be able to prove otherwise. Maybe it was Earth? The thought sent a shiver down his spine.

"What's up with you, Peter?" asked Miguel as he walked over and sat next to him. Peter was looking into the sky so Miguel joined him. "Yup, that's a cloud."

Peter laughed, "Yeah, but what kind of cloud?"

"Beats the hell out of me, I'm a spaceman."

"It's a cumulus cloud," said Peter. He sighed lightly and continued. "This place looks like Earth. I was just thinking about the past and flying in the at-mosphere, punching holes in clouds. I had a few flights a very long time ago where I just skimmed the ragged tops of cumulus clouds. I'd deviate slightly from my flight path and play in them, fly around them, or just pop through sections of them. That was fun."

"Sounds like it. Once the flight test is done I'll have to try that myself."

"You know, Miguel," said Peter as he looked to his left at a row of trees with some yellow flowers near them, "I don't like it here."

"This planet does kind of smell funny," shot Randy as he sniffed the air and began coughing.

"Not this planet, just planets in general. I spent thirty-three years of my life on one and wanted to get off. Now I'm actually living and working in space and I love every minute of it. Being down here brings back too many bad memories and it's making me uneasy and depressed. Give me the cold dark depths of oblivion any day of the week over this happy and sunny *Look, I've got gravity* crap."

Roger laughed loudly while shaking his head. "Never heard it put that way before. There is a rather famous poem that was written by a space merchant about half a century ago that sums it up quite nicely. Would you like to hear it?"

"Sure," replied the three pilots as all four of them looked up at the sky.

> "Deep, dark, and deathly,
> home to so few.
> Travel the universe,
> a job to do.
> Wandering happy,
> I'm so far from you.
> Goodbye you bitch,
> I hate you."

They laughed when Roger finished and Peter spoke first, "Wow, that's deep on so many levels."

"The man actually won a contest with that poem, made a lot of money too. He was on a four-day drinking binge at the time when somebody shot him. Everyone figured it was his ugly wife."

"Oh damn, now I get it," said Randy. "Or, at least part of it. Oh hell, poems are stupid."

"It's hard to explain," said Peter, "but when this war is over I really don't want to live on a planet. There doesn't seem to be anything there for me, anymore. If I have to become a *lifer* then I will if that lets me stay out in space. When I was enlisted I realized that military life wasn't for me, so when the time was right I got out and never looked back. Now I'm back in the military and I am loving it, minus the war part. It is much better the second time around."

"I know exactly what you mean," said Miguel. "As an enlisted simtech I figured that after the war, if I lived, I'd be done with the military and go to work for some software company or something. But, ever since I met you my life has been changing. I feel like I am somebody now. I feel that I can finally make a difference in the galaxy and damn it, I want to see that happen."

"Yeah, me too," said Randy.

"Me too," said Peter.

"Count me in on that plan. It's nice having a purpose. My original plan was to avoid the war at all costs and that was what I attempted when I requested a transfer off of Virginia Prime. I don't know how my orders changed but now I am glad that they did. I never expected that being a teacher could affect the outcome of a war so greatly," said Roger.

"Knowledge is power," replied Peter with a nod.

"There is always more than one way to approach fighting a war," said Miguel.

"The Art of Kicking Ass, by Roger Cleam," said Randy, causing the others to laugh.

"We need to get back to class," said Roger as he stood and collected his books. "This is it, then it's back to war."

"Back to the front," said Peter. All three of them nodded absently because Roger's classes on military history had explained that phrase to them.

They walked in silence to the building where the classes were being held. The classroom was full and became quiet as Peter, Roger, Miguel, and Randy entered the room. His friends took seats in the front row as Peter stood in front of the podium.

"Congratulations everyone, you all did a great job," said Peter. "Now the real work begins, training everyone else in the fleet one carrier at a time."

"A never ending mission," said one of the instructors.

"Yes, the training mission never ends, and it shouldn't. With the knowledge you have gained from these two weeks the entire operation of the Fleet will change. Then the war will soon turn in our favor. Not to burst the bubble but it won't last. As we change our tactics the enemy will learn to adapt to them. So what we need to do is constantly surprise them and change our tactics, sometimes midstream. We cannot afford complacency. To do so can only bring about death to us all. We must keep changing and pushing until the enemy buckles and surrenders, or is exterminated. The choice at that point will be theirs."

Everyone nodded but no one said anything in response. Getting the enemy to even converse would be a challenge for somebody else. The Bect had broken ties before, probably because they had always felt they had the upper hand. Maybe once that had changed, things on the political front would change. No one cared to speculate. Everyone in the room was a man or woman of war. War was what they knew and what they were trained to deal with. Bring death to the enemy so that we may live.

"I don't know everything," said Peter as he paced back and forth slowly. "I never have and never will. We are all on the same team so we must share information. If, during your training, you discover something interesting please pass that information along. Evaluate the enemy every chance that you get and use deception whenever you can. Use the tools you have been given in these two weeks of class to develop tools of your own. This bullshit class is now officially over. Let's go kick some alien ass!"

Cheers erupted and the class stood to applaud. As the officers filed out of the room they all took the time to shake his hand and the hands of Roger, Miguel, and Randy. Everyone made it a point to congratulate the newly commissioned second lieutenants as well. Peter was impressed that Lieutenant Colonel Nelson had stayed for every single class, including the simulator sessions. He was the last in line to leave the room.

"Great job, men," said Lieutenant Colonel Nelson as he shook their hands.

"Thank you, Colonel," said Peter. "I was surprised to see you go through all the classes and sim sessions."

"What the hell else did I have to do? If I stayed on the ship I would've been put to work doing something stupid," said Lieutenant Colonel Nelson. "Seriously though, I needed to be here so that I could become a better commander."

"True," said Peter with a nod.

"I hope my being here didn't make you nervous."

"No sir, it helps us in the long run. It also justifies all the surprises I kept giving you."

Lieutenant Colonel Nelson laughed and Peter joined him.

"Very true. Now let's get the hell out of here and back to the ship. This real gravity shit is starting to make me sick," said Lieutenant Colonel Nelson. He headed for the door with the four men of the training department behind him.

They stopped by the officer quarters and recovered their gear. The spaceport was still crowded and Peter looked at the small shuttle in the berth that Emily's ship had been in. He could not stop thinking about her.

Lieutenant Colonel Nelson found a dockhand and was directed to the berth where the Ticonderoga shuttle was due to arrive. They still had another thirty minutes to wait so they stood quietly while watching the activity around them. Cargo ships were being loaded and unloaded as soon as they touched down. As soon as the doors dropped the loaders went to work immediately.

"Here it comes," said Lieutenant Colonel Nelson as he continued to watch the sky.

"How can you tell, sir?" asked Randy as he tried to see what the Lieutenant Colonel was looking at.

"I see a glint of the sun off of a metal surface," Lieutenant Colonel Nelson replied with a wink in Peter's direction.

"Wow, good eyesight sir. I can't see shit," said Randy as he struggled to see the mysterious shuttle.

The shuttle arrived three minutes early and was unloaded eight minutes later. They boarded and took seats at the forward part of the shuttle. It was not due to depart for another thirty minutes but they were tired and just wanted to sit on something one step closer to the carrier. Once the door closed the loadmaster walked around with barf bags for everyone. When he stopped at the pilots Peter waved his right hand and shook his head.

"Pilots?"

"For the most part," said Peter indicating the five of them.

"Good," replied the loadmaster. It was that much less vomit he would have to clean up afterward.

"I'll take one," said Miguel with his hand held out.

Peter, Roger, and Randy gave him an odd look while Lieutenant Colonel Nelson was already fast asleep.

"What?" asked Miguel.

Peter laughed and leaned his head against the side bulkhead. It did not take long for him to fall asleep. It had been a long two weeks and he was exhausted. He never heard nor felt the launch and slept right until the impact of docking with the carrier. He felt a little disoriented upon waking since he was weightless.

Miguel was spinning the barf bag in circles like a pinwheel in front of himself. He would start the bag turning and would then lean back to watch it. This caused the poor Private across from him to use his bag heavily. In space any object could float about inside the cabin, including vomit. Very rarely did someone projectile vomit but when they did the vomit would impact the wall, ceiling, floor, or some poor human. Barf bags had a small vacuum insert that reacted when wet to draw in the fluid.

Peter reached over and tapped the spinning bag and its motion and path changed slightly. He found himself watching the floating bag in fascination as it dawned on him that he was weightless. The rear door opened and the loadmaster, along with several other people, assisted everyone leaving the shuttle into the cargo bay. Once everyone had disembarked, the external door was closed and gravity was slowly introduced. Peter reveled in the weight-lessness as much as he could. He was soon standing on the floor as gravity returned. Two more people used their barf bags while kneeling on the floor. Some people could not handle the floating feeling but Peter liked it. He always wondered what it was like and now he knew. He was weightless for his only mission in a Stiletto but he was too busy to really enjoy it.

"Ah, home sweet home," said Randy as he sniffed the air. He began coughing as his face cringed. "Smells like puke and engine oil, just like I remembered."

"When are we leaving orbit?" asked Miguel of nobody in particular.

"Tomorrow at oh-seven hundred," replied Lieutenant Colonel Nelson, loud enough to be heard by all in the room. "Better get a good night of sleep because tomorrow we are back in the war business."

"Yes sir," said Miguel.

The cargo door opened and the crowd dispersed into the hallways of the carrier. At every hallway branch people peeled off to find their bunkrooms. The five of them headed for their rooms in Flight Ops. Peter tossed his duffel bag on his bed and sighed heavily. He did not want to unpack it, so he left it there. He turned and walked out of the bunkroom and into the hallway.

It was a short walk to the observation deck where he had watched the first battle and there was no one there, as usual. He walked to the window and watched the planet turning below. Continents were the dominant feature of this world, with very few oceans worth mentioning. There was still a lot of activity in orbit. He followed two Stilettos making their way between two capital ships. He could not help but wonder if one of the cargo ships was Emily's but he knew she was nowhere near this solar system.

An hour passed and Peter remained at the window. He heard movement behind him and saw the white uniform reflection grow in the window as he watched a storm churn in the planet's northern hemisphere. Peter refused to acknowledge the presence of the newcomer and wondered who it might be as the person stopped next to him.

"Not such a bad place," said a familiar voice.

"But not worth staying on," responded Peter as he turned to discover

Captain Washington.

"I've been wandering around the ship looking for you. Captain Cleam said you might be here. He said that this has become your favorite spot when you have a free moment."

"Yes sir," said Peter as he returned to watching the planet. "When I was in the Twenty-First Century there was virtually no chance that I would ever leave the planet. I used to dream about it and hope for it, but it would never happen. I was dying to leave, just didn't realize that I would have to die in order to leave it."

"You are here by some odd circumstances, son. Are you unhappy here?"

"No sir, oddly enough I'm totally happy here. I hate war but I feel like I have a real purpose here. I'd rather stay in space than be trapped on some planet."

"Spoken like a true spaceman," said Captain Washington with a chuckle. "I left my home planet a long time ago and have never gone back. If you are happy here why do you seem depressed?"

"I'm just remembering my past a little bit too much lately. Everyone I knew, family and friends, are all long gone. If they could only see me now, the new me."

"Was the old you that bad?"

"No, it wasn't anything like that. The old me was just me. I had a small circle that really didn't impact that many lives. My leaving probably went barely noticed, just a flash in the pan," said Peter. He paused as he searched for the words and Captain Washington waited, sensing there was more. "My being here seemed so surreal, almost like watching a movie, until I stood on that planet. I knew it wasn't Earth but it sure looked like it."

"Gravity," replied Captain Washington.

"Being down there ..." Peter slowly shook his head back and forth. "I didn't like it. Not one bit and I don't want to go back."

"That's why I refuse to go planetside unless I am ordered to, and luckily that doesn't happen very often."

"But you showed up to pin the bars on Miguel and Randy."

"Miguel and Randy deserved them and I wanted the honor of being the first to congratulate them. They are both with the examiner in the simulator right now. It should be a very uplifting day for the two of them, I've seen them fly."

"Why didn't I have to take a written or flight test?" asked Peter.

"Terry and I worked that out. It's not that you didn't take a written or flight test, because in essence you did. It's the method of the tests that you apparently missed. We figured that due to your previous flying experience, even though it was atmospheric, formal testing would be a waste of time. All of your long conversations with Terry about the Stiletto were your oral tests in lieu of the written. When we submitted the paperwork for your wings we included the amazing simulator session when I had given you your commission. It all works out in the end."

"Yes, I guess it does," replied Peter.

Captain Washington and Peter stood silently and watched the planet turning below. The storm had made its way across their view and was in the process of disappearing to the left. One of the planet's three moons appeared on the far right of the planet. It was a small green ball about half the size of Earth's moon. Peter watched as it grew in the distance.

"Was she nice?" asked Captain Washington, breaking the silence.

"Who?"

"The cargo ship commander. I heard you visited her ship twice while you were on the planet."

"Good intel, sir."

"It's a captain thing."

"She was very nice. Met most of the crew too, shook their hands. I am a genuine hero to them," said Peter without emotion, "except for the dead ones."

"You can't save them all, son, but you saved the ones that you could. War is a sad business, a business of death dealing and death taking. Be glad that you did save some and were able to meet those that you did. Most of the time you don't get that opportunity."

"I am glad, sir. That's why I overextended my evaluation flight. I had to do something, even if it killed me in the process. I was the only one out there that could have done anything to help them, so I did, and I'd do it again without hesitation."

"I wouldn't have expected anything less from you. You are a born leader."

"Well, not the first time around. But this time, I feel I'm in the right place. Right where I want to be and right where I need to be. I'm still not sure of my main purpose here other than to help win this war."

"None of us ever are," said Captain Washington. "Was she pretty?"

Peter thought about the question before answering. He knew exactly whom he was asking about but wondered at the Captain's line of questioning. Why was the Captain spending his free time talking to me when there must have been so much more to do to prepare the ship for departure? Why all the sudden interest?

"Very."

"I take it you had that beer the two of you talked about after the save."

"Yes, and spent the night together ... but not in that way."

"Did she offer?" asked Captain Washington.

"Yes, but I turned her down. I didn't want sex with her to be a reward for saving her and her ship. I would like it to be on more equal terms, if that makes any sense."

"Well, look at it from her perspective. She commands a ship of people she cannot have intimate relations with because it's against regulations. Plus it's just bad for everyone aboard. So, she had a good looking hero on her ship and used that as an opportunity to enjoy life just for the sake of being alive. Just for once in this futile war to step away from being a commander and to be just a woman. Odds are she didn't want to sleep with you because you saved her and her ship. That just presented her with the perfect opportunity and excuse to do so."

Peter remained silent as he continued to look out the observation window. He was no longer seeing the activity in orbit. He was replaying all the events with Emily, trying to make sense of things. Captain Washington was right. Emily had been honest and straightforward with him. He suddenly felt like he had cheated her out of what she had needed and wanted.

"Most men would have taken her offer," said Captain Washington quietly as he watched Peter's reflection in the window.

"I'm an idiot."

"I wouldn't say that. You both had your reasons and things played out as they did."

"Yeah, I know. We did sleep together and I really liked waking up with her arm around me. I didn't ... it just ... the situation ... it felt wrong."

"Well, you made your point to her and your impression. She probably likes you a lot more now and respects you too. Women are the most confusing things in the universe but, sometimes, they make perfect sense. Try to think about that when you see her in two weeks."

"I will ... two weeks?" asked Peter as he turned.

"Yes, we are meeting up with Cargoes One through Five, two cruisers, a battleship, some marines, and a squadron of support fighters. I'm going to invite the commander of each ship aboard for dinner when they arrive. Just thought you might want to know ahead of time."

"Thanks Captain, for everything."

April
2348

CHAPTER
24

W hat do you make of that?" asked Captain Jeff Washington of his First Officer, Commander Frank Mito, while pointing at the long-range scanner. The largest group was marked as the cargo compliment on their way to rendezvous with them. Behind them and a bit further out were an unknown bunch of dots that were shadowing the Cargo Group.

"Can't be good, sir. Most likely a Bect assault force either preparing to attack them or following them to us," replied Commander Mito.

"Communications, get Colonel Nelson up here on the double," said Captain Washington. His eyes never left the screen and he continued speaking but in a whisper. "How good is the Bect intelligence?"

"No one knows for sure, sir," said Commander Mito while shrugging. The two of them watched the screen as they pondered alternatives.

"How long until the Cargo Group reaches us?" asked Captain Washington.

"Two hours, sir."

"We need a plan and fast."

It took Lieutenant Colonel Terry Nelson two minutes to get to the bridge and he came through the door at a run. He approached the Captain at the scanner and stood at attention as his breathing tried to catch up.

"Colonel Nelson reporting as ordered, Captain."

"At ease. We've got a slight problem, Terry," said Jeff. He rubbed his chin as he continued informally in a whisper. "This is the Cargo Group heading our way. This other group might be Bect following them in the attempt to ambush us. Or maybe they are closing on our cargo friends to have a little massacre. What do you think?"

"Could go either way, Jeff. From what I know of Bect capital ship propulsion systems they very nearly match ours. We could leave a squadron here to protect the rest of our Carrier Group and head out there as fast as this carrier can go. Once there we drop all of our remaining squadrons and engage them."

"We don't know how big of a group they are," said Jeff, trying to spark further thought on Terry's part.

"True, and we also don't know if they are after us or the Cargo Group. I'd much rather see them after us since we are better equipped to handle it. Has the Cargo Group's fighter compliment had the upgrades and training?"

"Most likely not, they headed out our second day at Virginia Prime. They picked up a battleship, marine expeditionary unit, and marine squadron at Omega Prime. I've sent an encrypted message to the Group Commander to see if they know about their shadow. We should be hearing from them soon, I hope."

"Sir, request permission to assemble Squadron Commanders for briefing and options?" asked Lieutenant Colonel Nelson, knowing that it was time to be all business. He waited patiently for the Captain to respond.

"Go ahead, Colonel."

Lieutenant Colonel Nelson ran from the bridge and for Flight Ops as fast as he could. He stopped at each squadron bunkroom to yell orders for someone to find and have their commander report to the briefing room immediately. Junior officers began running around looking for their commanders to give them the orders.

Four minutes later Carlos, Peter, Major Silvio Brannick of Defend Squadron, and Major Allen Seller of Attack Squadron arrived at the briefing room. Lieutenant Colonel Nelson was standing at the front of the room examining a star chart on the view screen. He hit a button and the scene zoomed in. He hit it two more times until he was satisfied with the enhancement.

"Have a seat, gentlemen. We've got a problem," said Lieutenant Colonel Nelson. He began detailing what he knew about the Cargo Group and the Bect force following them. The view screen showed current data relayed from the bridge and it updated in real time. He changed the viewing angle a few times and zoomed in as much as he could on the unknown force.

Peter nodded absently, Emily would be in that Cargo Group. He had not heard from her in a couple of days.

"Is Second Alert Flight currently patrolling?" asked Lieutenant Colonel Nelson.

"Yes, sir," replied Carlos.

"Here's what I will offer to the Captain as a battle plan. First we will launch Defend Squadron to protect the rest of our Group and immediately recover Second Alert Flight. Then the carrier will intercept the Cargo Group. While we are launching Attack Squadron the carrier's rail guns will try to cause some problems for the Bect. Reserve Squadron will launch to assist Attack while Alert launches. We will take out the fighters and hopefully the capital ships will run, otherwise we will engage them as well. The marine Stilettos have not been upgraded nor have their pilots been trained so we will recover them. Any questions or comments?"

Peter rose his hand slowly and saw that no one else was going to challenge the Lieutenant Colonel's plans.

"Yes, Captain."

"Sir, what about having the marines stay out to protect the carrier as a last line of defense. Hopefully we don't need them but we can help them save face that way."

"Save face?" asked Lieutenant Colonel Nelson.

"Honor, sir. Having them run away from the Bect to be recovered and protected by the carrier is calling them a bunch of worthless pilots. By having them protect the carrier they still feel like part of the team even though they don't join in battle. Maybe issue the orders under the assumption that they are tired from a long flight and we didn't want them to throw their lives away needlessly."

"Makes sense, anything else?" asked Lieutenant Colonel Nelson as Peter's hand raised again.

"Sir, I'm the only pilot to have engaged a capital ship. What about launching Alert Squadron second and Reserve last. As crazy as this may sound I volunteer Reserve Squadron to attack all the enemy capital ships as soon as we launch."

"That is crazy, but what about all the fighters?"

"I think Captain Mendez and Major Seller can keep them all busy. Their sim work has been impressive even though we've only been at it for two weeks."

"What do you two think?" asked Lieutenant Colonel Nelson.

"Count me in," said Carlos. He had not been in a real dogfight in a while and the sim was getting him excited about it. Being able to go against twenty Bect with your entire Flight was better than rolling around naked with Delilah. Ever since he had been promoted to captain his free time had almost disappeared. Add upon that the sixteen-hour days in the training department and the only end in sight was the end of that relationship. For him it was no great loss. His attitude changed considerably the day that John died.

"Me too," said Major Seller. He was in his late twenties and completely bald. He blamed it on the whiskey and cigars but everyone knew it was because of his wife. She had the skill to piss off everyone she met almost instantly. Her arrogance and demeanor annoyed everyone in the room within seconds. Nobody understood why he kept her around, especially since she was not worth looking at. War was the best thing to happen to him because he could finally get away from her without having to need an excuse the length of the Milky Way.

Major Brannick nodded slowly as he realized that he hated being in

Defend Squadron. There was nothing like having the rest of the carrier run off for a good fight while leaving the children behind. He needed to find a way to change that but kept coming up empty.

"All right, get busy, you have fifteen minutes to warn everyone. Captain Mendez, get your pilots recovered. Major Brannick, get your squadron launched. When the klaxon goes off it will be party time. Let's go."

Everyone stood without saying a word and began running when they exited the briefing room. Lieutenant Colonel Nelson ran to the bridge and wondered if he was getting too old for this. When he entered the bridge Captain Washington was still standing in the same place, watching the view screen.

"That was quick," said Captain Washington without looking up. He knew that it was Terry because he was the only person that typically ran onto the bridge. Jeff really liked that in an officer.

"Yes, sir. We have a plan and the ball is rolling on part one. We're going to launch Defend Squadron and recover Second Alert Flight. Once that is complete, Flight Ops will be ready for rapid deployment upon relocation."

"Controller, notify me when Defend has launched and Second Alert Flight is recovered," yelled Captain Washington.

"Aye aye, sir," responded the controller.

"So, what is the next part, Colonel?"

"Once we arrive at the Cargo Group, the rail guns can keep the Bect busy while Attack and Alert Squadrons launch. They will engage the Bect fighters and bombers. We can recall the marine pilots to fly cover for the carrier since they are not trained nor are their ships upgraded. Reserve Squadron will launch and engage the capital ships."

"Damn, that sounds like a death wish," shot Captain Washington.

"Peter's idea, sir."

"Is that man trying to get himself killed again?"

"Sir, the impression I get is that he knows his limitations. Since most of his flying is in the sim and not actual combat, well, I guess it could be a death wish."

Captain Washington nodded as he pondered the plan presented to him.

One minute later he was told that Second Alert Flight was recovered and Defend Squadron was in place patrolling the rest of their Group. He issued the order to turn and proceed to intercept the Bect force at maximum speed, which was five SU for a carrier-class ship.

Captain Washington still had not received a response from the Cargo Group and wondered what was going on with them. He was fairly certain that the transmission should have been received and a response transmitted by now. He guessed it was also possible that the Bect forces were jamming all transmissions to and from the Cargo Group. Things were going to get messy if their targeting computers were being jammed.

"Prep the rail guns, have all forward batteries standing by," said Captain Washington as he turned to Lieutenant Colonel Nelson.

"Aye aye, sir, notifying rail gun batteries," said the Lieutenant Junior Grade on duty.

"We still don't know what we are up against," said Captain Washington.

"Time to put all of Peter's training to the test."

"Yes, it will be educational. This appears to be the largest force we've ever engaged."

The Ticonderoga approached the Cargo Group rapidly and there was still had no response from them. The Bect force had actually closed the distance and was almost within striking range of the Cargo Group. It was going to be close.

"Captain, hostile forces confirmed and we've got a ship count," said Commander Mito.

"Go ahead."

"Signatures indicate approximately fifty fighters, three cruisers, a tanker, and what might be a destroyer-class capital ship. The tanker is near the destroyer and might be refueling it and is slightly obscuring our scanners in that area."

"Fifty fighters and four capital ships? Damn," Captain Washington remarked as he walked to his chair. If they failed here, the Bect would massacre the remainder of his Group. Was this going to be another Cori Prime? "Push a high-intensity secure flash message to the Cargo Group Commander.

Tell him we'll need the marine pilots to cover the Ticonderoga because we're hitting the aliens with everything we have."

"Aye aye, sir," responded the communication officer.

"Time until rendezvous?" yelled Captain Washington.

"Twenty-three minutes, sir."

"Brief your people," said Captain Washington to Lieutenant Colonel Nelson. "Have Peter concentrate on that destroyer first, it will present the greatest threat to all of us. Have both Alert and Attack Squadrons hit the fighters. God help us."

"Yes sir," said Lieutenant Colonel Nelson as he exited the bridge and ran to Flight Ops. When the war was over the last thing he would ever do is run. War was a strange beast that wore away at your mind and body. There would be weeks with no sight of the enemy and everyone would slack off from the normal routines. Then a battle would occur and fire everyone up. Then the cycle would begin again. It was an endless struggle between boredom and near death experiences.

Lieutenant Colonel Nelson ran into the Reserve Squadron bunkroom and saw all sixteen men and women pilots getting into their flight gear as fast as possible. The room was quiet as they prepared their minds for the coming fight. It would be the first real combat for most of them and they had been told of their mission, to attack the alien capital ships. Sure, their commander had taken one out single-handedly, but this was different. They argued about it in their minds trying to justify why this was an insane idea but could only come up with reasons why it would work. They were the best-trained pilots on the ship. Well, at least half of them were. The other half of the squadron were newcomers since Virginia Prime but they were paired with the more experienced pilots as their wingleaders.

"Peter," yelled Lieutenant Colonel Nelson, out of breath and bent over.

"Sir," said Peter, "are you okay?"

"Shit, I should have used the intercom."

Peter laughed as Lieutenant Colonel Nelson tried to catch his breath. That was what he liked about the Lieutenant Colonel. He was a real person and one that commanded respect.

"But just think of all the exercise you're getting," shot Peter.

"Screw that. I'll take the tram back to the bridge and have a nap."

"What brings you down here in such a hurry, sir?"

"Take out the destroyer first. One destroyer, three cruisers, and a tanker."

"Yes sir, piece of cake," said Peter as the new pilots looked on in shock. They had seen the video of Peter saving the cargo ship and were surprised to see the look on his face at that moment ... he was smiling.

"Piece of cake?" asked Lieutenant Colonel Nelson through deep breaths.

"Sorry sir, more slang. I mean, not a problem."

"Okay then, good luck," said Lieutenant Colonel Nelson. He turned to leave, walking away slowly this time while holding his right side.

"Okay everyone," said Peter loudly. "You've had the training, now it's time to earn your pay."

"We get paid?" asked Randy seriously. This caused a stir of tense laughter within the group.

"You know, I don't recall ever seeing any money," said Peter. "That's it, I'm outta here!"

The group laughed again and the tension slowly lifted from them. Peter finished putting his flight gear on.

"All you new pilots, remember your training and follow your wingleader. We've been training for a while and now it's time to prove to the rest of the Group that we aren't a bunch of simulator rejects. Do what you were trained to do and do it to the best of your ability."

The other pilots continued dressing as Peter climbed onto the table. He put his hands on his hips and surveyed the room.

"Target one is a destroyer. We want to take it down as quick as we can which will be an interesting endeavor since nobody in the entire Fleet has ever flown against one. What is the plan? We'll split into two flights and attack it from two angles. We have no idea what this thing has for firepower so it could get pretty hairy."

"Like Miguel?" asked Randy. Another round of laughter passed through the room as Miguel raised his middle finger for Randy.

"Miguel, you have command of Second Flight."

"Thank you, sir."

"Maneuver your flight behind the destroyer and fill its engines with missiles. Seven missiles disabled the cruiser I fought so plan on firing two each. I'll have my flight also fire two missiles each. That will put thirty-two missiles on target. If that doesn't cause some serious problems for it then I don't know what will."

"You got it, sir."

"Remember everyone, I want radio chatter at a maximum. They are used to our being quiet, so let's flood the airwaves with so much bullshit that the enemy doesn't have time to translate any of it. I want to confuse the hell out of them. Let's go find our Stilettos."

"All right!" everyone shouted out as they entered the hallway. It was a short run to the flight deck and the general quarters klaxon began going off as they entered. They would be the third group launching so they had some time to prepare mentally for the coming battle.

A squadron of Stilettos was placed on floor panels that tilted forty-five degrees downward before the green light went on. Then the engines were started and the throttles eased forward for the fighter to shoot out of the bottom of the carrier. Once the ships were gone the panels would close up and the deck crew would move the next squadron of fighters into position. It was an efficient operation and took only two minutes between launches. Recovery of a squadron of fighters was a much longer process.

*

"Sir, targets in range," said the gunnery officer on the bridge.

"Fire," said Captain Washington.

"All batteries fire," said the officer into the boom microphone in front of his mouth. The carrier shook as the rail guns launched their projectiles down pulsing magnetic tubes and across space toward the enemy ships. A few burst-style projectiles caused minor damage to the approaching enemy fighters in an attempt to thin them out.

"Launch Attack Squadron," said Captain Washington. The controller gave the order as all but one of the rail guns switched their firing to the capital ships. The rail gun projectiles were fast and the firing rate was one round every fifteen seconds. The Captain almost cheered when a projectile impacted one of the cruisers and a stream of flames shot out to immediately extinguish into space.

"Sir, Attack Squadron has launched. Alert Squadron is moving into launch position," said the controller.

"Good," said Captain Washington as he surveyed the Cargo Group. A few of the cargo ships were spewing wreckage and debris but they were still moving. One of the Cargo Group's cruisers was badly damaged and rolling slowly. They were taking damage from the alien destroyer and it would not be long before the cruiser had no chance of survival.

"Get those batteries laying some fire on that destroyer," shouted Captain Washington as he pointed to the offending ship in his front window.

"Aye aye, sir," said the gunnery officer as he relayed the order. There was a slight pause in the rail gun activity as the targets were switched. One of the rail guns continued peppering the alien fighters trying to reduce their numbers.

"Sir, Alert Squadron has launched," said the controller.

"Have Attack and Alert engage those enemy fighters," said Captain Washington as he slowly shook his head. The front window was almost full of activity and it would only fill up further.

"Aye aye, sir," said the controller and then relayed the order. Thirty-two Stilettos appeared from under the Ticonderoga and headed for the group of enemy fighters.

"Helm, bring us up one incline and slow to point one SU," said Captain Washington. "Keep the pressure on those capital ships."

The damaged human cruiser took another few hits in the engine compartment and split in half as the entire aft end of the ship broke into dozens of pieces. Several escape pods shot out of the side of the cruiser and floated aimlessly in space. The rest of the cruiser broke up as various internal structures failed and collapsed. Captain Washington sighed, they had lost one ship and the battle had only just begun.

"Where are those marine Stilettos?" shouted Captain Washington as he checked the scanners.

"What marine Stilettos, sir?" asked the controller.

"Don't give me that shit, what happened to them?"

"Sir, since we have arrived there were no other Stilettos on our scanners," replied the scanner operator.

"Comm, any success contacting anyone in the Cargo Group?"

"Negative, sir."

"Wonderful."

*

Captain Carlos Mendez glanced at his short-range scanner and a lump grew in his throat. The screen was full of enemy activity. There had to be more than fifty alien fighters out there. Off to his right he saw a friendly cruiser burst wide open as several escape pods shot out of it. One down and it most likely would not be the only one.

"Alert Squadron, down two inclines and going right," said Carlos over the command frequency. He was having problems trying to use as much chat as possible. After so much time of being quiet over the frequency he could not just change overnight.

"Attack Squadron, up one incline and going left," said Major Seller.

"Let's pick em and pluck em," said Carlos with a laugh. Peter had used that one during a sim session and it quickly became Carlos' favorite. There were enemy fighters all over the place so he began putting ICIS to work. As soon as they were in range he fired two missiles and switched to a secondary target.

Every single pilot did as he was trained and announced their call sign followed by, "Missiles fired."

Thirty-two missiles streaked toward their targets as the second volley was queued up. As soon as ICIS flashed *Ready,* Carlos hit his weapon release button twice more and the next two missiles leapt from his wing pylons. He glanced quickly to the left and the entire area of space between them and the alien fighters was filled with two volleys of missiles. One hundred and twenty-eight missiles created a cloud of screaming white metal between them.

The impact from the first volley did not take very long at all. Four missiles failed and kept going past all the activity. The remaining sixty missiles impacted and destroyed twenty enemy fighters and wounded seven more. The next volley of missiles had seven failures that wandered out into space. The remaining fifty-seven missiles slammed into the wave of alien fighters and destroyed eighteen while damaging twelve more.

*

"Damn," said Captain Washington, "what a sight."

"Sir, Reserve Squadron has launched," said the controller.

"Do we have a total enemy count yet?" asked Captain Washington as he watched the battle in morbid fascination.

"There's too many of them, sir," replied the scanner operator. "Best count so far is roughly eighty fighters and twenty bombers."

"My God," said Lieutenant Colonel Nelson as a look of shock appeared on his face. He stared at the view screen in stunned silence wondering if his pilots could handle that many ships. A few months ago the answer would have been a resounding *No*.

"How many did the missile volley take out?" asked Captain Washington.

"Sir, about forty of them and maybe twenty more damaged."

"Well, we've got a long way to go," said Captain Washington. The ship shook again while the rail guns continued suppression fire. The Bect destroyer had backed off and the three Bect cruisers moved in to continue their laser fire at the various cargo ships, cruisers, and battleship. The battleship was very busy and needed help, several enemy bombers were swarming around it wreaking havoc.

"Damn bombers," shouted Captain Washington. "Redirect Alert Squadron to hit the bombers attacking the battleship."

"Aye aye, sir," replied the controller.

*

Carlos barely heard the call come over the command frequency. He was not quite sure what to make of it but knew that he could not see the entire battle, so it must have been important.

"Alert, break off. Follow me," yelled Carlos over the short-range frequency. He found the battleship and noticed the cluster of bombers moving around it. Laser fire filled the area with deadly light as Alert Squadron approached.

"We have some fighters on our six," shot the First Lieutenant in command of Second Alert Flight.

"Take them out, we're heading for the battleship," shot Carlos.

"Roger that, good luck," replied the First Lieutenant as he had his flight break off from the rest of them.

"You too."

Carlos began targeting the nearest bomber with ICIS. As soon as he had a firing solution he depressed his weapon release button twice and his two missiles shot forth. The rest of his flight did the same and soon the sky filled with flashes of light as several bombers took hits. Of the eight bombers targeted only five of them were destroyed, the other three took damage and were finished off by the battleship.

Carlos watched as secondary explosions appeared on the battleship, it was still taking heavy damage from the remaining alien bombers. He picked out his next target and released his last two missiles as the rest of his flight fired theirs. Four of the bombers burst open while the other four took the hits, only one missile failed.

"Let's go mix it up," shouted Carlos over the short-range frequency. "Split into twos and let's pop the rest of these freaks."

"Roger that!" came the shouts of agreement. It was almost comical in nature to blab like they did over the radio. He found it very relieving in an odd sort of way.

Carlos picked a nearby bomber and sprayed it with laser fire. "Damn, these new lasers kick ass!" yelled Carlos over the short-range frequency. He put ten shots into it and probably only needed three, he figured the gumdrop must have lost its shields earlier. He moved to the next one and soon the area was clear of bombers. The bombers were very focused on the battleship as their target and they just let the Stilettos waste through them. That concerned him a little bit but he still had a job to do.

"Scratch the bombers, let's go play with the fighters," said Carlos over the command frequency. As he turned toward the fighters he saw Peter's squadron heading for the destroyer.

*

"Destroyer my ass," said Peter over the command frequency. "That's a damn Bect carrier." He watched as another wave of slugs exited the left side of the ship.

"A very juicy target then," said Miguel.

"And then some. Same game plan everyone. Remember your training and let's blow this bastard back into the Stone Age." Peter pushed his throttles forward and started ICIS on a firing solution. He selected the ports on the side of the ship that he saw the fighters coming from and launched one of his missiles. The other fighters in his flight did the same for the other ports. Then Peter selected what he figured would be the bridge of the ship and fired another missile with his flight following his lead.

Miguel brought his flight around behind the enemy carrier and they launched their two missiles into the engines. The carrier began firing its lasers in response to the human fighters around it. A few of the Stilettos took hits but nothing major as they evaded and kept their distance. The further they were from the carrier the better the chance of avoiding the lasers would be.

Eight missiles slammed into the launch bays of the carrier and lit up the entire left side with secondary explosions. Several slugs in the process of launching were trapped in the blast and disintegrated. The next volley of missiles had one failure that still impacted the suspected bridge area with the rest of them. Those eight missiles ripped open a large hole that sucked a bunch of debris, and most likely alien bodies, out into the vacuum of space. It was a perfect hit and Peter hoped that that actually was the bridge.

Miguel's volley of sixteen missiles tore into the engines on the alien carrier like hot knives through butter. The entire aft portion of the alien carrier erupted violently and caused the last fighter in Miguel's flight to spin out of control into his wingleader. The two Stilettos exploded killing both pilots instantly. Enemy fighters that had previously launched from the dying carrier headed in their direction.

"We've got bandits," said Peter over the short-range frequency. "That carrier is wasted. After we get the fighters we'll go finish her off."

"Don't bother," said a new male voice over the frequency, "we could use some payback."

"All yours then, good buddy. Make a mess to write home about," said Peter as he targeted the first fighter.

"Roger that, you crazy bastards," said the voice again. "Thanks for the help, that was one ballsy move."

"Balls, we've got. Brains ... that's optional," said Miguel.

*

"Look at that carrier burn," said Captain Washington in awe as secondary explosions on the enemy carrier split it into two halves. "So that's what an alien carrier looks like. We need to get a classification of that ship."

"Sir, in progress," said Commander Mito.

"Captain, I have the Cargo Group Commander on a secure channel," said the communication officer.

"Finally. Patch him through."

"Captain Washington, this is Captain Victor Radcliff of the Battleship Reeds."

"Captain Radcliff, we've been trying to contact anyone from your Group for over an hour."

"Been kind of busy, glad to see you made it to the party."

"Glad to help out. What happened to your marine pilots?"

"Dead. Lost them with the first wave of fighters," said Captain Radcliff with a touch of sadness in his voice.

"Vic, keep this channel open while we mop up this mess."

"Okay, Jeff."

*

Carlos had more enemy fighters on his combat computer than he could count. He could tell from the laser blasts ahead that Attack Squadron was in the heat of battle. He figured that the sixteen pilots of Attack Squadron were currently engaged with about forty enemy fighters. There were too many white and red dots on the scanner to come up with an actual count and he hoped that no white dots were missing.

"Let's go, Alert. It's time to thin out this herd."

Alert Squadron split into two flights and changed inclines before engaging. Several enemy fighters popped open before they knew what had hit them. Carlos lined up on a fighter and put four laser blasts into it and switched to the next one as it burst apart. They were dropping the Bect fighters easily, the only problem being the shear number of them in the area.

"Get this freak off me!" yelled a pilot in trouble. He had two alien fighters chasing him and filling his tail with laser fire. The pilot from Second Attack Flight panicked and turned into the Second Alert Flight fighters. He clipped Alert Seven and the two of them spun into his wingman. The three ships exploded and only one ejection compartment exited the twisting pile of wreckage.

Carlos cursed loudly but did not press his transmit button to share his flowery comments with the rest of the Group. It was a useless waste of life. He turned his Stiletto and removed a few more slugs from space as his wingman took out one more.

*

Miguel finished off the last fighter and formed up alongside Peter's flight. They looked out of their cockpit windows and waved to each other.

"Hey, I know you," said Peter over the wingcom.

"I think I took a wrong turn somewhere," replied Miguel.

"Let's mop up these cruisers," said Peter over the command frequency. "We'll use Plan B with a twist and a side of fries."

Peter targeted the nearest cruiser and Miguel angled his flight to the right so as to come in behind it for his missile volley.

"One at a time and then next. Breaker, come back," said Peter almost laughing out loud at the bizarre phraseology. He wanted his squadron to put one missile each into the first cruiser, then move to the second one and do the same. Then on to the third one with one more missile each. That gave each cruiser thirteen missiles to deal with. Then they would break off, come back around, and finish off whatever was left alive. This way they could quickly and efficiently cause the most amount of damage to the cruisers in the least amount of time. He hoped this tactic would keep the cruisers from causing any more damage to the Cargo Group and his lady.

"Roger that," said Miguel as he wondered where his boss came up with that crazy command. The man was brilliant and sometimes he was just another man. That was what Miguel liked most about him. No matter how good he was he never rubbed it in anyone's face.

"Firing missile," said Peter as he depressed his weapon release button. Thirteen missiles streaked for the cruiser and he did not bother watching them go in. He switched to the next target and repeated his actions. Thirteen more missiles inbound for the second cruiser.

The third cruiser was chasing a friendly cruiser and causing some serious damage to it. From the angle they were approaching the cruiser it looked like all of his squadron's missiles would enter its engines.

"Take this in the ass you alien freaks!" shouted Peter as he launched his missile at the enemy cruiser. Miguel was right below him and his flight also fired. They watched as thirteen missiles entered the engines of the enemy cruiser. The flash of light was so brilliant that they had to close their eyes. When they opened them the cruiser was gone, completely. There was no wreckage anywhere that they could see.

"Did anybody see what happened to that cruiser? I can't find it," said Peter over the command frequency.

*

"Looks like it had some technical difficulties," replied Captain Washington. The smile on his face was unusually large. No, it was not another Cori Prime for them. It was the Bect's version of Cori Prime. He never expected the outcome of this battle to be as devastating to the enemy as it had been.

"Oh, all right, I'll go find someone else to play with then," said Peter's voice over the loudspeaker.

"They had technical difficulties as well," said Captain Washington. Peter's training had paid off better than he had ever imagined it could.

"Damn it, is there anything left to blow up?"

"Not really," replied Lieutenant Colonel Nelson. "Alert Squadron, you've been on duty the longest so we'll recover you first."

*

"Acknowledged," replied Carlos as Alert Squadron returned to the carrier. His flight had finished off what remaining fighters they could find and were pleased to see no further red dots on their scanners.

Peter had his squadron climb to a positive three incline as he surveyed the battle area. He watched in fascination as the two cruisers they had hit broke apart. Thirteen missiles each were overkill, but it was better that way. The Battleship Reeds had finished off the Bect carrier and was busy making the big pieces a lot smaller. They would not be satisfied until every piece of that alien carrier was small enough to fit into someone's pocket.

Attack Squadron dropped to a negative three incline and patrolled opposite from the Reserve Squadron. There was a lot of recovery and repair work to do before they could get underway again. Several escape pods had launched and Peter wondered how many safe ejections had taken place.

Battleship Reeds had taken heavy damage but was still functional. It was the Cargo Group's command ship. Over seven hundred people had died on that ship. One engine was damaged beyond repair while another one was operating at fifty percent total output. The hull was breached in thirteen locations and thirty-eight compartments were now exposed to space. It would need three weeks in a space dock to repair the damage but they would not see that for a while.

One cruiser was destroyed and nine hundred or so lives lost. The other cruiser took heavy damage with two hundred lives lost and several hull breaches. One engine was crippled but repairable and would require a space dock to complete the repairs.

The marine expeditionary unit avoided any serious damage since its ship was the most vulnerable and it had the best speed. The captain of that ship used high-speed hit-and-run tactics against the alien capital ships, inflicting only minor damage, until the Ticonderoga showed up.

Of the five cargo ships all of them had taken damage. A total of thirteen hundred lives were lost between them. Cargo One had lost both of its engines and would need to be abandoned. Cargo Two had a severe hull breach that threatened to break the ship in half. Cargo Three had four hull breaches and one engine damaged beyond repair. Cargo Four had laser damage to the entire right side. Cargo Five had a hull breach due to several missile hits to its bridge, killing the commander and the rest of the command crew.

Alert Squadron lost six pilots and seven Stilettos. Two of the Stilettos were lost to friendly fire and luckily one of those pilots had a successful ejection. He was found after three hours of floating around the battle wreckage. Four other Stilettos were damaged and would need to be repaired.

Attack Squadron took the heaviest losses of the battle with eleven pilots and Stilettos lost. Major Seller was killed in action along with the captain in charge of Second Attack Flight. All of the five remaining Stilettos were damaged. One of them serious enough that the pilot had to eject and the craft was destroyed.

Reserve Squadron had the least amount of losses with only three pilots and Stilettos lost. Two of the remaining Stilettos were damaged, one of which needed serious repairs and the other was barely noticeable.

It took two hours for the remainder of the Carrier Group and Defend Squadron to arrive and they were immediately placed on patrol. Recovery of Attack and Reserve Squadrons commenced while the cleanup continued around the clock. All of the escape pods and ejection compartments were recovered and the area was searched for any remaining survivors. Emergency ship repairs were begun so that the Group could vacate the area as soon as possible. The estimated time until they could move was stated at twenty-four hours.

CHAPTER

25

C aptain McCabe reporting as ordered," said Peter as he stood at attention in front of the desk.

Lieutenant Colonel Nelson looked up from his paperwork and opened his middle desk drawer. He withdrew a handful of first lieutenant bars and a small box. "Open the box first." He motioned for Peter to take a seat. Peter picked up the box and sat, opening it slowly.

"A Silver Star for gallantry in action," said Lieutenant Colonel Nelson as he leaned back in his chair. "One was also given to Captain Carlos Mendez and another to Major Allen Seller, posthumously. The Cargo Group Commander, Captain Victor Radcliff, put in the paperwork for them, because of your actions while in command of the fighters that protected his Group. You can thank him tonight at dinner."

Peter closed the box and picked up the six sets of single silver bars that were on the desk. He was still a bit shocked that he received a medal for doing his job. So many lives were lost in this battle it seemed wrong that he should benefit from it in any way.

"Your squadron did an excellent job and all of your pilots are second lieutenants. I'll let you have the honor of promoting six of them to first lieutenant so they can have their proper place in the command structure. Just give me the list of names."

"Thank you, sir," replied Peter.

"Peter, Attack Squadron has lost its commander. Could you recommend a suitable replacement?"

"Yes sir, Miguel Rodriguez," said Peter in quick response. He did not need to think about it because that former simtech was an incredible pilot and wingleader.

"All right, promote him to first lieutenant and give him the good news. He'll also need a Second Flight leader. I suppose you'll suggest his friend Randy Taylor?"

"Yes sir, they work well together and he is also a damn good pilot. I'll promote him as well."

"As you can probably tell I'll be pulling pilots from your squadron to fill the other ones. This will leave you with a single flight again until we can get some replacements," said Terry as he lifted the pad of paper he had in front of him.

"Can I make another suggestion, sir?" asked Peter.

Lieutenant Colonel Nelson laughed, "When don't you?"

"Sorry sir, I'm just full of ideas sometimes."

"Go ahead," replied Lieutenant Colonel Nelson while smiling and shaking his head.

"I saw the look on Major Brannick's face when he was told that he needed to hang back to protect the rest of the Carrier Group as we headed for battle. He was not a happy man despite no complaints while doing what he was ordered to do. I suggest rotating the squadron's duties for the purpose of cycling pilots through training. Maybe make Major Brannick's squadron perform Alert functions for a week, and move Attack Squadron to Defend duties, and Alert to Attack duties. Reserve Squadron could then take over the patrols, which would lessen the duties for Alert Squadron and get the junior pilots more actual flight time. We could get more people trained this way and, I feel, this would increase morale."

"Makes sense to me, I'll go ahead and implement that immediately," said Lieutenant Colonel Nelson as he made notes on his pad. "Good job against those capital ships, I didn't think you'd be able to pull that off as well as you did."

"I had a lot of help, sir. There are some really talented pilots on this ship. Some of them have the potential to be better than I am."

Lieutenant Colonel Nelson looked at Peter and nodded slowly. He could not believe that to be possible but it was arrogant to think it unlikely. Peter had a good head on his shoulders and he was glad to have him under his command.

"Any other requests while I have you here?"

"Yes sir. I would like permission to offer promotion to several of the maintenance technicians that have been training in the simulator part time. I have identified six people, four men and two women, that show exceptional promise as pilots. They could use full-time training to hone their skills and get them ready for actual combat. This would be the first real batch of enlisted people to make the transition and may entice more to strive for the attainment of their wings."

"I'll have to ask the Captain about that. Give me a list of the technicians and I'll go and have a chat with him," said Lieutenant Colonel Nelson. "Anything else?"

"No sir," replied Peter. "I think I've pestered you enough for one day."

"Good, now get the hell out of my office so I can get some sleep."

"Yes sir."

*

Peter watched Emily exit the shuttle cargo bay wearing her full dress uniform. The brass was shined to perfection and the white cloth was bright and pressed. Her hair was held tightly against the back of her head and the smile on her face when she saw him standing there excited him. He waited patiently for the rest of the commanders to exit the bay and pass him in the hall with greetings and salutes. Peter saluted her out of respect of her rank and she returned it followed by a playful jab to his stomach.

"Another medal for saving me," she said. She lightly passed her fingers over the Silver Star and then caressed it between her fingers. Since he was wearing a full dress uniform the full medals were displayed instead of just the rack of ribbons.

"Yes, I'm going for the full set," responded Peter as Emily laughed quietly.

"I don't get in that much trouble, do I?"

"I certainly hope not," replied Peter as he turned and held out his left arm for her to grab hold of. They walked down the hallway in silence for a few minutes as they made their way to the diplomatic dining room.

"You look great," said Peter, breaking the silence.

"I wondered when you'd notice," replied Emily. Her smile held humor, satisfaction, and playfulness.

"Oh, I noticed when my heart skipped a beat as I saw you in the cargo bay."

"I wouldn't want you failing your flight physical because of me," said Emily.

"It'd be worth it."

Emily glanced at the man whose arm she held and felt his warmth through the dress jacket. It was hard not to compare him to other men she had been with or to other men of this time period in general. He was so different that it was refreshing. She found herself puzzled yet pleased.

As they approached the dining room, Peter saw Lieutenant Colonel Nelson chatting with a Commander. The Commander shook his hand and disappeared into the dining room as they approached. Lieutenant Colonel Nelson was about to follow the man when he glanced in their direction, smiled, and waited.

"Peter, I was wondering when you'd show up," said Lieutenant Colonel Nelson as he glanced at Emily. He never remembered seeing such a beautiful woman with Peter before.

"Colonel, I'd like you to meet Commander Emily Conrad, from Cargo Three," said Peter. "Emily, this is my commanding officer, Lieutenant Colonel Terry Nelson."

"It's a pleasure to meet you, Colonel," said Emily as she released her grip on Peter's arm and shook the Colonel's hand.

"Likewise, Commander," replied Lieutenant Colonel Nelson. "I think about half of those invited are already inside. Shall we join them?"

"Absolutely," replied Peter. "We don't want to keep the Captain waiting. He doesn't like that."

"No, he doesn't," said Lieutenant Colonel Nelson. He ushered them into the room before following.

Once they entered the dining room they were led to their seats by an Ensign. Peter was elated to see that the Captain thought of him when it came to the seating arrangements. Peter pulled the chair back and allowed Emily to sit before taking his own seat next to her.

"And they say chivalry is dead," whispered Emily into his ear.

He turned to her and leaned over, wanting to kiss her but whispering a response instead. "No, it was just in cryogenic sleep for a few hundred years." She laughed and peered at him from the corner of her eye.

Within fifteen minutes all the commanders of the various ships in the Carrier and Cargo Groups were seated at the table. Major Brannick, Captain Mendez, and First Lieutenant Rodriguez were also there at the request of Captain Radcliff. Captain Washington entered the room and everyone stood.

"At ease everyone and welcome aboard."

"Thank you, sir," replied everyone in unison.

"It's nice to have you all here tonight," started Captain Washington. "I don't get to do this very often so it is a pleasant change. I understand that recovery and emergency repair operations have been completed?"

"Yes, Captain," replied Captain Radcliff. "It took almost a week but all personnel have been accounted for in some way, shape, or form."

Captain Washington nodded, knowing full well what that statement implied.

"Let me introduce my Group and Squadron Commanders. To my left is Commander Frank Mito, my First Officer. Next is Lieutenant Colonel Terry Nelson, Flight Group Commander. His squadron officers, and raise your hands please since you're scattered about; Major Silvio Brannick, Captain

Carlos Mendez, Captain Peter McCabe, and First Lieutenant Miguel Rodriguez."

Captain Washington continued to introduce the other Carrier Group ship commanders while Emily's hand found Peter's hand under the table. He looked at her and she kept a neutral expression on her face. Peter almost made a funny face at her but this was neither the time nor the place.

"My First Officer was killed and I have yet to appoint a new one. I hate starting this off on a somber note, my apologies," said Captain Radcliff. He named the officers of the surviving ships as he made his way around the table.

"With your permission, Captain," started Captain Radcliff while standing. "I'd like to start this dinner with a toast."

"By all means, my old friend," replied Captain Washington.

"To those that lost their lives recently in the line of duty." Everyone raised their glasses of wine in front of themselves and lowered their heads in a quick prayer. After thirty seconds of silence, Captain Radcliff spoke again. "May you all find your way home." All of the officers took a sip of their wine and placed the glasses on the table in front of them.

The wine was a red wine and since Peter preferred beer he had no idea what kind it may have been. It tasted like any other wine he had ever had so he did not think twice about it. The most memorable thing about the wine was how light and fruity the aftertaste was. It was probably the smoothest wine he had ever remembered tasting.

"With our reluctant and sad duties behind us, let us enjoy dinner and the evening together," said Captain Washington.

"Yes, sir," was the combined response.

Several stewards exited from the attached kitchen and brought appetizers to the table. Peter recognized some of them while others looked rather bizarre. He tried a few of them and they were delicious.

Conversation around the table was friendly and centered on getting to know something about everyone. Captain Radcliff questioned the Carrier Group people one at a time while Captain Washington questioned the Cargo Group commanders.

"Captain McCabe, what's it like being ... frozen?" asked Captain Radcliff, catching himself before using the word *dead* instead of *frozen*.

Peter was munching on an appetizer that required both hands and jumped slightly when Emily placed her hand on his thigh and squeezed gently. His eyes opened wide and he swallowed the piece in his mouth before answering.

"Rather boring, actually, sir," said Peter as he reached for his wineglass.

"How does our current world compare to the world you remember?"

"Sir, I much prefer this world than the one I left. I don't care much for war but I have a purpose here. I never felt like I had a purpose in the other one."

"So, you never want to go back?"

"Hell no," shot Peter a bit too loudly, "sir." Peter smiled as others around the table laughed. Captain Radcliff laughed and nodded.

Next out were the salads as the questioning continued. Captain Radcliff was surprised to learn that Miguel started the war as an enlisted man and had commanded Second Reserve Flight in cooperation with Peter against the capital ships. Because of his actions Miguel had been given the command of a squadron along with a promotion and medal.

Major Brannick was quiet and said very little until the questioning turned to him. Peter was sitting next to the Major but was not sure what to say to him so he ate his salad in silence. Anytime Emily was not using her left hand it was on his thigh, and he liked it there.

When the questioning was on the other side of the table, Major Brannick leaned over and whispered into Peter's ear. "Was it you that suggested to the Colonel that the squadron duties rotate once a week?"

Peter thought about it a bit, wondering what the Major was after. It was hard to tell if this man was sincere or angry since his demeanor never changed. Peter finished his bite of salad and leaned over to respond.

"Yes, to better improve the training of all pilots."

"Whatever the surface reason, thank you," said Major Brannick. "It was a puzzle I could not solve."

Peter nodded and the Major actually smiled. It was a good plan, one that was certain to improve the morale of all pilots. The current setup for cycling pilots around was archaic and needed to be improved for the good of the entire Fleet. Expecting one squadron to be the seasoned veterans while the others sat in waiting all the time was a death sentence for most of them.

The main course came out next and the smells assaulting his senses made him salivate like Pavlov's dog. Emily squeezed his thigh lightly and he turned to look at her. Her warm brown eyes beckoned him, and he could smell the light perfume she was wearing despite the smells of dinner.

"Commander Conrad," said Captain Radcliff as he watched the interaction between her and Peter. He was no fool and thought it was rather refreshing to see happiness amongst all the death. "How did you happen to be seated among all the handsome young pilots?"

"Sir, I requested to be seated near my hero," replied Emily while nodding at Peter. She related the story in a shortened version as the stewards were distributing the main course around the table. When she finished the story the officers that had never heard of what had happened were impressed while the others just dug into their meals.

"You are one hell of a pilot, Captain McCabe," said Captain Radcliff.

"Thank you, sir, but I'm not the best in this Group," replied Peter.

"Really? Who is?"

"Sorry sir, that's information I'll never divulge. Pilots have a big enough ego as it is and that information in the wrong hands would cause more damage than good."

"Understood. I just can't fathom a better pilot out there."

"Well, sir, the really surprising thing is that I know of more than just one. There are some truly talented individuals out there just waiting to make their mark."

Conversation trailed off while everyone enjoyed the main course. Peter's best guess was a surf-and-turf of some sort. The fish was extremely tasty, the best he had ever had. The steak was a cross between beef and venison. He did not know which he liked better as he finished both of them. When he sat back in his chair he realized that he might have had too much to eat. All of it was excellent. The potatoes were a sort that he just vaguely recognized albeit much more tasty. They must have been seasoned or something along that line. The strange vegetables were a pink color and an odd shape as well. He wanted to know what they were but did not want to interrupt and ask.

A steward poured more wine for Peter and Emily as he made his way around the table. Peter drank slowly, making sure not to have more than one glass worth of wine. That was proving to be difficult since the steward's mission was to keep everyone's glass full.

After the meal was completed, the stewards came around to collect the plates and bring anyone more wine or coffee if they wanted. Peter switched to his glass of water and ignored the glass of wine. He kept his right hand under the table so he could hold hands with Emily as the conversation continued in a more relaxed atmosphere.

An hour later a few of the officers asked to be excused since they had an early morning ahead of them. Once a few more stood to leave Peter decided it was time for him to go as well. Emily stood when he did and followed him out the door. They walked in silence down the hallway and after they turned a corner Peter stopped and leaned against the wall.

"Do you know where my room is?" asked Emily.

"No," replied Peter, "but I'd like to find out."

Emily gave him an evil grin and the two of them began hurriedly walking down the hallway. It took them a few minutes to find the diplomatic staterooms and her particular room. She opened the door and turned on the lights as she quickly surveyed the room. It was a lot bigger than the one on her ship, maybe three times the size. It had a double bed, a small desk, a bureau, and an adjoining bathroom. As soon as her door closed she turned and embraced Peter.

"You're still my hero," whispered Emily.

Peter pulled away from her quickly and she frowned, remembering their last time together. "I can't ..." started Peter as he lowered his head and looked at her belt. "I just can't ... get your clothes off fast enough." Peter grabbed her belt while the kissing turned to the expeditious removal of clothing.

They barely made their way onto the bed and laughed as they rolled into the wall. The kissing progressed to making love like two animals in a feeding frenzy. Both of them needed the release more than anything else and quickly got that out of the way. They held each other with mild caresses until they made love again and fell asleep in each other's arms.

CHAPTER
26

The general quarters klaxon woke them abruptly and Peter yelled out, "Lights, time." The lights came on and he was told that it was oh-four-twenty-three hours. He jumped out of bed naked and slid his boxer shorts on. The rest of his clothing could only slow him down and he would need to remove them to put on his flight suit anyway.

"Be safe," said Peter as he kissed her gently on the lips.

"You too," replied Emily as she climbed out of bed and tried to rub the sleep from her eyes. She had a ship and crew to attend to as well.

Peter grabbed his ID card and opened the door. He stepped into the hall and looked back at Emily, giving her a smile that she returned. The door closed and he ran down the hallway in his bare feet. He made a few turns and was soon in Flight Ops, holding his ID card up as he approached. The guards looked at him oddly with big smiles on their faces and held the door open for him to pass. He entered the Reserve Squadron bunkroom and three other pilots were suiting up. He opened his locker and grabbed his flight suit, not thinking twice about two of the pilots being female. They did not seem to notice that he only wore boxer shorts and had no shirt or shoes on. He climbed into his flight suit quickly and pulled on his socks and boots.

"Status?" asked Peter of anyone that listened.

"Not sure, the rest of our flight have been on patrol and we're the only squadron being scrambled. Defend is on launch standby once we get up," replied the female second lieutenant.

"Let's get airborne then, I mean spaceborne."

They followed him out of the bunkroom at a run. The two guards opened the door to the hanger and snapped to attention as he approached. He saluted as he ran past them and grabbed his environmental suit. The technicians present helped him suit up and then climb the ladder of his Stiletto. Once he was seated he started his engines while the tech fastened his five-point harness.

"Good luck, sir," said the tech while patting the top of his helmet. Peter gave the man a thumbs-up and hit the switch to lower the canopy. He watched as the other three Stilettos lowered their canopies at the same time while the techs exited the hanger launch area in a hurry. Once the doors were sealed the floor canted at a forty-five degree angle and the green launch light came on. Peter pushed the throttles forward and shot out of the bottom of the carrier. He retracted the landing gear and fired up his combat computer.

"Ticonderoga, Reserve One. What do we have?" asked Peter over the command frequency.

"Reserve One, Ticonderoga. There's a large alien force at our six o'clock and approaching fast," said the controller on duty.

"Form up," said Peter over the short-range frequency as he increased to a positive five incline. The other seven Stilettos formed up on his wings as he realized that he was now commanding a bunch of greenies that had less than a dozen hours in the actual spacecraft. They all had many hours in the simulators and he had comfortably trained them since their arrival. Three of the pilots, all women, were excellent pilots and currently flying in the positions of wingleaders. One of the wingmen was a screw-off that was just hours away from spending the rest of the war in the kitchen, but there was nothing Peter could do about him right now.

Peter surveyed the area and tried to come up with some kind of plan for this new mess. The most notable feature being that the Group was passing the moon of a small red planet. His mostly-useless long-range scanner showed a massive cluster of red dots indicating Bect ships. It was the largest clustering of red dots he had ever seen. There were also quite a few large red dots that were probably capital ships, most likely hiding a carrier in there as well. It was an attack force vastly larger than the force they had recently defeated.

"Ticonderoga, Reserve One. Launch Defend," said Peter as a plan formed.

*

"Acknowledged Reserve One, Defend is being launched," said the controller.

"Peter, what do you think?" asked Captain Washington.

"I think we have hit the mother load, my friend," replied Peter over the loudspeaker.

"Is that a good thing?"

"Not one bit. Bug out and we'll keep them busy."

"Can we take them?"

"Doubtful. There are more than last time, a *lot* more. It's not worth the risk, we've already lost too much as it is."

"But Peter, what about you and your flight?" asked Captain Washington. He already knew the answer but was not really sure he wanted to hear it. He was concerned that Peter's voice was so calm in such a stressful situation. This was not a normal man to choose the ultimate sacrifice this readily.

"All part of the game, Captain. We'll be here when you get back."

"Raise some hell, son."

"Tell her," was Peter's last transmission over the command frequency.

"Acknowledged," replied Captain Washington as a wave of sadness rushed over him. There were not many people he met in life that made such a huge impact on him. This unlikely man that he recovered from a coffin floating in the depths of space managed to become his friend. He hoped that the inevitable would not occur as he silently wished his friend a good trip to the afterlife.

*

Peter watched as the Carrier and Cargo Groups continued for deep space as fast as their slowest ship could manage. He stared at the small moon and a plan snapped together in his mind.

"Follow me," said Peter on the short-range frequency. He eased his throttles forward as he angled the flight between the moon and the planet. He brought his ship to a stop once he was where he wanted to be. "Close up and go to wingcom one."

"What are we gonna do?" asked Second Lieutenant Cindy Forstal. "I don't want to die like this." She was a talented pilot with better than average skills. What Peter liked the best about her was that she had an innate situational awareness that surpassed everyone he knew. She always knew where she was and what was around her. She had a very promising future, until today.

"I'm not going to lie to you," started Peter as he talked slowly in an attempt to calm everyone. "This does not look good. I suspect that the enemy force is massive so I told the Captain to get out of here in a hurry. We, us eight, are all that stand between an insane amount of Bect and our friends. Our mission is to keep the Bect busy long enough for our Group to get away."

"But we're all gonna die," said another officer whose voice Peter could not quite place. Most likely it was the worthless wingman and aspiring cook.

"It's a sacrifice. The eight of us die here and now or tens of thousands die when this Bect force reaches the Group. Plus, who said we were going to die?" said Peter as he waited to hear if anyone else would say anything.

The eight Stilettos floated behind the moon and Peter watched the red planet below him. He tried to compare it to Mars and found it too difficult to think about at the moment.

"You have all been trained, you all know your mission, you all know what I'm capable of. If I thought we stood no chance in hell do you think I'd dive into this headfirst?" *Okay*, thought Peter, *so I lied*. But it was a good lie and one that would hopefully calm his pilots and allow them to do their jobs to save the lives of thousands. They needed some small piece of hope to latch on to.

"So, what's the plan?" asked Cindy, breaking the silence. She always saw the big picture and the tone of her voice indicated that she too had accepted the fact that this mission could really only end one way. She knew he was lying.

"I expect to see at least one carrier in that mix," started Peter as he tried to formulate the rest of his plan. He really had no plan, just a rough idea of something to try to reduce the enemy force enough to make them think twice about continuing against the human forces.

"Our mission is to take this entire enemy force by surprise and cripple them so badly and so quickly that they decide against following our friends. Once that has been achieved our mission is accomplished and we will bug out. Is everyone okay with that?"

"Yes sir," were the replies over the wingcom.

"All right, we'll wait for the enemy force to pass the moon as they follow our friends. Then we'll come around the moon and appear behind them. I'll call the targets on ICIS. We have eight missiles each so we'll plan on there being two carriers. Everyone will launch four missiles at each of the carriers. That puts thirty-two missiles into each carrier, which should ruin their day. If there are actually two carriers, we should be able to destroy both of them with that onslaught. I doubt the Bect will continue with that kind of damage from just a handful of fighters. Knocking their fighter support out in seconds might cause them to reconsider their plans."

"Then what?" asked a female voice he did not recognize.

"Then we get the hell out of there in a hurry."

"Amen," said Cindy.

They sat silently in waiting as they watched their combat computers plot the course of the enemy. The Ticonderoga Group was on the outskirts of their long-range scanners as the enemy force was passing by the moon. Peter hoped this plan of his worked, for the Group's sake.

He figured things would come to this at some point. It was sadly fitting that he traveled three hundred some-odd years into the future just to sacrifice his life for the greater good of the human race. Well, not really. He did not want to die when things were looking so good for him. He had an exciting and rewarding career as a combat fighter pilot, in space, and a woman he loved. Finally, after years of suffering in his previous life, he had a life worth living and now he had to sacrifice that life. It was not fair. Unfortunately that was something that had made the transition from one time to another with him. Just one more slap in the face before he left this universe forever.

He thought about various aspects of his past. His lack of luck with women somehow led to his marriage to a woman that would later destroy their relationship. Then he spent years looking for another woman to share life with, to no avail. Peter went from job to job changing careers as he searched for something that made him completely happy, but found nothing. He did crazy things and spent many months with a death wish, but remained alive. He could never find the answers he was looking for.

But none of that mattered at the moment. The past, the present, and the future were a blur. The only things he cared about in life were always forcibly taken away from him in some way or another. Sadly enough he continued onward because to him there was no other alternative. *Take the pain*, a good friend had once said to him. Now it all made sense.

Peter thought about the good times and the bad times in his past. If he had to die here and now he was ready for it. He had died before and had accepted death a very long time ago. If he had to choose the way he would die it would be just like his current situation, a battle he could never win against an enemy force one hundred times his size for the purpose of saving thousands. The ultimate sacrifice was the ultimate gift to those you truly cared about. He had friends here too, really good ones, and a woman he loved. His real family was long dead and he missed them but these people had treated him like family ever since taking him from a frozen entrée to an accomplished officer.

He watched the enemy force appear on the far side of the moon and decided that it was time for them to make their assault. ICIS tracked the enemy ships and, with the updated categorization of the Bect craft, he saw three carriers indicated.

"Three carriers," said Peter. He targeted the two carriers on the outside that they would fire upon, leaving the middle one. The other pilots around him highlighted the targets and locked them in. He throttled up his Stiletto and rounded the far side of the moon.

"Split into two groups, combat spread, one incline separation, and let's go in hot. Ready?"

"Ready," responded the flight.

"All right. Our time flying together has been short but it has been an honor to fly with you. Let's get this job done and get the hell out of here. Keep radio silence until we've launched our first missiles. Good luck, everyone. Remember your training. Let's go."

The Stiletto flight moved around the moon and appeared behind the large enemy force. According to ICIS there were three carriers, fourteen cruisers, two tankers, and three capital ships that had yet to be classified. *What a mess that would have created*, thought Peter as he pushed his throttles to the stops. The Stiletto flight approached the Bect force rapidly and he waited until the range was well inside the useful envelope of the missiles.

"Fire," said Peter over the short-range frequency. He depressed his weapon release button four times in rapid succession and switched to the next carrier to repeat his actions. He saw the two volleys of missiles streak toward the targets as he turned back toward the moon. The missiles brought the enemy group to a rude awakening as the ships turned rapidly to confront the threat. As far as Peter was concerned their mission was successful. The enemy group had turned around and was no longer following the Ticonderoga Group.

"Bug out," yelled Peter as he pushed his throttles over the stops and began accelerating to four SU. He watched the missiles impact the two large targets in his rear view screen. The first carrier flashed rapidly in several spots before it violently burst wide open, taking out two cruisers and severely damaging one other unknown ship. The second carrier took thirty of the missiles directly in the engines and kept going. It began to shake and shimmy as internal explosions blew the entire front portion of the carrier off and split the remainder down the middle. Both carriers were instantly destroyed along with two cruisers and another unknown ship that had sustained critical damage to its hull. The spray of resulting shrapnel peppered the remaining assault force causing considerable collateral damage. The third carrier, being between their two targets, received sprays of shrapnel from both of the dead carriers. The targeting plan worked better than Peter had hoped it would.

Now it was time for them to get out alive, hopefully. Laser fire filled the area around them and Peter watched his wingman take several of the high-energy beams before exploding. Two other Stilettos succumbed to heavy fire before disappearing from his side. Several blasts impacted the rear of his Stiletto and he jinked reflexively as his Master Caution light came on to indicate system failures.

"Go evasive," yelled Peter over the short-range frequency. He glanced at his caution annunciator panel and saw three lights flashing: Right Fuel Cell, Right Wing Thrusters, and Right Pylons. None of the systems were critical so he reset the Master Caution system and the flashing annunciator lights changed to being solidly lit as the Master Caution light extinguished.

The five remaining Stilettos separated and fended for themselves as they tried to avoid the incoming rain of laser fire. Initially they gained some distance but the Bect capital ships were outrunning them. Reports always indicated that the Bect ships were slightly slower than the humans, but here they were the same if not a bit faster. Once again the human intelligence reports were erroneous. The only logical choice at this point was to turn and engage, otherwise death would certainly befall them.

"Can't outrun them, let's engage that last carrier. Maybe we can take it out too."

"Do you think we can?" asked Cindy.

"No, but what the hell else do we have to do but get our tails shot out from under us. I'm tired of taking it in the ass," said Peter, forcing a laugh.

"Good point," laughed Cindy. "Let's take even more of the bastards with us."

"Roger that," said Peter as he executed a rapid turn. He felt the slight sloppy nature of the turn due to the failed right thrusters and it was annoying. He watched as the other four Stilettos turned and he blinked as one of them blew apart before his eyes. There was no turning back now and no chance for them to escape. Their new and final goal was to remove as many enemy ships as they possibly could before they joined their friends in the afterlife.

They approached the remaining Bect carrier as fast as possible, which was twice as fast as normal due to the closure rate. This maneuver caused a lot of confusion on the enemy's part. They never expected four little fighters to turn on a force that was insanely greater than theirs. The Bect laser fire ceased for fear that they would damage their own ships. This allowed the Stilettos to get off a barrage of laser fire on what appeared to be the bridge of the third alien carrier. A large explosion signified a direct hit on something juicy so they continued to assault it.

Slugs soon joined the battle once the carrier had slowed enough to launch them. Peter's combat computer was so full of red dots that he ignored it. He coaxed his Stiletto around and blew apart four slugs in rapid succession before placing more laser blasts into the damaged carrier. Another internal explosion shook the carrier as a fire erupted into space for a brief few seconds before extinguishing. He turned once again to see Cindy and her wingman take out two slugs as they flew past him. They had half a dozen fighters crawling up their tails so he sprayed the slugs with laser fire, destroying five while the sixth one spun out of control into a cruiser that got too close.

The fighting conditions improved when the enemy capital ships restrained from firing their large cannons into their own midst. That gave his flight a fighting chance in a futile situation. As the slugs slowly disappeared from the screen the cruisers became anxious and fired at the Stilettos. Several cruisers took friendly damage but their gamble was successful in taking out one of the Stilettos.

With three Stilettos left, the humans were surprisingly holding their own against the massive amount of alien forces. The remaining Bect carrier was sparkling and burning in various places, which was why very few bombers had shown up. That would have shifted the fight against them.

Cindy turned to find a lone bomber lining up on Peter's Stiletto. She and her wingman sprayed its tail with laser fire and quickly ate through the shields. The Bect bomber turned to evade but it was too late as Cindy's lasers ripped the hull wide open. She smiled and turned once again to bear down and lay some fire on the remaining carrier. She took a few hits from some passing slugs and her Master Caution light came on. She checked the caution annunciator panel and saw that her outer hull was breached, which did not matter at the moment. She reset the Master Caution light and got back to work.

Peter passed Cindy and her wingman's Stilettos and fired at the collection of slugs following them. He tried banking sharply to the left and miscalculated the extent of the damage to his right thrusters, causing his Stiletto to flip over. He flew through a waterfall of enemy laser fire trying to find its way to Cindy's ship. One blast cracked his cockpit window as the others splattered across his upper fuselage and wings.

"Mayday," yelled Peter over the short-range frequency as his engine noise diminished. Immediately after his transmission he lost all electrical power as a large puff of white smoke filled the cockpit before being sucked out into space. His Stiletto kept tumbling forward in the frictionless expanse of space as he examined his circuit breaker panel.

Cindy heard the call and quickly found Peter's Stiletto slowly spinning across the battlefield. She tried calling him but he was not answering. She headed for his ship and destroyed whatever Bect craft was stupid enough to get in her way. As she neared his Stiletto she saw that he had no power, making him an easy target. Movement in the cockpit signified that he was still alive so she needed to give him some time.

"Let's cover this area and give Peter a chance to fix himself," said Cindy over the wingcom.

"Roger," replied the Second Lieutenant, happy to still be alive. He kept reassuring himself that if he followed his training he would be okay.

Cindy picked the nearest slugs and began methodically destroying them. A few blasts impacted her lower fuselage and shook her ship violently, setting off another few lights on her caution annunciator panel. Her Left Wing Pylons and Left Main Landing Gear were damaged, both non-essential systems so she reset the Master Caution light.

Peter found the problem almost instantly, the Primary Bus circuit breaker was missing. A massive electrical short must have melted the Primary Bus and blew the circuit breaker apart. He pulled the isolation circuit breakers and was relieved when emergency power from his battery pack came online. He restarted the engines and applied maximum power as he pressed the Essential Bus circuit breaker in. Bect laser fire entered the space he recently vacated and Peter breathed a sigh of relief.

He pushed in two more circuit breakers and his weapon system came online along with his radios. The Master Caution light was blinking so he scanned the caution annunciator panel before resetting it. There were over a dozen of the caution lights now lit and he wondered how he had survived.

"Damn, that was close," said Peter over the short-range frequency.

"I thought we lost you," replied Cindy. She destroyed another cluster of slugs that were chasing Peter's damaged ship. Peter turned sloppily to the left and Cindy cut the corner to shorten the distance between them.

"Yeah, me too."

"Form up," said Cindy over the short-range frequency, hoping her wingman was still out there somewhere.

The battle was going very badly for the Bect at this point so they opened fire with no regard for their own ships. An unknown capital ship blew apart when it took several direct hits to something critical.

"Roger," replied her wingman. He located her fighter and struggled to avoid the intense enemy fire. Two more cruisers were ripped apart by alien fire before the front of his Stiletto disintegrated around him. He never knew what hit him as he died with a smile on his face, satisfied that he had done the best he could and saved thousands of people he did not know.

"My ship can't take much more of this," said Peter.

"Mine either," replied Cindy.

"Emergency bug out," yelled Peter as he strafed a nearby cruiser.

Cindy strafed the same cruiser and smiled as its guns were silenced. She looked for her wingman and a lump grew in her throat as she watched a Stiletto tail section vaporize in the middle of a nightmarish concentration of enemy fire. She turned back to the job of staying alive and followed Peter's Stiletto. The two of them pushed their throttles over the stops and full forward, and then they flipped the guarded switch for emergency power. Emergency power gave an added boost to the engines, taking the Stiletto from a maximum of four SU to almost six SU for a brief period of time, until the engines melted.

I should have used emergency power earlier, thought Peter. He could have saved some of his flight's lives had he done that. Why did it slip his mind? Was his subconscious mind trying to sabotage his future and end his life? It would be one way to take away all the pain. Maybe his decision to re-engage the Bect was to gain some insurance for the Ticonderoga Group by destroying even more of them. That made more sense to him than having a self-destructive tendency. They had already succeeded in causing the Bect serious pain and probably deterred them from their mission. But with alien races, could you ever really know what motivated them? Besides, burning out their engines earlier and ejecting could have only led to their capture or slaughter. His brain hurt but he knew there was an answer to this question, he remembered reading it somewhere. *What was it?*

"Head for the planet," screamed Peter into the wingcom, "and jink like you mean it."

Peter and Cindy moved their control sticks at random intervals and in random directions as they approached the planet. The bulk of the Bect force floated aimlessly in ruins while the laser fire coming from the remaining capital ships was intense and filled the area with blue light. The confusion the humans had created would give them very little time to gain some distance. He hoped they could get to the planet before the Bect force caught up.

But then what? He never checked to see if that planet was even habitable. What if the Bect landed a force to hunt them down and capture them? Then what would they do, become Bect prisoners of war? Did the Bect eat their prisoners? He had too many questions that he would rather not have an answer for and more immediate concerns.

"Nice show, boss," said Cindy as they left the Bect behind them.

"Very nice. Good job Cindy, and thanks for the save," said Peter. "We've gotten this far, let's try to live through this one, okay?"

"I'm with you, boss."

"Up two," said Peter as they initiated a positive incline change to confuse the Bect. They leveled off and the alien capital ships had to redirect their fire. "Down one, then up two, go."

Peter watched his engine temperature gauges climb to the danger point and wondered how much more they could take before exploding. The flight manual never mentioned much of anything about it. It was probably an untested feature. That was when the obscure text he was trying to remember hit him.

The planet grew in the distance and he glanced at the small inset screen on the right multifunction display. It was habitable but the oxygen content at sea level would be like a higher elevation on Earth. It was good enough as far as Peter was concerned since he had no other choice in the matter now.

"I'm burning up, Peter," said Cindy.

"Me too. According to the manual if we pull the circuit breaker for the breaking thrusters we can eject now and the forward momentum should get us into the planet's atmosphere. At least ... in theory."

"Then what?"

"Then we pray that the heat shields and parachutes on the ejection compartment actually work since I doubt they were ever fully tested either."

"Wonderful," replied Cindy.

"Also pull the emergency beacon circuit breaker. Then maybe the Bect won't search for survivors to violate."

"Makes sense."

"Cindy, it's been a pleasure flying with you, you're a damn good pilot. See you on the planet."

"Thanks Peter, see you soon."

Cindy pulled the appropriate circuit breakers and initiated the ejection sequence. Her engines turned a brilliant red and began melting through the nacelles as her power plant approached critical mass. Her ejection compartment separated from the ship and floated carelessly while the thrusters remained dormant. A bright flash signified the explosion of her ship and caused her ejection compartment to tumble.

Peter pulled his breaking thruster and emergency beacon circuit breakers, ejecting just as his Stiletto blew apart. He was glad they had waited as long as they did and hoped that the lack of thrusters and emergency beacons on their cockpits would cause the Bect to write them off instead of looking for corpses to defile. His ejection compartment began tumbling and it was almost sickening to watch his view go from black space to red planet. He wanted to close his eyes and let the inevitable happen but had to watch to see if the Bect followed them or not. Because of the turning motion he found it difficult to tell a planet from a moon, so he closed his eyes and prayed for the best.

The temperature inside his suit climbed greatly and he figured he was nearing the atmosphere. It was a good run, a good life, and a very successful mission. Eight brave combat fighter pilots went against the odds and destroyed a huge part of a force much greater in size. Two enemy carriers were destroyed and another was either crippled or destroyed, he was not sure which. He could not remember how many other capital ships had fallen either. At one point in the battle he was certain that he had seen some of the enemy cruisers destroy their own ships. That thought made him laugh as the spinning increased.

Did he finally make a difference in life? Peter felt that he had. He could have accepted mediocrity and stay a civilian on some random world that would soon have been invaded by the Bect. But that was not who he was. He could never just sit around and watch what happened, that was his former self. Peter had the chance to be the man that he had always wanted to be and he grabbed it with both hands. It was ironic that his new beginning turned into an early ending, but it was a good ending.

His time spent on the Ticonderoga changed the thinking of every person that he had met, and probably many more to come. He had passed valuable information on to others and it would be in their hands now, for them to use and continue the fight. The war would have been lost had he not appeared and helped as he had. Was dying for a second time, and more permanently, worth all of that? Yes, and he would gladly do it again.

It was then that he realized that for him the war was now truly over. He may never know the final outcome of the Sol-Bect War but he hoped that in the afterlife he would at least be granted that knowledge. At least going to the afterlife he knew for a fact that his actions today, and those of his flight, would save the lives of thousands. That, in and of itself, made it all worth it.

The ejection compartment shook as it entered the planet's atmosphere. New warning lights flashed but went unnoticed as the spinning intensified. Peter's helmet bounced off the left side of his canopy and he drifted into unconsciousness.

Paul was born in Western Massachusetts in 1966. He joined the Air Force at 18 as an aircraft electrician and became interested in aviation. In 1988 he began flying, earned his private pilot certificate in 1992, and moved to Colorado Springs to complete flight school. Paul currently lives in Maine where he is a charter pilot and co-owner of Lost Luggage Studios, with his brother Jamie.

ABOUT TERRAN SHIFT

Terran Shift is an open universe project created by Jamie and Paul Belanger. The main goal is to construct a science fiction universe like the creators of Star Wars and Star Trek did, but without the universe itself being owned by any corporation.

There is no fan fiction in Terran Shift. Or, rather, no need for it. You can use events and places in the Core Canon, combined with your own characters and ideas. Create new planets or races, and contribute them back to the project for others. Create any fiction, comic books, games, music, TV shows, or movies you want. Everyone can contribute to the universe and everyone's work will help to promote everyone else's work. There are no restrictions on what you can do, and no need to pay royalties or request permission to be a part of the project. Anything listed in the Core Canon is done so with a Creative Commons license. Create your media, attach the Terran Shift logo, and join the open universe revolution.

The Core Canon has been designed by Jamie and Paul Belanger for use in their novels and future Lost Luggage Studios computer games. Beyond that, the universe is open to your imagination. More details will be released on the project's website in the months ahead as we announce and release the projects and stories we've been working on.

Visit http://www.TerranShift.com for more information.

www.ingramcontent.com/pod-product-compliance
Lightning Source LLC
Chambersburg PA
CBHW070853180626
46817CB00003B/760